Alan Gibbons

Alan Gibbons is a full-time writer and a visiting speaker and lecturer at schools, colleges and literary events nationwide, including the major book festivals. He lives in Liverpool with his wife and four children.

Alan Gibbons has twice been shortlisted for the Carnegie Medal, with *The Edge* and *Shadow of the Minotaur*, which also won the Blue Peter Book Award in the 'Book I Couldn't Put Down' category.

The Lost Souls Stories Book 2

SETTING OF A CRUEL SUN

ALAN GIBBONS

Orion
Children's Books

First published in Great Britain in 2006
by Orion Children's Books
a division of the Orion Publishing Group Ltd
Orion House
5 Upper St Martin's Lane
London WC2H 9EA

1 3 5 7 9 10 8 6 4 2

The Orion Publishing Group's policy is to use papers that are natural,
renewable and recyclable products and made from wood grown in sustainable
forests. The logging and manufacturing processes are expected to conform to
the regulations of the country of origin.

A catalogue record for this book is available from the British Library

ISBN 10 – 1 84255 179 5
ISBN 13 – 978 1 84255 179 0

Typeset by Geoff Green Book Design, Cambridge

Printed in Great Britain by Clays Ltd, St Ives plc

www.orionbooks.co.uk

To Paul Foot –
rise like lions from your slumbers.

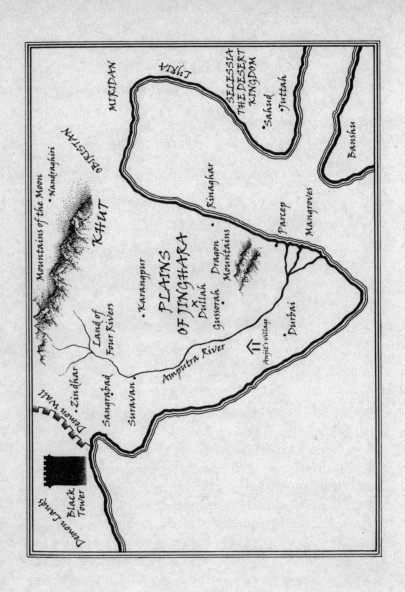

CHAPTER I

The Nine

I

It was the day the sun began to die, the tenth day of Hoj, in the year 675. After that day, nothing would ever be the same again. On Jinghara Plain two mighty armies clashed. Hour after hour, in thunder and pounding rain, man and demon fought their pitched battle. The carnage was terrible to behold. War elephants fell with piteous roars. Horses screamed as their riders tumbled from the saddle, dead by the time they struck the ground. In return the hands of men struck down the demon predators. Black blood sprayed through the murk and chaos of battle. But nothing slowed the assault of the night breed. Millions strong, they fought without concern for their own safety. Without conscience, without thought, they were mere tools of a superior, but hate-swollen intelligence. These legions of the undead, minds swirling with blood lust, attacked and attacked, then attacked again. Mired in mud, slithering through the blood and filth of battle, the two sides wore each other down.

But it wasn't the ocean crash of war that changed history. Just as the great Sol-ket army, pride of the Muzal Empire, started to waver, just as the oceanic press of the undead threatened to engulf the beleaguered ranks of their foe, the battle ended. At the moment of their triumph, for no apparent reason, the demons dropped their weapons. Some fell to the ground, wailing and gnashing their yellow, rotting teeth. Others chose self-slaughter. Before the astonished eyes of the Grand Army of the Empire, their ferocious enemy dissolved into a wretched, despairing rabble. There was no breakthrough, no final rally, no heroic charge to break their ranks. There appeared to be no reason for their collapse. Strange to say, the demon host just stopped fighting.

The cause of the battle's unexpected end was not to be found among the struggling combatants, but on a desolate crag miles away. In a dark tower, high on a bare mountain, an unlikely band of nine travellers severed the bond between the demon lord and his night breed. The Nine overcame him through courage, wisdom and faith. They did what many thousands of soldiers had failed to do by force of arms: they ended the demon plague that had terrorised the land for many generations.

As dawn broke over Jinghara, two of the Nine appeared in the doorway of the Black Tower, barely able to believe that the fight was at an end. The first to step out into the morning light was Gardep, a boy of sixteen summers. Though he was a warrior Sol-ket, he had not fought at Jinghara Plain. Losing faith in his god and his code, he had given up allegiance to the Empire of the Sun. Inspired by strange new ideas, he had fought in the Black Tower. His opponent was the general of the demon masses. It had been a savage struggle. There was fresh blood on his tunic and a scar on his face, evidence of the arduous journey he had undertaken to reach this place.

A young woman followed him out onto the mountainside. She was Cusha, the slave-girl who had set these events in motion. Though, by law, Gardep could have purchased a slave-girl like her any time he wanted, she would never be his property. She was unique. She was the woman he loved. Gardep had given up all his privileges, everything he had ever known, to protect her from evil. He had fought battles, suffered torture, all to be by her side.

'Is it really over?' Gardep asked, lifting his face to feel the sun's rays.

'Yes, it's over,' Cusha said, darting a look towards the top floor of the tower where they had fought the demon lord. 'We have conquered the Darkwing and broken his power over the Lost Souls. Their long servitude is over. We have liberated them from the horror of living death.'

Hope was in the air. By dusk however, the joy of victory would have been replaced by bitter despair.

'This is a strange kind of freedom,' Gardep observed, pointing across the bare mountainside that led to the Black Tower.

The demon lord was defeated. Now the aftermath was unfolding before their eyes. Ghosts were circling the tower like a stream of Lyrian fire. They were prising open the mouths of the undead. The translucent phantoms then forced the Lost Souls to swallow them whole. Immediately the faces of the night-striders, the foot soldiers of the undead, changed. For centuries, these monstrous predators had terrorised the land. No longer.

They had become bewildered men and women, appalled by their own condition. Against their will they had been raised from the grave and trapped in the slimy, decomposing shells of the night breed. The bestial hunger that normally lingered in their eyes faded, replaced by something that was recognisably human. First, they registered confusion. Then came a fearful understanding.

'Look at them,' Cusha said. 'They have recovered their consciousness. They know that they were once mortal men and women, like us. I pity them.'

She was right to feel pity. Rational thought did not bring joy to the night-striders. Out of the fog of primal blood-lust came the bright, searing light of shame. One turned his own sword on himself. Driving in the blade, he slashed open his belly. His entrails spilled like so many wriggling eels on the stony ground.

'Poor creature,' Cusha said. 'He can remember what the Darkwing made him. He can remember how he was resurrected from the cold clay to kill and maim the innocent.'

The night-strider's fading eyes met hers.

'Imagine his feelings,' she said. 'All those years, his mind was shrouded in ignorance. He obeyed the demon lord, becoming the monster's unthinking tool. By breaking the Darkwing's power, we have brought it all flooding back.We have shown him the full horror of what he has done.'

All around them, the night breed were wailing and moaning, clutching their faces, beating their heads and chests. Cusha and Gardep had heard them moan before, but not like this. It wasn't the dismal chorus that had filled the night hours, promising the living a wretched, agonising end. This was a piteous whine. The once merciless creatures were begging for an end to the thoughts that had

4

begun to torture their newly-conscious minds. One of them fell to his knees, palms flat, forehead thumping the floor. That's when it happened. The night-strider lifted his head and met Gardep's eye.

'End my suffering,' the creature begged. 'I can't bear this any longer.'

Gardep recoiled in horror. 'You spoke!'

Gardep had never heard the creatures formulate human speech. A snarl, a screech, yes, but not intelligent communication. Ignoring Gardep's cry of astonishment, the night-strider grabbed for his ankle. 'Please, Lord. End my torment.'

Gardep shot Cusha a querying glance. She nodded. Gardep then unsheathed his sword and beheaded the tortured soul kneeling before him.

'He spoke to me,' Gardep said.

Cusha didn't answer. It wasn't clear to Gardep whether she understood what was happening. He was wiping the black blood from the blade when he saw one of his comrades, a giant by the name of Oled Lonetread.

'Oled,' he said, calling him over, 'where is everyone?'

Oled was a full head and shoulders taller than any man Gardep had ever met. He was powerfully built, like a lumbering mountain bear. Little wonder. Oled was one of the last of his kind, a Tanjur. The Tanjurs were known as the people of the dragon, shape-shifters who could assume the form of wild beasts. Sometimes their beast-form was reflected in their human gait. Once they had been nomads, wandering the length and breadth of the Jingharan Plain. Now there were just three remaining survivors of this once mighty race.

'They are employed in the same grim task as yourself, Gardep,' Oled answered. 'The night-striders want to die. We decided to give a merciful end to those that asked.'

Cusha's eyes glistened with tears. 'To think, they have suffered the fate of the living dead. Now this.'

Oled shrugged. 'Nobody said the world was fair, Holy Child.'

Cusha knew the truth of Oled's words. 'Take us to the others,' she said.

The Tanjur led the short walk to the cave where the others were taking what rest they could get. It wasn't easy. For as far as the eye could see, hundreds of demons were exposing their flesh to the sun, allowing themselves to be consumed by fire. Such was the multitude of the risen dead that the whole world seemed to be ablaze.

'Here they are!' Harad shouted gleefully.

He came running, his eyes flashing a joyful greeting. Harad was Cusha's adoptive brother, a boy of almost fourteen summers. Cusha was a year older.

'You've finished then?' he asked.

Cusha smiled at Gardep. 'We haven't even begun.'

Harad frowned then turned to watch the Lost Souls. 'Did you ever see anything like it?'

Cusha shook her head. 'It's terrible.'

'Terrible?' The word was spoken by Qintu, Harad's best friend. 'I don't see what's so terrible about demons killing themselves,' he grumbled. 'They've killed enough of us in their time.' He scowled, remembering one such day of blood. 'Good riddance, I say.'

Cusha listened. Yes, good riddance to the Lost Souls. A shadow crossed her mind. It was the Darkwing. Yes, and good riddance to him, too.

2

But Cusha had dismissed her nemesis too easily. The Darkwing did not die in the Black Tower. He fled. Leaving the ancient building far behind, he flew far and wide across Jinghara, alone in defeat, desolate in exile. As the sun rose in the cloudless sky, burning away the few wisps of morning mist, he saw roving bands of his Lost Souls, utterly disoriented by their new condition. Once or twice he called to them, just as he had for many years, summoning them to implacable war on mankind. But they did not obey. If they looked at him at all, it was with eyes full of hatred, loathing their former master for the countless crimes he had made them commit. There they were, the unthinking, obedient creatures he had once formed into an army of many millions. But they had understanding. They had consciousness. Damn them, they had free will. In their new condition, they rejected him, spitting their contempt, glaring their hatred.

The Darkwing saw the Demon Wall. The Muzals had erected it as a barrier against his hordes. It was abandoned now. He had driven the defenders from its battlements and keeps, slaying most, driving the rest into the arms of their comrades, gibbering with nerve-shredding tales of butchery and horror. There, a little way beyond, was the fortress of Zindhar. He had triumphed there too, killing the garrison to the last man before torching it. He almost smiled at the memory. But smiles don't come easily to ruined faces such as his.

Once, so many years ago, he had been a prince of the Muzal Empire, a darling of the court. Possessed of charm and courage, dashing good looks and a ready wit, it was only a matter of time before he ascended to the Imperial throne in his father's place. But he had fallen from grace.

An evil priesthood had summoned the dark arts, subjecting him to an ordeal that cocooned his body and soul in a shroud of torture and decay. That made him what he was today, a monster. The Darkwing closed his eyes for a moment, conjuring his own form in his mind's eye. His body was encased in a scarlet and black carapace, a giant insect shell. Vast, leathery wings gave him the power of flight. Lethal claws tipped his fingers and toes. His head was repulsive to all living things, a bare, raven-black skull from which a pair of merciless eyes stared, inky with vengeance. Surrounding him, no matter where he went, no matter whose company he sought, there was the putrid aroma of decomposing flesh. He was the distillation of death, cruelly denied the escape of oblivion. His only succour was revenge.

Revenge. He slowed the beat of his wings. Of course. Defeated I might be for now. Exiled too. But I will not be destroyed. He circled, pondering his next move. He imagined the Holy Children, reunited, swapping stories of the lives they had led while apart.

'Enjoy your triumph,' he snarled. 'It will not last long.'

3

Atrakon Ebrahin sat apart from the others. He had fought alongside them against the Darkwing. But they did not trust him. Why should they? He was a late convert to their cause. Atrakon was an assassin by trade. But for the Holy Child, he would be a mercenary still, taking lives at the behest of the Imperial priesthood. He gave Cusha a sideways glance. She had rescued him from his former life. His brown eyes welled with gratitude.

'Will you eat with us?' Cusha asked, catching his eye.

'Will your comrades accept me into their company?' Atrakon asked.

Oled speared him with a suspicious glare. He'd cast his vote already.

'Come and join us, Atrakon,' Shamana said, ignoring her son's hostility. 'Cusha vouches for you. That is good enough for me.'

Shamana was old. Atrakon didn't know how old. But she had the agility and power of a predatory beast. She was a shape-shifter like her son.

'Thank you.'

Atrakon sat as far as he could from Oled. The cook, Murima, Cusha's adopted mother, was serving what food they had. Atrakon found himself staring at the small band. It was a long time since he had broken bread with a family (for that's what adversity had made this strange group). He watched Murima fussing over everyone. She was Harad's natural mother. She had also taken Qintu under her wing. Cusha, the orphan brought to her by Shamana, also called her Mama-li. The shape-shifters ate in silence. Besides the priestess Shamana and her son Oled, there was Aaliya, third and last survivor of a proud race. Finally, there was the boy-warrior, Gardep.

'Can I ask you something, Gardep na-Vassyrian?' Atrakon asked.

Gardep turned his head. 'Ask your question, Selessian.'

'When I look around those assembled here, I understand their motives. They are slaves, shape-shifters. They have no stake in this Empire. For years, the Sol-ket has treated them as beasts of burden. They have a reason for fighting for their freedom. But why you? You are Sol-ket. You were raised to serve the Imperial cause.' He turned in the direction of the great battle. 'Why are you not over there, fighting alongside your brother Sol-ket?'

Gardep chose to answer simply. 'I have chosen to act according to my conscience.'

'Or your heart,' Shamana said, a mischievous glint in her eye.

Gardep felt Cusha's hand steal into his. 'What Shamana says is true,' he admitted. 'It has been my love for a woman that has changed me. I have served the Empire all my life. Until just a few months ago, I was Sol-ket, raised as a member of the warrior caste and content to remain part of it until I died. The garrison barracks was my home, the prosecution of war my sole horizon. The Sol-ket put a sword in my hand and taught me to cut throats and break bones. They made me a man. Cusha has done something more important. She has made me a man with a soul.'

Gardep thought of his great friend Kulmat, still serving in the Imperial Army. When would he too take the first step to freedom?

'What now?' Atrakon asked.

There was a brief silence.

'You have conquered the Darkwing,' Atrakon said. 'But the job is only half done. The Empire still stands.' He could feel everyone's eyes on him.

'The Selessian is right,' somebody said behind him. It was the final member of the group, Vishtar, the boy they had come so far to free. 'I have been eight years in this prison,' he said. 'Young as I am, I have a right to speak. The Darkwing is broken, but the Muzals still rule. Have you forgotten so soon that the Helat masses have two enemies, not one?'

'Nobody has forgotten,' Shamana said. 'We have come far, Vishtar. We have fought many battles. Soon we will resume our quest. What Atrakon says is true. For freedom to endure, the Empire must fall. But that is for the future. Now it is time to rest.'

Atrakon shook his head. 'The Empire will not rest. Within days the Sol-ket will be scouring the countryside for you.' He hesitated, aware that he had said *you*, not *us*. Oled would surely have noticed the slip of the tongue. 'Already the Hotec-Ra will be drawing up plans to destroy you.'

At the mention of the Imperial priesthood, Oled spoke. 'You should know, Selessian. You served those saffron-robed thugs.'

Atrakon did his best not to react. 'You're right, Oled Lonetread. I served them. But I did not do it for money. A great injustice was done to me and my family. I sold my soul to avenge the wrong.'

Judging by his face, Oled was far from convinced. Atrakon was in no mood to appease him.

'I will not plead with you to accept me,' Atrakon said. 'Ask me to go and I will leave this minute.' He indicated Cusha with an outstretched palm. 'This Holy Child redeemed me. I accept criticism from her and no other. She made me see what I had become. The night-striders are not the only Lost Souls.'

With a fierce stare, Shamana prevented Oled interrupting. 'You are welcome among us, Atrakon Ebrahin. You turned from the Hotec-Ra when you could have bought your freedom from them and returned to your own land. You chose to turn your back on the oppressor and bring our dear Cusha back to us. In my eyes, you are a man of honour.'

Gratitude showed in Atrakon's face. He knew Oled didn't trust him. Changing the giant's mind would take time.

'Then I will stay,' Atrakon said. 'Until your quest is at an end, my sword will be at your service.'

4

At the site of the battle of Jinghara Plain, the council of war was about to end. Linem-hotec, Lord-priest of Rinaghar, the second most powerful man in the Empire after Muzal himself, was speaking. At his side stood Timu-hotec, his new deputy. Linem indicated the demons that were staggering aimlessly across the battlefield.

'The legions of the Lost Souls are disintegrating as we speak. But a far greater threat may yet rise in the east, at the heart of the Empire. All these years, the Blood Moon has cowed our slaves and made them obedient. Ask yourselves this, gentlemen: what will hold them down now?'

He fixed the officers around him with a stare. 'The Helati will not rise this day or tomorrow. They have neither the leadership nor the organisation. Indeed, the servile masses do not even know what has happened here. But understand this, we must track down the Darkwing's conquerors. Though they are few, they may soon become thousands. We must find them and exterminate them before they can spread their message.'

He finished his speech and dismissed the Council. The senior generals, Rishal and Barath, were about to go when Linem called them back.

'Would you accompany me to my quarters?' he asked. 'There is somebody I want you to meet.'

Rishal and Barath followed Linem to his tent. There, they found a junior officer, Murak.

'What's this all about?' Rishal demanded. 'As General of the Grand Army, I am a busy man.'

Linem gave him a superior smile. 'You are keen to capture the rebels, are you not?'

'You know I am.'

'Then this is the man to help you do it.'

Rishal eyed Murak with suspicion. 'I don't understand.'

Linem savoured the moment. 'Meet priest Murak of the Hotec-Ra.'

'Priest!' Rishal exclaimed. 'But I've seen you before. You were at our side during the battle. You're just a cavalry captain.'

'That's what you were meant to think,' Linem said. 'My apologies for the deception, commander.'

'Do you want to tell us what this is all about?' Barath demanded.

'I have been following the Helat plot for many years,' Linem said. 'We in the Hotec-Ra have not been idle. We employed Atrakon to track Shamana and the Holy Children. We rather hoped he would deal with this traitor Sol-ket of yours. Unfortunately, the Selessian has proved a great disappointment to us.'

Rishal scowled. He didn't like being reminded about Gardep. Before he went over to the enemy, the young warrior had been Rishal's own squire.

Linem watched the effect of Gardep's name on the commander before continuing. 'Murak here was our second line of attack. The Hotec-Ra always have several irons in the fire. He was assigned to follow Oled Lonetread's every move.'

'Why was I not informed?' Rishal wanted to know.

'The Hotec-Ra can't afford to be too transparent, General Rishal,' Linem replied. 'One of our roles is to gather intelligence. That requires secrecy.'

'Go on,' Rishal said. He was developing a grudging respect for this priest. A strong right arm wasn't enough to rule an empire. You needed cunning and ruthlessness too.

'I have had my eye on Oled Lonetread for some time,' Linem said. 'I hoped he would lead us to his mother, the

13

She-wolf of Tanjur. This Shamana has been a burr under our saddle for some time. Sadly, the son is as incorruptible as the mother. During his time as a scout at Zindhar, my agents attempted many times to sway him to the Imperial side. He refused every time. We had to find a different way to draw him into our web. We decided to use his soft heart against him. I employed Murak to gain scout Lonetread's trust.' He glanced at Barath. 'You, General, were an unwitting pawn in the game. When you took such an obvious dislike to Oled at Karangpur, Murak saw his chance. He pretended to take Oled's side.'

'By Ra, you're devious!' Barath exclaimed.

'Thank you,' Linem said, revelling in the compliment. 'Trust me, Murak will deliver the heads of the Helat plotters.' He then explained his plan. 'We could move against the Nine. But why rush? We are in a strong position. We can insert Murak into their ranks. Then every time some Helat malcontent rushes to their banner, we will have his name. Why settle for crushing one rebellion when we can behead all future rebellions?'

Rishal and Barath swapped glances. The idea of weeding out potential rebels appealed to them. This priest was a master strategist.

'You have our support,' Rishal said.

'Thank you,' Linem said. 'I will set events in motion.'

Rishal and Barath left satisfied. Linem watched them go then turned to Murak. 'They are pleased.'

'So they should be, Your Holiness,' Murak said.

'You understand what I must do?' Linem asked. 'This has to look convincing or the rebels will not accept you.'

Murak nodded. 'I understand.'

'And you subject yourself to this trial of your own free will?'

'I do, Your Holiness.'

'Before we begin,' Linem said, 'let me give you this.'

He passed Murak a ring. It was embossed with the symbol of the Hotec-Ra. Timu's eyes flashed. This he hadn't expected.

'Your Holiness?' Murak said, allowing it to nestle in his palm.

'Oh, no false modesty, please,' Linem said. 'You understand the significance. It is the seal of the Hotec-Ra, the eyes and ears of the Sun God. My adopted son Shirep wore this ring until his untimely death. Oled murdered him. I want you to take Shirep's place at my right hand. I am making you second lord-priest of the Hotec-Ra. If anything happens to me, you will take my place.'

Timu was staring in horror. So soon after taking the dead Shirep's place at Linem's side, he was being usurped, tossed aside like a discarded garment.

'This is a great honour,' Murak said, his heart pounding with joy at his sudden advancement. He noticed Timu standing just behind Linem's right shoulder. As attendant to the lord-priest, Timu clearly believed he should have received Shirep's ring next.

'You will not be able to wear it until your mission is completed,' Linem said, taking the ring back and handing it to Timu. 'It will be kept for you at the Ziggurat of Ra.'

Timu put the ring away. His resentment was obvious. Murak made a mental note. His rival would not forgive this slight.

Linem snapped his fingers. A dozen saffron-robed Hotec-Ra, led by Timu, lined up to their right and left. Timu passed Murak a phial of green liquid.

'Drain it to the dregs, Murak,' Linem said. 'It will lessen the pain.'

Murak drank the potion. He showed little emotion.

Linem admired him for that.

'You will give me the Helat plotters,' Linem said. 'In return, I will give you a place at my side.' He drew Murak to one side, leaving Timu to seethe with impotent rage. 'Now that you are my adopted son, I wish to share something in confidence.'

Murak waited, barely breathing.

'The Emperor is in his seventy-third year,' Linem said. 'He will not live for ever.'

Still Murak didn't speak but his throat was dry with excitement.

'The army is the Empire's strong right arm, Murak. We, the Hotec-Ra, are its brain. I assume you know which is the more important.'

'Obviously it is the head, Your Holiness.'

'It is. We are taking our first steps towards the Sun Throne, Murak. The defeat of the Darkwing and the Helat conspiracy have given us our chance. We must seize the opportunity before Muzal throws the Empire away.'

He guided Murak back to the waiting priests. He didn't stay to see them give Murak his beating, a beating in which Timu took special, almost sadistic, pleasure. Instead, he slipped out of the tent.

He didn't notice the bat-like shadow that was sweeping towards him.

5

Cusha and Vishtar were sitting side by side, watching the knots of night-striders in the distance. Though they were brother and sister, they had been separated for eight years. They had been talking for an hour, maybe more, rediscovering this or that childhood memory.

'I was the lucky one,' Cusha said. 'Unlike you, I didn't have any memories of a happier time to torture me. But for the memory lamp, I would still be in ignorance.'

'What was it like,' Vishtar asked, 'living without a past?'

'Every waking moment I ached to know who I was,' Cusha told him. 'The day I breathed the vapours of the memory lamp, my heart sang for joy.'

'My memories caused me no pain,' Vishtar said. 'Thinking about you, knowing one day we might be reunited, was the one thing that kept me alive.'

'You must have been so afraid.'

Vishtar nodded.

Cusha hugged her knees. 'We conquered him. We defeated the demon lord.'

Vishtar smiled. For someone who had changed the entire world, his beautiful sister sounded so much like a child.

'All those years in that prison,' Cusha said, 'it must have been terrible.'

Vishtar agreed. 'But I had my books. Just imagine the things I learned during all those hours of study. I can speak ten languages: Khut, Miridan, Selessian, Obir, many more.'

Cusha noticed that he was blinking continually and his eyes were streaming. 'Does the sun hurt them?' she asked.

'I am not used to it,' Vishtar admitted. 'For eight years I have lived in a perpetual twilight. The only source of illumination was a line of flickering candles. Sitting here, beneath the golden sun, it is as if a fire has been lit inside my brain.' He squeezed Cusha's hand. 'For all that, I would not want to return to my cell. Listen.'

Birdsong was welling up from the lower slopes. Together, the Holy Children listened to the chorus of finches.

'Up there!' Vishtar cried excitedly.

A crane was drifting across the sky. To Vishtar, after eight years in a windowless cell, it was impossibly beautiful.

'But for Shamana,' Cusha said, 'none of this could have happened.'

'She is a great sorceress,' Vishtar agreed.

'She wouldn't thank you for saying that,' Cusha told him. 'She is a priestess of the Scales. Sorcery, she says, is for the dark forces of this world.'

Vishtar nodded. Sorcery had given the world the Lost Souls. Who knows what future horrors the dark arts were preparing. The twins talked this way for a long time. Suddenly, without any warning, Vishtar's body went rigid. He convulsed, a glassy stare in his eyes.

'Vishtar!' She took his hand. It was clammy with fear. 'What is it, my brother?'

Then she felt it herself. Though it was not yet noon, she could feel tendrils of darkness coiling around her, constricting her throat, invading her soul. A sliver of ice entered her heart. Vishtar's eyes cleared. Slowly, he straightened his back.

'You sense him too, don't you?' he asked. He didn't need to speak the demon lord's name. 'I can feel his shadow advancing across the land.'

'But we defeated him,' Cusha cried.

'Maybe not,' Vishtar said. 'He has no army. That does not mean he is finished.'

In a gesture of panic, Cusha wound her fingers through her hair. 'Tell me it's not true!'

Vishtar shook his head. 'I am not going to tell you lies, sister. We both sense him. We see the shadow world behind this one, you and I. We hear the chorus of the dead. We feel the pulse of hell throbbing beneath our feet. You must accept the inevitable, Cusha. The monster is not done with us yet.'

Cusha turned away, as if willing the evil presence to fade and die.

'Our companions talk as if the Darkwing's time is over,' Vishtar said, refusing to let her avert her eyes from the truth. 'It is as if they believe there is one less player in the game. We know that to be false, don't we, sister?'

Cusha nodded grimly. 'In spite of all we have done,' she said, 'still his shadow is everywhere. Though his demon army is destroyed and only scattered fragments wander the land, he haunts us still. Somewhere, far from here, he is plotting his revenge.'

They sat there for a long time, imagining the Darkwing.

Vengeful.

Waiting.

6

Linem had two groups of priests to see. The first were the spies. He listened to the reports. It was true. Everywhere, the Lost Souls had become aware of their true nature. They realised that they had once been human, that they had died and risen again to commit countless evil acts. Their memories had reduced them to pathetic wretches, whimpering helplessly as their memories haunted them.

'Have the messenger pigeons returned?' he asked.

'Yes, Your Holiness.'

As yet, there hadn't been a single sighting of the rebels. They hadn't moved from the Black Tower.

'Instruct your men,' Linem said. 'They are to keep watch. The moment the rebels start to move, I am to be informed.'

'Yes, Your Holiness.'

Linem watched the smoke from the funeral pyres climbing to the sky. A battle was over. The war was about to begin. He had been expecting something like this. With each year that passed without news of the Holy Children, he had sensed disaster approaching. The Sol-ket were fools. They thought everything could be resolved by the sword. He knew that knowledge, magic and faith were more powerful tools than any weapon. He turned to a second group of priests.

'I hear you have something to show me,' he said.

'We have,' they confirmed, excitement in their voices.

'Continue,' Linem said.

One of the priests carried a terracotta pot towards him. Linem noticed the way the man walked. He seemed nervous of the pot's contents.

'What is it?'

'Fire Dust. This simple red dust may one day change the world, especially on the field of battle.'

'What does it do?'

'Let me demonstrate.'

The priests dragged in a struggling Helat. Gingerly, the head priest scooped a spoonful of the dust. Then, with a deferential smile in Linem's direction, he showered the dust over the slave. The moment it touched his flesh, the man burst into flames. Within moments he was reduced to a charred corpse.

'Excellent,' Linem said. 'How much of this material do you have?'

'Very little,' the priest admitted. 'It is important to get the mixture right. We have lost ten men during our experiments, all roasted like this poor wretch.'

'Speed up its production,' Linem said. 'This concoction of yours will give us an enormous advantage over our enemies.'

'Yes, Your Holiness.'

The business of the day concluded, Linem set off in the direction of his quarters. On the way, he reviewed progress. Murak would fulfil his mission. Of that he was sure. Not since Shirep had he seen so much promise in a young priest. Linem knew how Timu felt, of course. This was part of a Hotec-Ra's training. Your loyalty wasn't to the priesthood but to holy Ra himself. To become lord-priest, you had to kill your rivals. Either Murak would slay Timu, or Timu would slay Murak. It didn't matter which. The fittest would survive. The victor would come out of the experience stronger, more equipped for high office. What was one dead priest when the entire order would be strengthened by sacrifice?

He thought of the Nine. All the rebels were together now. There were no loose ends. He would use them as bait to catch all the Empire's enemies. Yes, he had good cause to feel satisfied. He was halfway back to his tent when he heard something. He paused and looked around. The bodies had been cleared from this part of the battlefield. It was deserted. Dismissing the noise as an old man's imagination, he continued towards his tent. That's when the noise came again.

'Who's there?' he asked. He turned all the way round. He saw nothing. 'Who's there?'

Before the words were out of his mouth, he felt the rush of wind, glimpsed the shadow looming over him. Instinctively, he shot a look skywards.

'You!'

A moment later the priest was gone.

7

The Holy Children reported their fears to Shamana. In spite of the heat of a Jingharan afternoon, they were both possessed by a deep, numbing cold. Sensing their fear and their almost physical misery, Shamana immediately took them seriously.

'I didn't expect him to move so quickly,' she said.

'So you knew it wasn't over?'

'We are talking about the Darkwing,' Shamana said. 'He is a creature who has ruled the entire western world. Did you really think he would quietly accept defeat then simply fade? No, somehow he will pursue you. His heart has space only for vengeance. It will go on until either you or he is dead.' She hesitated. 'There is a verse in the Book of Scales. I did not understand it until now.'

Cusha's teeth were chattering. Instinctively, though he too felt the primal bite of an impossible winter in his bones, Vishtar slipped an arm round her shoulders.

'This is what it says,' Shamana told them.

> 'From one arid land to another,
> the final struggle will spill.
> There, in the dying light,
> an innocent and generous heart
> must learn to redeem the irredeemable,
> or perish in the attempt.'

'Is there no end to this?' Cusha cried. 'Did we cross the Empire from Parcep to the western lands for nothing?'

'For nothing?' Shamana said. 'What a short memory you have. The demon lord's army is broken. Your brother is restored to you. Is that nothing?' There was anger in her voice.

Cusha regretted her outburst. 'I'm sorry, Shamana. I spoke out of turn.'

'There is no need to apologise,' Shamana said. 'You reported your fears to me right away, that is the main thing. We must inform the others.'

The Nine were soon discussing the unexpected development.

'But what does it mean?' Gardep asked. 'What can he do, one against the world?'

'If he were a mortal man,' Shamana answered, 'I would say very little but I am disturbed by the prophecy of the Scales. It is this reference to the dying light.' She looked at the Holy Children and sensed the bleak, glacial shadow that still had them both in its grip.

'You're right,' Murima said, picking up Shamana's thread. 'He is inhuman. The danger is real. We must watch over the Holy Children night and day.'

Oled frowned. 'I agree that we should guard Cusha and Vishtar. Somehow, that is not sufficient. I don't believe that mere vengeance is enough for the Darkwing. He very nearly won the world. Why would he now settle for revenge against these two? Surely he has greater ambitions.'

'You're right,' Shamana said, deep concern veiling her green eyes. 'Yes, you're right.' She pointed at the Holy Children. 'Just look at these two. Look how they tremble. There is some larger scheme. There has to be.'

'But what *can* he do?' Atrakon said. 'When he still commanded the Lost Souls, all Jinghara trembled before him. He broke bodies like bread and drank blood like wine. He was the consumer of men. But he is alone. I say we put him to the back of our minds and concentrate on raising an army against the Sons of Ra. It is the Sol-ket who crush the peoples of the world under the heel of their

23

boot. They are our first concern, not one solitary, broken creature of the night.'

Oled bristled. 'Since when did the assassin have a voice here? Only yesterday, he was our enemy. Have you forgotten so soon? He kidnapped Cusha. Mere days before that he would have slit your throat without a thought, mother.'

Shamana listened to her son. 'This is true. Atrakon and I crossed swords in the caves of Suravan. But let me ask you this, Oled, is any man beyond redemption? He did everything you say. He also brought Cusha back to us. He fought courageously at our side against the demon lord. Cusha is the Holy Child. I trust her instincts in this.'

Cusha spoke next. 'Don't let suspicion poison you, Oled. I have seen into this Selessian's heart. Atrakon is a changed man.'

'I've said my piece,' Oled concluded gruffly, turning to Shamana. 'Make your Selessian first among men if you wish. I remember what he was. I also remember an infamous day forty years ago. Slave and Tanjur combined to fight their common oppressor. Great Shinar led a revolt that made the Empire tremble. Who changed sides and betrayed the Army of the Free, Selessian? Tell me if you dare. The Empire could have fallen that day but you stabbed our people in the back. That one act gave us forty years of oppression.'

Atrakon reacted angrily. 'You don't need to quote history to me, Oled Lonetread. I know all too well what happened at the Battle of Dullah. The name of Ehut Haraddin, leader of the Selessians that day, is cursed among the great mass of our people. It is the great shame of the desert kingdom that we fought for the Muzals. The clans of Selessia have been regretting it ever since, wishing there was a way to right the wrong.'

'A pretty speech,' Oled retorted. 'There is just one thing wrong with it, Atrakon. After Dullah, your people got to live in peace, their pockets jingling with imperial coin, their mouths stuffed with gold. It's a lucrative business, treachery. You were able to trade and build houses. You were able to have families and break bread with your kinsmen. What happened to the peoples represented here? The Helati have groaned ever since under the yoke of slavery. The Sol-ket beat them, sell their children, kill them. We Tanjurs have been all but exterminated. Three, that's how many survived the manhunt. Talk until the sun grows cold if you want, Selessian, I'll never trust a single one of your kind. Damn you to hell, desert rat!'

With that, Oled stalked away. Aaliya watched him go, then rose and followed.

'I apologise for my son,' Shamana said. 'He grew up suffering for the terrible consequences of Dullah.'

'He spoke his mind,' Atrakon said. 'I hold no grudge against him.'

Murima shook her head sadly. 'We are nine against a cruel monster and an Empire of millions of souls. If we are not united, how can we hope to win?'

Nobody tried to answer her question.

8

Linem opened his eyes and screamed in terror.

'Scream all you like,' the Darkwing said. 'Nobody can hear you.'

Linem looked around. He was in a temple carved out of solid rock. 'Where am I?'

'Don't you recognise it?' the Darkwing said. 'Your priesthood ordered that the monks be evicted from this sacred ground. If I remember correctly, they were all murdered for heresy.'

Linem groaned. 'Nandraghiri.'

'Yes, this is the temple of Nandraghiri. Ironic, don't you think? When your foul priesthood destroyed the old ways and created the cult of Ra, there were two great sites of resistance. There was the Black Tower.' He waved his arm. 'Then there was Nandraghiri.'

In the land of Khut there is a range of colossal mountains. Each peak is like a column supporting the vault of heaven. They are the Mountains of the Moon. High on one such peak, Mount Sangra, there is a long-abandoned monastery. The ancient building is perched just below the summit. It is as bleak as it is remote. The only access to it is by a flight of thirty vertiginous steps, similarly carved into the sheer face. These exposed, slippery steps lead to a hoist. The ropes have long since decayed or been swept away. Once they lowered the monks and visitors hundreds of feet to a broad granite shelf below. But the monks are long gone.

'What do you want?'

'What does any demon lord want?' the Darkwing said, indulging in sour humour. 'World domination, vengeance, perhaps the end of all things?'

Linem rephrased his question. 'What do you want *from me*?'

The Darkwing chuckled. 'I want your magic.'

'I don't understand,' Linem said.

'You have immersed your arms in the vapours of living death,' the Darkwing said. 'Only a score of men have entered the shadow world between life and death. Your power is great. There is something I want you to destroy.'

Linem wondered at his captor's words.

'Cast your mind back forty years,' the Darkwing continued. 'You were a young priest and I a rebel prince.'

'I remember,' Linem said. He could smell the rank odour of his own fear.

'They called me Sabray then,' the Darkwing reminded the priest. 'I adored a woman, a princess of Banshu. But my father . . .' He shook his head. 'Father, is that the word for him?' He leered, his black eyes boring into Linem's brain. 'Lord Muzal, Emperor of all the Peoples, coveted my sweet Kewara. He wanted her for himself. Imagine that, Linem, a father who takes his own son's betrothed. But he did not take her. Princess Kewara defended her honour. She leapt from her window. She died.'

'For Ra's sake!' Linem cried. 'I know the story. I know my part in it, too.'

The Darkwing seized the priest's face with his steely claws. Linem's protest died in his throat. 'If it entertains me to tell my story, then I will tell it.'

Linem held his tongue.

'I raised an army against my father,' the Darkwing said, 'but I lost. So he gave me to you. You used all your arts, didn't you, Linem? I was . . . an experiment. You turned me into this.'

Linem saw his handiwork and his heart stopped for a moment. 'What are you going to do to me?'

The Darkwing seemed genuinely confused. 'Do to you?' He considered Linem's words for a moment then chuckled. 'I understand. You think this is about the way you tortured me.'

'Isn't it?'

'Do you think my ambitions are so limited, priest?' the Darkwing asked. 'Do you think I care about your miserable fate?'

'Then what?' Linem croaked.

The Darkwing started to explain. 'You Hotec-Ra have a great understanding of life and death. You can harness dark magic from the House of the Dead. You used it to make me what I am. But that is such a trifling project. I have powers too. Together we can do something truly . . . final.'

In spite of the mountain cold, Linem's face was covered in a sheen of sweat. 'I don't understand.'

The Darkwing drew closer. 'Then let me explain. The purpose of your order is to serve the Sun God, holy Ra, is it not?'

'You know it is.'

'And you use sorcery to protect your god?'

'Some call it that.'

The Darkwing nodded. 'What I am asking is that you turn those powers inside out. You are going to reverse your life's work.'

Linem shook his head. 'What are you saying?'

'You will endow me with power over your god. I will be the dark lord of eclipse.'

The Darkwing explained his momentous scheme. Linem listened for a few moments then twisted his head round to meet his tormentor's eyes. 'You're insane!'

'Only because you made me so,' the Darkwing said.

'You want me to give you power over the light of the world!' Linem cried. 'It's blasphemy.'

The Darkwing sneered. 'Look at what you did to me, priest. You are no stranger to blasphemy.'

'But every living creature on Earth will die.'

'You're wrong,' the Darkwing said. 'The lord of darkness will survive. Night is my true home. I will have an eternity to spend in its black realm.'

Linem sensed the Darkwing's murderous thoughts.

'You can help me of your own free will,' the demon lord said, 'or you can force me to torture you.' He stroked the lord-priest's throat with a steely claw. 'Believe me, I am good at torture, even better than the Hotec-Ra. Now stop talking. We are about to begin.'

9

The Nine waited in the Jingharan twilight. They were expecting news of the Darkwing.

'How do you know he will speak?' Murima asked Shamana.

'There is a bond between this monster and the Holy Children,' Shamana said. She looked at them. 'Are you ready?'

Cusha and Vishtar nodded.

'Open your minds to him,' Shamana said. 'He is one of the half-dead. You can summon that part of him which is ghost. He will not resist you. Already this day he has teased you with his presence. He is eager to speak.'

'No!' Harad protested. 'You can't ask Cusha to face him again. Hasn't she suffered enough?'

Shamana stood in his way. 'It must be done.'

Murima supported her son. 'Do you want to put them in danger again?' she asked.

'If we do not act,' Shamana said, 'all mankind will be in peril.' She glanced from Murima to Harad. Qintu lingered in the background.

'It isn't fair,' Harad said. 'They have only just escaped from his clutches.'

'I agree with Harad,' Qintu said. 'Let them at least rest.'

'There are three votes against the course of action you propose, Shamana,' Murima said. 'It is too dangerous. Don't make the Holy Children open their minds to him. It could destroy them.'

'Very well,' Shamana said. 'Murima demands your opinions. Oled?'

'We must listen to what the Darkwing has to say.'

'Aaliya?'

'I agree. Do it.'

'That makes three for summoning the demon lord's voice, three against. What about you Atrakon?'

Ignoring Oled's scowling face, Atrakon turned to Cusha and read the message in her eyes. 'We have to know.'

She nodded. 'We do this of our own free will.' She held out her hand to Murima. 'I'm sorry, Mama-li.'

Without another word, she took Vishtar's hands. They stood facing one another and closed their eyes. After a few moments a polar wind rose. It started to gust and whip around them, throwing up stinging dust. Strangely, despite the warmth of the day, everyone felt the arid howl of the wind. It swirled and growled around them, gathering speed, until it was roaring into their faces. That's when the Holy Children reopened their eyes. They resembled the pure obsidian of the Darkwing's.

'Show yourself, demon,' Cusha intoned. 'Your spirit speaks to us. Tell me what you want.'

Gradually a translucent form emerged from the writhing column of wind. Cocooned in the spiralling currents of air, the Darkwing's image floated, initially oblivious to the watching rebels.

'We summon you,' the twins said, 'you who were lord of Lost Souls.'

Reacting to her voice, the Darkwing turned. 'So you wish to speak to me,' he said. 'I am almost flattered.'

'We have both felt your presence,' the Holy Children said. 'You have something to tell us.'

'I have something to tell all mankind,' the Darkwing said. 'I could have been all. So many years I have watched this mortal race of yours as it plundered, tortured and murdered. Mankind is not worthy of its pre-eminent place in creation. You foiled me in this. For that I can never forgive you.'

Murima edged protectively towards Cusha. She had been a mother to her for eight years, ever since the child was found wandering in the fields north of Parcep. It was her deepest instinct.

'If I can never rule the land,' the Darkwing continued, 'if I can never be restored to the man I was, if I can never hold my dear Kewara ever again, then there is only one course of action left to me. There must be atonement. All are fallen; all are corrupt; all must die.'

Shamana stepped forward. His words were like a sliver of ice in her heart. 'What have you done?'

The Darkwing turned lazily. 'Ah, the She-wolf,' he said. 'We are a pair, you and I. I am a lord of Lost Souls and yet I am lord of nothing. You are a queen without a people. What does that make us, Shamana? I'll tell you, it makes us the loneliest creatures in this cold, heartless world.'

'But what have you done?' Shamana cried.

A second image appeared beside the Darkwing's. 'Do you recognise him, She-wolf?'

Though his eyes had been torn from his sockets, Shamana knew Linem-hotec immediately. For half a century he had been the spiritual leader of the Children of Ra. He it was who had ordered the extermination of her people. He had very nearly succeeded in his mission.

'I see you do,' the Darkwing continued. 'I asked Linem to help. It took a little persuasion, but he has been more than generous. He has given his eyes, his blood . . .' The Darkwing squeezed the priest's jaw, making his mouth gape open. 'He has even given his tongue.'

'But to what end?' Shamana cried.

'You disappoint me, She-wolf,' the Darkwing said. 'I thought you would have worked it out by now. The demon lord, sick of life, weary of mankind, abducts the lord-priest of Ra. Put them together, the lord of Lost Souls and the Sun's representative on Earth. What do you have, Shamana?'

Dense grey clouds started to boil behind the Darkwing. Membranes of ice crawled down the granite walls behind him. Tortured faces floated behind the translucent sheets, mouths wide with horror. A blazing, golden orb bobbed amid the raging tide of cloud before sinking into an ocean of whiteness. Finally, all that was left was a black, starless night. Shamana's eyes widened. Now she understood.

'What is it?' Oled demanded. 'What has he done?'

But Shamana ignored her son's question. She had one of her own. She addressed it to the demon lord. 'How long?'

'Such work as this,' the Darkwing said, 'will not be achieved overnight.'

Shamana repeated her question. 'How long?'

The Darkwing's image started to fade.

'How long?' Shamana screamed.

Finally, the Darkwing gave her his answer. 'You have until the first day of Kukhala-Ra. I think it's a good choice, don't you? It gives you a hundred days. On the first day of the month of the sun, the day the Empire was founded, this cursed world will perish.'

Shamana sank to her knees.

'He can't do it, can he?' Oled asked. He turned to the Holy Children. 'Well?' They were recovering from their trance but they did not answer him. He tried one last time. 'Is this possible?'

'It begins from this moment,' Cusha said. 'The Darkwing has drawn upon all the powers of the Hotec-Ra to destroy the thing they venerate and worship most. In the next two months, the sun's power will wane. Its warmth will fade, abandoning the world to a cruel, barren winter. On the first of Kukhala-Ra, the sun will set for the last time. Yes, Oled, it is possible. On that day the world will die.'

CHAPTER 2

The Nine Become Ten

1

'I see them,' Atrakon said.

'So do I,' Gardep confirmed. He noticed Atrakon watching him.

Both of them were gazing through an identical Selessian spyglass. Atrakon recognised the instrument Gardep had in his hand. It had belonged to Atrakon's apprentice Zahar, whom Gardep had killed. Atrakon's eyes remained fixed on the spyglass. If you had killed him for the spyglass, the Selessian thought, I would have had to settle accounts with you. But Zahar had been on a mission to slay the boy-warrior. There would be no more killing. Sensing the tension between them, Shamana made a hasty intervention.

'How many do you see?' she demanded.

It was noon on the eleventh day of Hoj. Already, Commander Rishal ax-Sol had his men out scouring the lands of the west for some sign of the Nine.

'Twenty horsemen,' Gardep replied.

'Twenty-five,' Atrakon said, correcting him.

'We would be foolish to engage them,' Shamana said. 'Even if we won the skirmish, we might sustain disastrous losses. No, we must skirt round them to the south.'

Oled grunted. 'We'll have to fight sometime.'

'Yes,' Shamana said, 'but not yet.' She gestured to Aaliya. 'Take bird form. See if there are any more patrols.'

Without a word, Aaliya transformed. Instantly, a hawk fluttered away through the cloudless sky.

'Where did you find her?' Oled asked, watching the bird vanish into the distance.

At his mother's bidding, he had lived apart from her for eight years, acting as a scout for the Sol-ket. He found this disciple of hers a fascinating creature, and a beautiful one.

'She was with a band of travelling entertainers,' Shamana told him, 'a circus. They kept her in a cage and made her transform to please the rich noblemen and their ladies. When I discovered her, she was filthy and illiterate. Over the years I have trained her in the ways of the Scales.'

'Then you have taught her well,' Oled said. 'She is a graceful and intelligent young woman.'

Shamana had little trouble reading the true meaning behind the words. 'Yes, my son, and of marriageable age.'

Oled gave another of his characteristic grunts. 'I hadn't noticed.'

'Then you're a fool, Oled my boy. I've seen the way she looks at you.'

Oled looked away for a moment. When he did speak, he could only manage this clumsy observation. 'She transforms easily.'

'Yes,' Shamana noted, before adding an acid rejoinder, 'rather more easily than you. I have taught her self-discipline. She hones her arts every day. She can take the form of the tiniest mouse or a rampaging elephant.' She gave him a long, hard look. 'I suspect that, while you have been away, you have been less devoted to the ways of the Tanjurs.'

'I was living among the Sol-ket,' Oled protested. 'They despise shape-shifters. I would have been a fool to risk my life.'

'All the same,' Shamana said, not entirely satisfied,' you have a lot of catching up to do.'

As they went south all that day, Cusha asked the obvious question. 'Why this way?'

'First,' Shamana said, 'we must evade the Sol-ket. No doubt Rishal will be keen to nip our revolt in the bud. When Aaliya returns we will know the scale of our task.'

'Can the Darkwing really kill the sun?' Harad asked.

'Yes,' Shamana answered, 'with the help of Linemhotec, I believe he can. I have witnessed the power of the Hotec-Ra at first hand. They are well practised in their unnatural arts.'

Gardep touched the scar on the side of his face. He remembered them well.

'But to kill the sun,' Murima said, 'to plunge the land into eternal night? How can that be possible?'

'You must remember the nature of the Hotec-Ra,' Shamana said. 'They save Lord Ra, god of the sun. Their devotions ensure his life-giving rays. But they know the deity's weaknesses. The darkness of the underworld can extinguish his golden light.'

'There has to be a way to stop this happening,' Murima said.

'There are two ways,' Shamana said. 'We could try convincing the Darkwing to spare the world.'

Gardep shook his head. 'Surely you're not serious. We have seen the demon lord at close quarters. He is without mercy.'

Shamana seemed to agree. 'The second option is simple. We destroy him.'

'Then we should already be looking for the creature,' Oled said, 'not wandering the land, hiding from Sol-ket patrols.'

'If only the world were as simple as you make it sound, Oled,' Shamana said. 'You can't sort out every problem with that battle-axe of yours. There are nine of us, nine against millions. We are not in a position of strength. Our task was difficult enough when we thought we only had the Sol-ket to contend with. Now that we know the Darkwing's plan, it will take a miracle to achieve our aims.'

'We have achieved miracles before,' Cusha said.

Vishtar supported her. 'We will achieve them again.'

2

The patrol the Nine had spotted did not belong to the Sol-ket. Concealed beneath the army uniforms were the saffron robes of the Hotec-Ra.

'Did they see us?' Timu asked his scouts.

'Yes, Your Holiness. They did as you expected. They turned south. We couldn't stay on their tail. The She-wolf has despatched her apprentice to reconnoitre the area. She would have sensed the trap.'

'Where is she now?' Timu asked.

'She flew east, towards the Grand Army.'

'That makes sense,' Timu said. 'They will be expecting

Rishal to hunt them down. Let's get this done quickly. If your reports are correct they will come this way within the hour.'

Four of the warrior-priests lifted Murak from the litter on which he was being carried. At the first movement, he groaned. His face was puffy and covered in blood. Both eyes were completely closed. Timu looked down at him and remembered the way Linem had given him the ring. It would have been so easy to remove the upstart. But Linem would have known. No, Timu thought, I will bide my time. It is between me and Murak now. One of us will succeed His Holiness. I must ensure it is me.

'Bind him to the tree,' Timu ordered.

The priests reached for Murak's wrists.

'Not like that. Hang him by the ankles.'

The priests registered shock at his words.

'A man's legs are stronger than his arms,' Timu said. 'If this plan is to succeed, he must survive.'

It wasn't the only reason for hanging Murak upside down. Timu wanted to see him that way. The upstart deserved this moment of humiliation. Soon, Murak was hanging suspended from the tree, tied by the ankles to a sturdy branch. He had lost consciousness again.

'Check that he's still alive,' Timu ordered.

The nearest priest pressed a finger to Murak's pulse and nodded. Suppressing his disappointment, Timu mounted his horse.

'Let's go,' he said. 'There is no more we can do here.'

3

Aaliya was returning from Commander Rishal's camp. In spite of the losses they had suffered, the Sol-ket remained a formidable force. Worryingly, they showed no sign of returning to Karangpur or Parcep. It looked as if they were going to remain in the field. By way of confirmation, their patrols were already ranging far and wide across the endless Jingharan Plain. She rode the warm air currents and found it hard to believe that what the Darkwing had said was true. How could the sun die? Yet Shamana was concerned and she, more than any living soul, understood the extent of the Hotec-Ra's power. Sweeping westward, Aaliya allowed her thoughts to fill with Oled. Did he notice her at all? She was still wondering about him when she saw something.

'What is that?'

Like a dark fruit hanging from a tree, there was the body of a man. Aaliya immediately feared a trap. But she had been brought up on the Book of Scales. It was her duty to aid her fellow man. Circling the area several times, she made sure there were no lurking assassins. Finally, still darting her eyes left and right, she settled on the branch of a neighbouring tree. After a further inspection of the terrain, she transformed and dropped agilely to the ground.

'Are you alive?' she asked, as she approached with care. There was no answer. 'Tell me,' she whispered in the bloodied man's ear, 'do you live?'

That's when she heard a low moan. Supporting his weight, she cut his bonds and lowered him to the ground. For the first time, she could see the extent of his injuries. He had been beaten senseless. Judging by the extensive bruising, more than one man had been involved in the vicious assault.

'By the Four Winds!' she gasped. 'Who did this to you?'

The man gave no answer. Aaliya produced a mixture of herbs from her belt. It would ease the pain. Knowing that her companions would soon be passing this way, she stayed with him until they arrived.

'He's in a bad way,' Shamana said, examining the victim.

'Is there anything you can do for him?' Cusha asked.

'It's hard to say. He's lost a lot of blood. Is this the way we treat our poor, suffering brothers?'

For all the horrors she had seen, Shamana had never got used to mankind's appetite for cruelty. Beside her, Aaliya was unbuttoning the man's tunic to examine him. She stopped abruptly.

'What is it?' Shamana asked.

Aaliya pointed out a scar in the shape of the rising sun. 'He bears the mark of the Ket-Ra. This man is a Warrior of the Sun, a Sol-ket.'

Her words raised a disturbing thought in the minds of two of those present. Simultaneously, Gardep and Oled leaned forward to take a closer look. Gardep, thinking for a moment it might be his childhood friend, Kulmat, was relieved to discover that he was wrong. It was Oled who saw something familiar in the battered features.

'Can you clean some of the blood away?' he asked.

Aaliya did as he had asked, gently cleaning the face before her.

Oled gasped. 'I know this man. We fought battles together. When I was a man alone, he befriended me. He is a Sol-ket officer.'

Aaliya wiped more blood from the man's face. 'Are you sure?'

'Yes, it's him,' Oled confirmed. 'His name is Murak.'

4

Timu hadn't even dismounted when he saw a cadet running towards him. He recognised Kulmat, Commander

Rishal's new squire.

'Your Holiness,' Kulmat panted. 'The commander requests your presence. Rishal-Ra has some terrible news.'

Timu followed without a word. When he entered Rishal's tent, he saw that General Barath was also in attendance. Two generals, Timu thought: this has to be important. His gaze settled on a third man, a young soldier from the ranks.

'Tell His Holiness what you saw,' Rishal ordered.

The Sol-ket hesitated.

'You have nothing to worry about,' Barath reassured him.

'I was in a cremation party,' the warrior explained. 'We were gathering the dead. We had just built our third funeral pyre. That's when I saw His Holiness, Linem-hotec.'

He had Timu's attention. 'This is about Linem?'

The Sol-ket started to babble. 'I tried to help him. I really did. But I was too far away.'

'Just tell your story,' Rishal said. 'I've already promised you immunity. You won't be punished.'

'I don't think Linem saw us,' the Sol-ket said. 'We were about to light the pyre. Linem was a hundred paces from me. I noticed him turning round as if somebody had spoken to him. Then I saw the reason. It was the Darkwing.'

'The demon lord,' Timu said. 'He was here?'

The Sol-ket nodded. 'I know I should have shouted a warning. I should have got my bow. But it happened so fast. I failed, Your Holiness. I just watched.'

Timu grabbed the warrior by the jaw. 'I don't want your excuses. All I want is the facts. Did the Darkwing take Linem-hotec?'

Frightened, bulging eyes stared back at him. 'Yes.'

'Get this fool out of my sight,' he barked. 'Is this how you train your men, Rishal-Ra, to gape uselessly while the first priest of the Empire is spirited away?'

Ignoring Timu's sleight, Rishal dismissed the Sol-ket. Relieved, the warrior scurried away.

'Now you know why I had to see you,' Rishal said.

Timu frowned. 'What could the Darkwing possibly want with Lord Linem?'

Something in his tone made Rishal wonder whether he knew more than he was saying.

'Who can read a demon's mind?' the Commander said. 'He abducted my own daughter, Julmira. She has only just been restored to me, after an ordeal that could have taken away her sanity.'

Timu wanted to tell Rishal that, compared with Linem, his daughter was of no importance whatsoever. But he knew it would have been a foolish, possibly fatal, thing to do. Rishal was the greatest warrior in the land. He also had a famously foul temper.

'I know the priesthood has certain tricks up its sleeve,' Rishal said. 'Is there anything you can do? We need to know why he took Linem.'

'It will be done,' Timu said. 'Come to Lord Linem's quarters tonight.'

5

Only Atrakon was against establishing camp.

'Are you mad?' he demanded. 'You are taking on an entire Empire and fighting for the survival of the world, yet you stop for one man.'

'The ways of Fate are complex,' Shamana said. 'This

event may be important in the wider scheme of things. If you want to care for all mankind, you must start with one suffering soul.'

Atrakon shook his head. 'I'll never understand you, She-wolf. Sometimes I think you are the wiliest creature on this Earth. Other times you seem both innocent and gullible.'

'Maybe it is good that we are so different,' Shamana said.

A few paces away, Aaliya was tending to Murak. Beside her patient there were the tools of the surgeon's trade: needles, a mortar and pestle, turmeric to heal wounds and garlic to kill bacteria.

'Is he any stronger?' Oled asked, looking down at his sleeping friend.

'It is too soon to say,' Aaliya answered. 'None of the wounds is fatal. He is young and strong. His body must be given time to return to harmony and balance. He needs rest.'

Oled nodded. 'Tell me when he wakes.'

He was about to go when he heard Murak's voice. 'Oled,' he croaked through blistered lips, 'is that you?'

'It is.'

'Thank Ra.'

'Did Barath do this to you?' Oled demanded, remembering the way the general had looked at them together.

'He ordered it,' Murak said. 'The Hotec-Ra carried out the punishment.'

Oled's green eyes flashed. 'Why would they torture one of their own?'

'You've just answered your own question,' Murak said. 'You knew I had doubts. I no longer serve the Empire of the Sun.' Aaliya offered him a cup of water. He paused to take a sip. 'You know how I feel about the cruelty of the Sol-ket. That's why we became friends.'

A frown creased Oled's forehead. It was a long journey from doubt to rebellion. What had brought about the sudden conversion? Oled had served as a scout in the Imperial Army. In all that time he had only known one man to break from the Sol-ket. That was Gardep. But he was a most exceptional case. A warrior like him only emerged once in many generations.

'But you chose your path, Murak. You could have come with me when I left Karangpur. You had only to ask.'

Murak took another sip of water. 'What do you want me to say, Oled?'

Oled came straight to the point. 'I want you to tell me the truth.'

Murak nodded. 'I owe you that. I thought I could continue in the service of Ra. I fought the demon host at the battle of Jinghara Plain, though it meant standing shoulder to shoulder with a man like Barath. But our friendship opened my eyes, Oled. I found your words running through my mind. I envied you your faith in the future, the strength of your conviction. You made me believe that there could be another, better world where no man held another as a slave. You made me question every belief I ever held.'

Still Oled was wary. 'You chose to remain with the Children of Ra,' he observed. 'You did that of your own free will, even though I had offered you an alternative. You could have come with me. What changed your mind?'

'It was Barath. The man is a monster.'

'Yes,' Oled murmured. 'Barath.'

Like all the Sol-ket elite, Barath detested shape-shifters like Oled more than any living creature. Maybe he detested those who befriended the dragon-people just as much.

'Do you remember Karangpur?' Murak asked. 'He tried

44

to kill us – you for daring to stand up to him, me for being your friend.'

'Even so, you remained Sol-ket.'

'I did,' Murak said. 'At first I thought I had made the right choice. Barath acted as if we were reconciled. Then, after the Battle of Jinghara Plain, came the reckoning. The moment the threat of the Lost Souls was lifted he denounced me as a traitor and handed me over to the Hotec-Ra for interrogation. He told them that I would have important information regarding your whereabouts and those of the other rebels.'

'What did you tell them?'

'Nothing,' Murak said. 'There was nothing to tell. I didn't know where you were.'

Oled turned the story over in his mind. He wanted to believe Murak. 'The Hotec-Ra rarely let their prisoners live,' he said, still cautious.

'Do you really think they intended me to live?' Murak cried. The effort caused him to cough and double up in agony. 'Look at my wounds, Oled. They hung me from a tree in the middle of nowhere. They meant me to die.'

Aaliya caught Oled's eye. 'Oled, he is still weak.'

Murak waved her away. 'Say you believe me. We are friends. Surely you know I am telling the truth.'

'Are you done with the Warriors of Ra?' Oled asked.

'I despise them,' Murak said. 'Give me the chance and I will devote myself to the cause of freedom. You must believe me.'

Oled hesitated for a moment then seized Murak's outstretched hand.

'I believe you.' He glanced at Aaliya. 'Now we are ten.'

6

The order to retire to bed sounded over the camp as Rishal and Barath entered Linem's quarters. Timu greeted them by pressing his palms together and giving a little bow. There was incense in the air and one of Linem's robes was hanging outstretched above a flaring brazier.

'What's that for?' Rishal asked.

'Watch,' Timu said.

He sprinkled a fine powder on the fire. Immediately the flames leaped and started to consume the saffron robe. As they burned away the thin material, purple wreaths of smoke started to curl towards the roof of the large tent. Within these ribbons an image formed. Barath was the first to spot Linem.

'By Ra, the creature has mutilated the Lord-priest! See his bloodied features.'

Seemingly unmoved, Timu peered into the flickering picture of a place far away. He saw the columns that helped support the roof, the painted frescoes on the walls. 'I know this place,' he murmured.

Rishal opened his mouth to ask a question. Timu silenced him with a raised hand. 'The frescoes are damaged,' he said. 'See, there is Lord Ra. But a second figure has been chiselled away. It is the moon god, Sangra. Yes, I can name this place. It is the monastery of Nandraghiri, one of the main sites of the Scaline heresy.'

'Explain,' Rishal ordered, nettled by the impudent way Timu had treated him. It was the second time this priest had offended in this manner.

'Many generations ago,' Timu began, 'there was a strong Scaline strand in our faith, blathering about peace and a community of equals. While the dominant Hotec-

Ra proclaimed that there was only one true deity, the Sun god himself, the followers of Udmanesh preached a different view. They set it down in the Book of Scales. In their eyes, all must be in balance, light and dark, sun and moon, male and female. My predecessors all those centuries ago responded to heresy in the only way possible. The blasphemers would have weakened our stock and condemned us to inferiority among the peoples of the world. So our ancestors rooted out the false prophets, putting the heretics to the sword.'

'This monastery of Nandraghiri,' Rishal said, tiring of the lesson in theology, 'where is it?'

'It is in the Mountains of the Moon,' Timu told him. 'It was built high on Sangra Peak. The followers of Udmanesh thought that they would be safe there.' He smiled. 'They were wrong, of course.'

Barath saw movement. 'Look,' he said, 'somebody's coming.'

A shadowy figure stepped over Linem's bloodied corpse. A scream tore through the gloom of the monastery.

'It's the demon lord,' Timu said.

The priest and the two generals watched the Darkwing stalk across the chamber, folding his leathery wings. He carried two struggling figures, one under each arm. The first was a young man of about twenty summers. The Darkwing shackled him to a wall. The second was a Khut maiden in her eighteenth year, recognisable by her patterned woollen dress. The Darkwing inspected her for a few moments before adding her to his collection. A dozen men and women, some near to death, others untouched, sat manacled to the wall.

'You know what he does with his captives,' Barath said. 'He feeds on their blood.'

Rishal clenched his fists. His own daughter was very

47

nearly added to the list of the monster's victims. But Timu wasn't interested in the Darkwing's menu. He had seen something.

'Look there,' he said. He peered into the fading image. 'No!' he said, as the smoke thinned and danced away through the roof vents.

'What did you see?' Barath asked.

'Something was painted on the wall. It vanished before I could make it out.'

'I can tell you what that was,' Rishal said.

The other two men turned towards him.

'It was the sun symbol of the Hotec-Ra.'

Timu's eyes widened. 'Was there anything else?'

'Yes,' Rishal said. 'I saw a hieroglyph.'

Timu pushed a sheet of parchment towards him. 'Draw it!'

Though he resented Timu's tone, Rishal did as he was told. He drew a crude house with twin towers and a large door. There were no windows.

'By the holy face of Ra!' Timu groaned. 'No. No. Lord Linem, why did you succumb?'

'What is it?' Rishal asked. 'Why are you so frightened?'

'Don't you recognise the symbol of the House of the Dead?' Timu asked. 'By terror, the Darkwing forced His Holiness to invoke the Spell of Eternal Darkness.'

Rishal was growing impatient. 'Meaning?'

'It is the greatest magic known to our order,' Timu explained. 'Nobody outside the Hotec-Ra is meant to know of its existence. From the day of its invocation, the spell will drain the strength of the sun's rays. One day soon, the sun will set, never to rise again. Life on Earth will perish.'

'Can this be true?' Barath asked.

Rishal had seen the priest's face. He knew the answer to Barath's question.

'Do we have long?'

'I must consult the holy texts.'

'Make it quick, priest,' Rishal said. Suddenly he felt very cold.

7

The Khut maiden was called Jinghirza Ghun, daughter of a Khut hammer-lord. The Darkwing had seized her and one of her father's attendants from their village that very day. She watched him, a shadowy, gliding figure, without mercy or humanity. Still naively unaware of what he wanted from her, she spoke innocently, thinking that she could appeal to his conscience.

'No,' she pleaded, 'please don't hurt me. I have done no wrong.'

The Darkwing examined her face. His prey did not usually speak. This one had spirit. 'Who said you've done anything wrong?'

'Then why am I here?' Jinghirza asked. 'My father is chieftain of our clan. We are poor but we have animal pelts and some gold. My family will pay a ransom for me.'

'Ransom!' the Darkwing snarled. 'Is that what you think? I am not some bandit to be bought off with ransom.' He leaned closer, his rancid breath making Jinghirza turn away in revulsion. 'I'll tell you what I want from you, my child.' He whispered into her ear before watching with pleasure as her face started to twist in horror.

'My blood! Please no!'

'Oh, don't plead,' the Darkwing said, disappointed. 'I thought you had courage. I thought you, unlike these spineless wretches, were worthy of my intentions.'

Grasping at any shred of hope, Jinghirza answered. 'Do you respect courage, my lord?'

She had his attention. 'It . . . interests me.'

'Then I will be brave.'

The Darkwing blinked, intrigued by the new strength in her voice. 'What are you saying?'

'Set me some challenge,' Jinghirza said. 'Put my courage to the test. Give me a chance to win the right to live.'

'You remind me of someone,' the demon lord said. 'She had courage.'

Jinghirza didn't know what to make of this, but at least he was speaking to her. Maybe, so long as she entertained him, she could delay the date of her execution.

8

Shamana waved away Oled's protests.

'We have to go,' she said. 'The sun has already risen. Soon the Sol-ket will be on our trail. We have cleaned and sewn Murak's wounds. There is no infection. He has a few broken ribs. They are bound and will mend by themselves.'

'Do you really think he is ready to be moved?' Aaliya asked, torn between her loyalty to Shamana and Oled.

'Normally I would say no,' Shamana answered. 'But we have no choice.'

Oled made a decision. He transformed into a water buffalo. Seeing what a struggle it was for him to manage even this beast, Shamana wrinkled her nose.

'Put him on my back,' Oled said. 'Aaliya, you will ride with him. Do what you can to ease his pain.'

Aaliya nodded. 'I have already mixed the herbs.'

Atrakon shielded his eyes against the rising sun. 'So we're going east now?'

Shamana nodded. 'It is dangerous, but the Darkwing is the first priority. We strike east, then north to the Mountains of the Moon. If the sun dies, there will be no world to win.'

Oled was still unhappy. 'And why did you need to strip him?'

'Do you remember nothing I taught you as a child?' she grumbled. 'There is an old Hotec-Ra trick. I have even employed it myself. They can trace their men through the pigment they dye into their robes.'

'So you think Murak's a spy?' Oled asked, accusation in his words.

'I didn't say that,' Shamana replied, 'but, in the Hotec-Ra, we face a cruel and brilliant opponent. I'm not going to take chances.'

'I don't know what you're complaining about,' Qintu said. 'You got the spare clothes for this Sol-ket from me and Harad. Why does he get our best things?'

'Oh, do stop complaining,' Shamana told him.

The exchange over, the group of companions, now numbering ten, set off.

'This is madness,' Gardep said.

'Why is it?' Cusha asked him.

'Are you serious?' Gardep demanded. 'On that plain, just beyond the Demon Wall, there will be tens of thousands of Sol-ket, every one of them looking for us.'

'What would you do?' Vishtar asked.

Gardep shrugged. 'I have been trained to command regiments of warriors. I would build an army.'

Slowed down to ease Murak's suffering, the band made only gradual progress but, by evening, they were within sight of the Demon Wall.

'Once we are through those gates,' Shamana said, 'we will turn north-east.'

'What about Sol-ket patrols?' Gardep asked.

'If they come,' Shamana answered simply, 'we will fight them.' The words were no sooner out of her mouth when a sword hissed from its scabbard. 'What are you doing, Atrakon?' she demanded.

Atrakon pointed with the point of his sabre. 'Over there,' he said, rummaging for his spyglass, 'on that ridge. Somebody's spying on us.'

Shamana trained her hawk's eyes on the silhouetted figure. 'You need have no worries about him,' she said. 'The watcher is a night-strider.'

9

Vishtar rose in the early hours of the night. He had only gone a step when Shamana stepped out of the gloom. She had taken first watch.

'Where are you going?' she hissed.

Vishtar's whispered answer held no surprises. 'I have to talk to that night-strider. It's me he wants. Shamana, I can hear his voice in the wind. He is calling me.'

'I heard nothing,' Shamana said.

'He talks only to the Holy Children.'

Shamana nodded. 'It makes sense. You have the power to end his suffering. What will you say to him?'

'I will ask why he continues to walk the Earth,' Vishtar replied.

'It is a good question,' Shamana said. 'I have been asking myself the same thing. Tell me his answer.'

'You expected me to do this,' Vishtar said. 'How did you know?'

'You and your sister are the Holy Children. You live in the regions between the living and the dead. If anyone should speak to the Lost Souls, it is you.'

'So should I wake Cusha?' Vishtar asked.

'No, let her sleep,' Shamana said. 'I sense that you are the one he wants. You can lay the Lost Souls to rest. Go to him.'

Without another word, Vishtar walked off into the night. He followed a trail of trampled grass all the way to the ridge where Atrakon had spotted the night-strider.

'You prepared a trail for me,' Vishtar murmured.

He continued along the makeshift path until he saw movement ahead. For a moment, aware of his own vulnerability, Vishtar glanced back at the camp where Cusha and the others were sleeping. That's when a skeletal figure stepped out in front of him, his haunted eyes flashing in the dark. When the creature emerged into the moonlight, Vishtar noticed that his exposed bones were blackened, as if by fire.

'Why did you take so long?' the night-strider asked. 'I have been waiting for you since sunset.'

'I was afraid,' Vishtar replied honestly.

'I am not the one you should fear.'

Vishtar felt an icy ripple down his spine. 'What do you want from me? Why did you not destroy yourself like so many others of your kind?'

'You tread the empty lands between life and death,' the night-strider said, echoing Shamana. 'You released us from our monstrous contagion. Because of you, the pollution of hell has cleared from our minds. You and your sister freed us from the demon night. We owe you a great debt.'

'But you have chosen to continue walking the land. Why?'

The night-strider touched the decomposing flesh on his face. 'Many of my kind chose self-slaughter. They could not live with their memories, the consequences of what they had done. I could not follow them. How could I leave a world blighted by horror and oppression? I have to put right my wrongs. I am not the only one of the night breed to think this way.'

To Vishtar's surprise, the creature bent his knee and held out a pair of beseeching hands. 'You must not leave a job half done. Help us compensate for our crimes. Lead us to redemption, I beg of you.'

'How do I do that?'

'Search your soul, Vishtar,' the night-strider said. 'You are the Holy Child. It is your destiny to lead the Lost Souls. United with your sister, you exercise great powers. You must find a way to lift the burden of guilt from our shoulders.'

'Do you know what the demon lord has planned?' Vishtar asked.

'I do.' The night-strider's suppurating lips formed something approaching a smile. 'I was in his service. When he invoked the spell, I felt the world shudder.'

'You say you want redemption,' Vishtar said.

'More than anything.'

'Then help us prevent this evil happening,' Vishtar said. 'Defeat your former master; save this world from eternal night; and I will give you peace.' The night was thick round them, like swamp water. It was as if streams of darkness were flowing out of the underworld and spreading through the silent land. 'How many of you are there?'

'So far,' the night strider replied, 'we are but a few score. But there are many more out there waiting to join us. Our tormented brothers and sisters are scattered far and wide.'

'Then these are my orders to you,' Vishtar said. 'Gather your forces. Return in your hundreds, in your thousands. When that is done, come and find me. Will you do this?'

'Of course,' the night-strider said. 'You are the Holy Child, my redeemer.' He turned to go. Vishtar could make out a line of shadowy figures waiting for him.

'Wait,' Vishtar said. 'I don't know your name.'

'There will be no names,' the night-strider said. 'Names belong to a man's mortal life. For me, all that ended many years ago.'

'I have to call you something,' Vishtar insisted.

The night-strider thought for a moment. 'I will take the name of the king of scavengers,' he answered. 'Call me Jackal.'

10

Far to the north, in the Mountains of the Moon, the Darkwing sat brooding in his lonely monastery. He wandered its echoing corridors, gazing at the broken statues of the god Sangra. He hated these moments of lucid thought. They filled him with humiliation, rage, bitterness, a mixture as corrosive as acid. How he loathed to be reminded of what he had been. The thought of what he could have become, the greatest of souls, the ruler of the entire world, tortured him. Even the world of nightmare was preferable to memory. He remembered his youth. He remembered falling in love. The scent of his loved one's hair was in his nostrils. Her voice sighed on the wind. Then he recalled the fall.

'Kewara.'

She had been so young, so wonderful and alive. He had adored her. He ached to remember the moment he had seen her body, broken on the stone square beneath her window. Once more, the demon lord saw the halo of scarlet blood, the still open, startled eyes. He had taken her in his arms, marvelling at how small she was, fragile as a baby bird fallen from its nest. Even now, he could not believe that the life had gone out of her. Then the torment of memory got too much for him. With his steely claws he slashed the walls, scoring deep gouges into the rock.

'No! No! No!'

His voice reverberated through the monastery, sending ripples of horror down the spines of Jinghirza and the other prospective victims. The madness of regret and loss seared through his veins. He saw it all: his rising against his Imperial father; his defeat; his ordeal in the torture chambers of the Hotec-Ra and finally his reincarnation as the Darkwing. In that moment he despised himself for what he had become, a creature so foul that he was abhorred throughout the land. But he despised the world more. He staggered towards the monastery's entrance and gazed out at the mist-hung mountain world. Turning, he fixed his eyes on the image of the sun, painted on Nandraghiri's walls in Linem's blood. For a moment, in his madness, he fancied he saw it sinking into the House of the Dead.

'I see you, Holy Child,' he screamed, imagining the girl with death in her eyes. Cusha's face danced in his imagination. 'You denied me,' he snarled, 'you and your whining whelp of a brother. You're what stood in my way, a pair of adolescents. Well, enjoy the moment of your triumph. It will be short-lived. Who can live without the sun? Only I. We are marching towards the day of reckoning, Holy Child. This will be my revenge. One by one, I will watch the death-throes of my enemies. I will walk between their funeral pyres. Then, when the last of them has perished, I will be master of the world.' Cusha's eyes filled his mind. 'I will be the thing you called me.' He roared it through the precincts of Nandraghiri. 'I will be lord of nothing!'

CHAPTER 3

First Blood

1

The goblet that Rishal hurled across the tent almost struck Kulmat in the face. The twelfth day of Hoj had begun badly for the commander of His Imperial Majesty's frontline troops.

'Say that again, priest!' he roared.

The supercilious smirk that most high-ranking Hotec-Ra usually wore had vanished from Timu's face.

'General Rishal,' he protested. 'There is no need for violence.'

'There's every need for violence!' Rishal bellowed. 'You tell me the world is going to end in a mere two months, you tell me the sun is dying, and you whine about a thrown cup? I should pull out your fool tongue and nail it to my battle standard.'

Timu did his best to reassure the commander. 'All is not lost, Rishal-Ra.'

Kulmat succeeded in reaching Rishal without injury. 'Please listen to what he has to say, Master.'

Rishal planted his hands on the table in front of him. 'Spell it out, priest. I'm a soldier. I need an enemy to kill, an objective to take. Tell me there is something we can do to stop the creature.'

'I spent the whole of last night reading Linem's notes,' Timu began.

Always the man of action, Rishal growled his frustration. 'The world ends on the first day of Kukhala-Ra and you sit up reading! Am I surrounded by lunatics?'

He glimpsed Kulmat's pleading eyes and made an effort to restrain himself.

'Very well,' he said. 'Continue, Your Holiness.'

'Again and again, Lord Linem stressed the importance of the Holy Children,' Timu explained, 'in destroying the Darkwing's hold over the Lost Souls. According to the journal, their power stems from their relationship to the House of the Dead. The female can call to the undead. She can summon their spirits from the House. The male has the power to redeem them and to give them rest. We have no choice. We must harness their power.'

Rishal's eyes bored into the priest. 'Are you going to get to the point?'

Timu gave a sigh. 'We need the girl Cusha. Her brother too. They alone can destroy the Darkwing.'

Rishal stared back in disbelief. It was a few moments before he said anything. 'We are talking about the same Cusha we left out there on the Jingharan plain?'

'That was before we knew what the Darkwing had

planned,' Timu said, a bead of perspiration working itself down his brow.

'Nonetheless,' Rishal said, with menacing calculation. 'What I say is true, is it not? We allowed the key player in the game to wander the plain. Though we need her to stop the Darkwing, we managed to let her wriggle out of our grasp.'

'You agreed to Lord Linem's plan,' Timu objected. 'We would insert Murak into the Helat conspiracy and tease out any prospective rebels. That way we would behead any future rebellions. It was a brilliant plan.'

'Oh yes,' Rishal said, his voice little more than a whisper, 'it was very clever, too clever in fact.'

'Commander . . .'

Rishal was in no mood to listen. 'Can you trace Murak?' he demanded. 'Maybe we could get to her through him. Is it possible to use that trick you used to find Linem?'

Timu shook his head. 'I tried. They seem to have destroyed his tunic. Nevertheless—'

Rishal held up a hand. 'I have heard enough from the Hotec-Ra for one day,' he said. 'Get out.'

Timu saw this as an affront to his dignity as a senior member of the priesthood. 'I really must protest!'

Rishal gripped the hilt of his sword.

'General Rishal,' Timu cried, 'you cannot draw your sword against a representative of the Hotec-Ra.'

'Then do as I say,' Rishal told him, beginning to slide the blade out of the scabbard. 'Get out of my sight.' He hurled a final comment at Timu's back. 'And don't come back until you have used your infernal tricks to contact His Imperial Highness. I need his permission to abort our original plan. We have two months to avert catastrophe. To hell with clever stratagems. I want the Holy Children and I want them now.'

Once Timu was gone, Rishal turned to his squire. 'How did it come to this, Kulmat? Why do all the threads of this tale coil around me? This Cusha once worked in my kitchens. She cut the onions and ground the cumin. I barely gave her a second glance. How did a mere slave-girl come to hold our destiny in her hands?'

2

The girl of whom Rishal spoke was standing on the Demon Wall, looking back towards the Black Tower, remembering the desperate struggle there. She sensed Gardep behind her. He lifted her plaited hair and stroked the nape of her neck.

'Don't,' Cusha giggled. 'Somebody might see us.'

'You amaze me,' Gardep said. 'Shamana tells us the world is dying and you are worried about a little thing like this.' His fingertips lingered on her back, marvelling at the softness of her skin. 'I want to be with you every moment of every day. Weeks may be all we have.'

'This is all so new,' Cusha said. 'It's . . . frightening.'

Gardep laughed. 'Can it be true? You face the demon lord with invincible courage yet you flinch at my touch.'

'I barely understand my own feelings,' Cusha admitted. She looked at him. The padded cavalry jacket he usually wore was spread over the battlements. He was wearing a light, armless, white tunic.

'Do I sound stupid?' Cusha asked.

'Not at all,' Gardep said. 'It is the same for me. We will unravel this mystery together.'

Cusha turned to look at him. 'Can that really be true? Am I more than a despised Helat to you? I used to hear the Sol-ket boasting about their conquests. You soldiers, you think you can do what you like with us.'

Earnest as ever, Gardep sought to reassure her. 'I am not like them. To me, you are every woman on Earth. This I swear: I will protect you till my dying day.'

Cusha looked around to make sure they were alone. Then, heart beating fast, she reached up and laid her palm against his face.

'No,' she said, 'you are not like them at all.' She ran her hands over his arms and paused. 'What's that?' There was a tattoo on his upper arm.

'Oh that,' Gardep said. 'I have had it since I was a child.'

'Let me see.' The tattoo was of a lion with a bull's head. 'Do you know what it means?'

Gardep shook his head. 'It is from my childhood in Vassyria, a time I can barely remember.'

Cusha was about to enquire further when Gardep's eyes hardened. His attention had been drawn to something behind her.

'What is it?' she asked, beginning to turn.

Before she could get halfway round she heard the jangle of harness. A Sol-ket patrol had just topped the rise and was galloping towards them. Already, arrows were clattering against the battlements of the Demon Wall. Stringing his bow, Gardep killed two of the riders. Simultaneously, Cusha ran to raise the alarm. Even as she reached the keep, her companions were already responding to the drumming hooves. Aaliya shot her bow with great skill, adding to Gardep's deadly volleys. Another Sol-ket thudded to the earth, lifeless. As one, Oled and Atrakon hurled themselves from the walls, toppling two of the enemy from their mounts.

'Draw your bows!' Shamana yelled at Murima, Harad and Qintu. 'Cover us.'

With that, she joined Oled and Atrakon in taking the

fight to the enemy. Cusha raced back to Gardep.

'Train your arrows on the rearmost riders,' Gardep told her, before vaulting from the walls after Shamana. 'You must prevent them surrounding us.'

The fight under the wall was a fierce one. Though, in the initial skirmish, they were just four against three times that number, Gardep and Atrakon, Oled and Shamana had halted the Sol-ket charge, clashing with the lead riders. The hail of arrows from the Demon Wall split the patrol in two, forcing the following cavalry to slow. Gardep killed his man and raced to engage the next. Oled and Atrakon had similar successes. Shamana alone was in a vulnerable position. Wedged between two horsemen, she was parrying their blows desperately. She succeeded in cutting one of them down but, as she spun round, the second was slashing downwards.

'No!' she screamed.

Even as the blade sliced through the air towards her, the attacking Sol-ket sagged in his saddle before tumbling to the ground.

'Whose arrow was that?' Shamana gasped. 'Who saved me?'

Oled pointed to the battlements. There, Murak was reeling backwards, exhausted by the effort of drawing the bow. In spite of his injuries, he had rescued the She-wolf with a single arrow.

'Do you trust him now?' Oled asked.

Shamana said nothing. She was troubled by the slowness of her reactions. Even a year ago, she would have transformed into some small creature and scurried out of danger. By the Four Winds, she thought, I'm getting old. She didn't dwell on the moment long. Her sword arm was needed. Soon the tide of battle was turning the way of the rebels. As the front riders fell, those at the rear swung their mounts round and started to retreat. Instinctively, the Tanjurs and their Helat allies lowered their weapons.

'What are you doing?' Gardep roared. 'Don't let a single one get away.'

He shot his arrows quickly, one after the other, killing three of the fleeing Sol-ket.

'Shoot,' he yelled, 'or they will be back.' He met Atrakon's eye. 'You understand, don't you?' he demanded.

Atrakon nodded and raised his bow. Reluctantly, their companions followed suit. Soon all the enemy lay dead. Without pause, Gardep gathered the horses. Some marvelled at the businesslike way he handled death. Others found him merciless, a dog of war.

'We must move the bodies out of sight,' he said. 'There must be no evidence of this fight.'

It was only when he had finished dragging the last body into the nearest keep that he noticed the way the others were looking at him.

'What's wrong?' he asked. 'It is first blood to us. We have fresh horses and there are no survivors to reveal our position.'

Oled shook his head. 'You may be right, Gardep. But you are more bloodthirsty than the assassin Atrakon. I just wonder whether you don't enjoy your work too much.'

3

As his troops engaged the rebel band far away, in golden Rinaghar, capital of the Empire, His Imperial Majesty Muzal ax-Sol was eating a light lunch of spiced lamb. Every mouthful was a trial. The Emperor, who was still robust for an old man, had bad teeth, the legacy of too many sumptuous banquets, too many sugary sweetmeats. Though his cooks were the finest in the land, even they couldn't make it so tender his gums didn't ache.

He downed a glass of *kinthi*, the strong Sol-ket brew, before pushing the plate away in disgust.

'Is there a problem with the food, Your Imperial Majesty?' his personal slave Sanjay enquired.

'Yes, there's a problem,' Muzal grumbled. 'The meat is tough and the spices haven't been fried properly.'

'Should I order the guard to execute the cook?' Sanjay asked.

'Yes,' Muzal said, 'make it slow. Pull out his teeth. Have the dog suffer as I suffer.'

Then, as Sanjay hurried away to give the command, Muzal called him back. 'No, let him be. He's the best of a bad lot. I've lost three cooks this month.'

Sanjay was still wavering when a page scurried past him across the marble floor.

'What now?' Muzal groaned. 'Will the demands of State never leave me in peace?'

The page flung himself to the floor, prostrating himself before the Empire's absolute monarch.

'Imperial Majesty,' he began, averting his eyes from Muzal's face, 'I have news.'

'It will be bad, I expect,' Muzal said.

'I am not privy to the contents of the communication,' the man said, continuing to grovel at Muzal's feet. 'It is from His Holiness, Lord Timu of the Hotec-Ra. Lord Asun took the message.'

'Then I want to hear from Asun.'

It was as if the page was trying to bury himself in the marble. 'To that end, Priest Asun respectfully requests your presence at the Great Ziggurat. He says the message is for your ears only.'

'Tell Asun to come here,' Muzal told him.

'Lord Asun fears that, outside the precincts of the Ziggurat of Ra, there may be spies. This communication must not fall into their hands.'

At this, Muzal relented. He was in his seventy-third year. The twenty-fifth monarch in the six-hundred-year-old dynasty had no heir. As a result, a virtual army of princes, priests and generals were eager to succeed him. They circled the Sun Throne like so many sharks and barracudas. Muzal knew that, should there be any news that reflected badly on his rule, he might succumb to the poisoner's phial or the assassin's dagger. Rinaghar had become a nest of cobras. With each year that passed, his rule was becoming more fragile, more vulnerable to their venom.

'Sanjay,' Muzal said. 'Send the Eternals to me.'

The Eternals were his palace guard, elite Hotec-Ra. They were sworn to give up their own lives to keep him safe. Once they were assembled, he crossed the elevated walkway which connected the Imperial Palace with the Ziggurat of Ra. Resplendent in white and gold robes, the Imperial crown on his head, Muzal entered the inner sanctum of the Ziggurat. There, Asun-hotec was waiting for him.

'Your Imperial Majesty,' he said, bowing, 'I apologise for the inconvenience. There was no other way to give you the news in confidence.'

'Come,' Muzal said. 'Walk with me.'

He wasn't altogether happy that he had to discuss such matters with a man who was only the third most senior man in the priesthood. They stepped out onto the steps of the Ziggurat. From their vantage point they could see all Rinaghar, the jewel of the Empire.

'Here is a transcription of Lord Timu's communication,' Asun said, handing Muzal the parchment.

Muzal started reading it. 'There must be some mistake,' he said. 'Linem abducted? I don't believe it.'

'You must read on, Majesty,' Asun said. He saw Muzal's eyes widen. His jaw went slack. 'Is this possible?' he asked. 'Can the sun burn out?'

Asun was silent.

'Well, speak, damn you!'

'When the priests of Ra opened the gates of the House of the Dead, we stared into the face of eternal night.' He hesitated. 'We had a great dilemma. What do you do with the knowledge that you can end all human life? Nobody ever dreamed it would come to this.'

Muzal felt like tearing out Asun's throat. 'Cut to the chase, priest!'

'This is the essential law of the universe, Majesty: all things will pass, even the sacred light that warms our world.'

'Blasphemy!' Muzal roared. 'The sun is the holy face of Ra. It will last for all time. Isn't that what your priesthood teaches in every temple throughout the land?'

'The Spell of Eternal Darkness had to remain secret,' Asun whispered, 'lest some enemy, your son for example, were to discover its existence.'

Muzal detested being reminded of his son, the foul traitor Sabray, now the Darkwing. 'My damnable son *has* discovered the secret!' he bellowed. He was beside himself with fury and terror. For long moments, he paced the Ziggurat. Finally, he spoke. 'Can nothing be done?'

'There is but one fragile ray of hope.'

'Tell me.'

'The Holy Children were able to tame the blood lust of the Lost Souls. They broke the Darkwing's power over his minions. Perhaps they can prevail against him one more

66

time.' Asun gave Muzal an enquiring look. 'Lord Timu awaits your orders, Imperial Majesty.'

'Find these Holy Children,' Muzal said. 'Harness whatever power they have. Send my miserable son to Hell.'

Asun bowed. 'It will be done, Imperial Highness.'

4

Kulmat waited until Rishal's lamp was extinguished. A short while later, sure that his knight was asleep, the cadet quietly made his way across the camp. He wanted to find a quiet spot where he could think. Soon he reached a spreading acacia tree. Sitting beneath its branches, he pulled out a scrap of bloodied bandage.

'Are you with her, Gardep?' he murmured.

The bandage was a memento of their childhood friendship, a bond of which he dared not speak, lest Rishal fly into a rage. Kulmat leaned back against the tree trunk and gazed up at the star-studded sky. He felt a sudden chill. Was that the first sigh of the dying sun? Kulmat remembered Rishal's question that same evening: how did a mere girl come to hold their destiny in her hands? It made him recall a sunset months ago in Tiger-gated Parcep. That night, Gardep had fallen in love with Cusha.

'Soon,' Kulmat said, with only the stars and the moon to hear him, 'the order will come to hunt you down, my brother. Flee, flee with all your cunning and all your strength. It would break my heart to face you on the field of battle.'

He pressed his hand to the sun symbol tattooed above his heart and prayed that they would never draw swords against one another. That's when he realised the futility of his wish. He was praying to a dying god.

5

Jinghirza Ghun was woken by a curious sound, a kind of wet mumble. For a few moments she peered into the darkness, trying to see what it was. Then she made sense of the crumpled figure chained to the far wall. A moonbeam caught his face. It made her shudder. The Darkwing had torn out his eyes and drained copious amounts of blood from his veins. By some miracle the saffron-robed priest was still alive.

'Why did he do this to you?' Jinghirza whispered, fearing for her own fate.

The priest tried to speak. Then Jinghirza understood how the sound had been made. The monster had cut out his tongue.

'By the gods of the sky!' she croaked, overwhelmed with the horror of the priest's tormented features.

'Don't speak to him!' a familiar voice hissed behind her.

The Darkwing stalked across the temple. His gaze swept the room, making his captives cower.

'If a single one of you dares address this priest or offer him succour,' the demon lord told them, 'you will pay the ultimate price.'

Some nodded, others simply hid their faces in shadow. Jinghirza alone found her voice. 'What has he done to be treated so?'

'You again,' the Darkwing said.

'Do you have no mercy?' Jinghirza asked.

The Darkwing gave a desolate chuckle. 'You are not the first mortal to ask me that question. The answer is no.'

Turning his back on Jinghirza, the Darkwing hauled Linem to his feet. The priest uttered a gurgling scream.

'Have you reconsidered your answer?'

Linem nodded.

'Then I will let you live another day.'

Jinghirza watched as the monster dragged his pathetic, broken captive away. She did not know what the Darkwing had asked him. She did know it could only lead to evil.

6

At dusk the Tanjurs sat together, breaking bread. There was precious little and nothing to accompany it. Hunger was becoming a major problem. Gardep was busy in the keep, aided by Atrakon. He had some plan.

'The boy-warrior is the most natural fighter I have seen,' Oled said. 'For all that, he has faults.'

Shamana chewed a spiced flatbread. 'We all have faults, my son. There are even some Tanjurs who struggle to take the form of a buffalo.'

Ignoring his mother's chiding, Oled persisted with his argument. 'Gardep's faults are great. When he fights, the blood lust takes him. He is not content with defeating his enemies. He wishes to annihilate them. This is not the way of the Scales. He lacks the quality of mercy.'

Shamana patted Oled's arm. 'Don't judge him too severely. He is young. All his life he has been immersed in the brutal ways of the Sol-ket. For all that, he has a great heart. He knows the ways of our enemy. His destiny is mentioned in the Book of Scales. He will be our general.'

'I will not oppose you,' Oled said. 'He is a leader of men, that is clear. He is loyal and true. I believe he has grown to love the cause of freedom. But he does not understand our ways. For there to be peace, all things must be in balance, light and dark, male and female. Do you think he can ever walk the path of reconciliation? Can he learn to live alongside his former foe?'

'We will teach him,' Shamana said. 'You are quiet, Aaliya. What is your view?'

'I understand what Oled says,' Aaliya replied. 'In battle, the gentler side of Gardep's character is lost. But look at him with Cusha.'

The lovers were sitting side by side, their heads together, sharing some secret.

'He loves her dearly,' Aaliya said. 'Surely his adoration for her will soften him.'

'It is a gamble we must take,' Shamana said. 'There has not been a rebel leader since Shinar with his qualities of generalship. Do you agree, Oled?'

'So long as we are ready to temper his excesses, yes.'

'Aaliya?'

'He will give us steel. We will give him heart.'

'Then it is agreed,' said Shamana. 'On the shoulders of this boy we will build the new Army of the Free.'

7

The Darkwing laid the semi-conscious priest on the stone floor, deep inside one of the caves that honeycombed Sangra peak. He gazed into the depths of a well. Here, the monks of Nandraghiri had drawn their water.

'It is time to do me one more service,' the demon lord said.

Broken, humiliated, Linem offered no resistance. The Darkwing dipped his claws into the well and watched the water trickle between them. Next, he upended a basket of cobras and watched them swarming in the black water. In the next few moments he deposited the contents of half a dozen more baskets into the well.

'Now the Lyrian fire.'

Linem craned to hear what he was doing. The Darkwing poured a thick stream of the pitch-like substance on the water's surface until it was entirely covered by a thick membrane of the stuff.

'One last ingredient,' he hissed.

He seized the priest, holding his head in a vice-like grip. At last understanding the direction of the Darkwing's thoughts, Linem gave a wet scream of despair, but the demon lord slashed his throat and deposited him into the vile soup. Then, with a razor-sharp claw, he sliced a vein and watched his own black blood ooze from the opening and spill into the well. The water immediately boiled and roared. Then he lit the Lyrian fire and watched. The bubbling mixture popped and hissed like a spitted bull. Clouds of scarlet and black smoke billowed across the chamber. Eventually, the flames burned down and the Darkwing could see the results of his experiment. He bathed in the foul concoction. When he surfaced, he roared across the mountains.

'Hitherto, there has been too much of the human in me,' he declared to the desolate peaks. 'I allowed the vestiges of the boy I was to cloud my judgement. Now I am made anew. I will not make the same mistake again.'

8

When Rishal's scouts reported the disappearance of one of his patrols, he marched them to the map that dominated his quarters. He tapped the line that symbolised the Demon Wall. 'Show me where they were last seen.'

'They broke camp here and turned north-west.'

Rishal examined the map. With his finger he drew a

triangle. 'Send every available man,' he said. 'Flood this area with light cavalry. We want soldiers who are mobile and quick. What trackers do we have?'

'There are the Khut mercenaries.'

'What about Selessians? They are the best at this kind of work.'

At this point General Barath interrupted. 'I hear that a fresh unit of Selessian cavalry was recently ordered to Karangpur. They are supporting the new garrison.'

Rishal nodded. 'I want them here as soon as possible.'

'Are you sure that's a good idea?' Barath asked. 'The Hotec-Ra tried to use the assassin Atrakon Ebrahin. They gave him good gold to capture the Holy Child. He repaid them by murdering Lord Shirep-hotec.'

'You can't judge all Selessians by the actions of one renegade desert rat,' Rishal said. 'He had the misfortune to meet the slave-girl Cusha. She has an uncanny ability to twist men's minds. No, the Selessians have served us well. Have you forgotten their role in our greatest victory? They turned the tide at Dullah.'

'That was forty years ago,' Barath answered. 'These are not the same men.'

Rishal was not swayed. 'Forget Atrakon,' he said. 'The warriors of the desert kingdom have been a mainstay of Imperial rule. We need them, Barath-Ra.'

Barath succumbed. 'As you wish.'

Having won the argument, Rishal strode out of the tent towards the horses. 'Tell the men to saddle up,' he shouted to Kulmat. 'We're going hunting.'

'At night?'

'That's right,' Rishal said. 'We're going after the rebels. When the Holy Children go to face the demon lord, it will be in our company.'

'What about their companions?'

'Why, they will die, of course.'

Kulmat ordered that the muster be sounded. As he watched the Sol-ket strapping on their armour and saddling their mounts, he could feel his heart kicking against his ribs. It was the moment he'd been dreading.

9

A dozen companies of Sol-ket horse were scouring the territory Rishal had marked out on the map. They rode together as far as the razed fort of Zindhar before splitting into separate units. It was Kulmat's northernmost patrol that discovered the bodies Gardep had had hidden.

'Cadet Kulmat,' one of his men shouted. 'You must see this.'

Kulmat followed him into the keep. By a shaft of moonlight, he saw the bodies. Though there had been an attempt to burn them, he recognised Gardep's hand in their destruction.

'Bring me a lamp,' he said.

Yellowish light bathed the room, illuminating the macabre scene. He discovered a Selessian sword-cut on one man, the effects of a Tanjur axe on another.

'It's them, for certain,' he said.

He made a search of the room. Once, fastening on some detail, he paused.

'What is it?' the soldier asked.

'Nothing,' Kulmat lied. 'I recognised one of the dead. He was in my dormitory at the Academy.'

The soldier didn't see him move one of the corpses with the toe of his boot, obscuring something. Returning the light to its owner, he climbed to the roof of the keep and surveyed the darkened plain. He had been scanning the area to the north and east when he saw a light. It was a faint glow, like dancing fireflies.

'Is that the best you can do, Gardep?' he wondered out loud. He heard the jangle of harness. Keen to keep Rishal out of the keep, he called to him. 'Commander, what do you make of this?'

Rishal raced up the steps to join him. 'It could be a campfire.' His brow furrowed. 'I thought I taught Gardep better.'

'The same thought occurred to me, Rishal-Ra.'

Rishal pondered for a while. 'What about the keep?'

'Nothing.'

'This fire,' Rishal said, 'it's got to be a ruse of some kind. Investigate the lights, Kulmat. The rest of our troops will ride in a line from the Great Wall to Zindhar. If we travel due north-east, we are bound to discover them.'

Kulmat nodded. Once Rishal's back was turned, he permitted himself a smile. Ten minutes after the Sol-ket left the keep, one of the bodies moved. It was covering a disguised hatch. Gardep was the first to emerge. Crouching low, he padded over to the door. After that, he checked the walkways and the bleak terrain either side of the Demon Wall. Was that really Kulmat's voice he had heard? Could it be his friend had protected him? Satisfied that the Sol-ket had gone, Gardep returned to the hatch.

'You can come out,' he hissed.

At that, one by one, his companions climbed out of the underground storage cellar. Oled appeared last, carrying Murak on his back. They then recovered the horses from a ravine on the far side of the Great Wall and rode due east, behind the Sol-ket lines.

10

It was mid-morning the next day when Rishal called off the pursuit. The light had been made by a flock of goats with lighted tapers attached to their horns. None of the companies had discovered any trace of the fleeing rebels.

'Somehow,' he said, 'they have outwitted us.' He scowled. 'These Khut trackers weren't much use, Kulmat. We need the Selessians.'

'I agree, Rishal-Ra.'

Rishal looked at his squire. For somebody who had been awake the whole night, he was surprisingly bright and cheerful.

'If I didn't know better,' he said, 'I'd think you were relieved that we've missed Gardep. I hope there are no divided loyalties.'

'My friendship for the traitor is over,' Kulmat said, a little too hurriedly for Rishal's liking.

'We will track him down, Kulmat,' Rishal said. 'When we do, I want to know you will do your duty. Would you have any hesitation in executing him?'

'None, Rishal-Ra.'

The prompt response seemed to appease the general, for now.

'Do you think there is a chill in the air this morning?' Rishal asked.

Kulmat thought for a moment, then nodded. 'I noticed it last night too, Rishal-Ra. Could this be the beginning? Is the sun's light starting to fade?'

The question hung. Neither of them had an answer.

'We will return to camp,' Rishal said. 'Before you take your rest, Kulmat, organise more search parties. The manhunt continues night and day until we find them.'

'Of course, Rishal-Ra.'

Again, Rishal noticed the cadence of happiness in his squire's voice. 'There's a spring in your step, Kulmat,' he observed.

'Do you think so, Rishal-Ra?' Kulmat asked.

Without another word, he fell in behind the general. In his mind's eye he recalled the search he had conducted in the keep. Step by step, he went through the events. He had seen the bodies and asked for the lamp. He had stopped suddenly, noticing a trickle of blood between the floor tiles. The soldier accompanying him had asked if there was anything wrong. Kulmat had dismissed the question, of course. There was nothing wrong, nothing at all. By over-looking the tell-tale trickle of blood between the tiles, he had just saved the lives of Gardep and his friends.

11

That same morning, through his window, General Ghushan ax-Sol, nephew of the Emperor and the new commander of Karangpur, saw one of his cadets climbing the steep flight of stone steps towards him. He closed the ledger in which he was writing.

'The signallers have just received this message by relay from the Grand Army,' the soldier said.

'Let's see it,' said Ghushan. He read the communication. 'Who commands the new Selessian regiment?'

Omar arrived ten minutes later. 'You sent for me, Ghushan-Ra.'

'Your presence is required at the front.'

Omar frowned. 'But we have barely installed ourselves at Karangpur. It is only four months since we left Juttah. My men are exhausted.'

'The order comes from General Rishal ax-Sol.'

'What is this about?'

'You're new to this land, aren't you, Selessian?'

'Yes.'

'Let me give you some advice, Omar. Never question an order. Just obey. What's your full name? I need it for my reports.'

'My name,' the Selessian said, 'is Omar Ebrahin.'

CHAPTER 4

The Spark

1

The fifteenth day of Hoj was a turning point. Hungry, relentlessly pursued by Sol-ket patrols, the ten companions made a fateful decision. With Sol-ket banners seeming to appear from every direction, they had gone two full days without food or rest. The close attentions of the Sons of Ra prevented even the resourceful Tanjurs from hunting. In the late afternoon the band took their rest in the shade of a tree while the horses drank from a stream. Shamana and Aaliya transformed into serpent eagles and flew away to search for food and pursuing troops.

'Did you see any Sol-ket patrols?' Oled asked on their return.

'You can't miss them,' Aaliya answered, anxiety crackling in her voice. 'They're everywhere. We have something of a lead on the nearest patrols but that is no reason for complacency.'

'I just wish the Four Winds would send us a sign,' Shamana said. 'Our wanderings are pointless. The Sol-ket are blocking our progress at every turn. We can't move north towards the Mountains of the Moon. There is no sign of revolt from the people. What is happening to our quest?'

Cusha felt the stirrings of unease. Shamana, usually so sure of herself, so steadfast, seemed to be losing hope.

'Maybe we should move on,' Vishtar suggested.

'I'm all for that,' Qintu said. 'I'd like to live to savour the delights of adulthood.'

Murima shook her head. 'You just want to savour the delights of good cooking,' she said.

'What's wrong with that?' Qintu asked. 'My stomach thinks my throat is cut.'

'The boy has a point,' Oled said. 'We've got to eat. We're bound to run into the Sol-ket again. If we cross swords with them while we are hungry and exhausted, we're finished anyway.'

Shamana shielded her eyes. 'The nearest patrols are still miles away,' she said. 'We've made good time. There's a village down there. Let's see if they can spare us some food.'

'Are you sure about this?' Cusha asked. 'For generations, the weaker of our people have sold runaways and insurgents to the Sol-ket simply to be able to live.'

'No,' Shamana said, 'I'm not sure at all. But does anybody have a better plan?'

A chorus of silence followed, deciding the discussion's outcome. On entering the village, the riders drew a small crowd of villagers. They looked apprehensive.

'Who is the village elder?' Shamana asked.

A tall, lean man of some sixty years stepped forward. 'I am Bulu. Who are you?'

There was some hesitation. How should they approach this? It was Murima who broke the silence. She was taking a great gamble. 'I am Murima-ul-Parcep,' she said. 'Everyone here has heard of my father. His name still echoes through the villages and towns. It was Shinar.'

Gasps erupted from the crowd. Even Shamana was taken aback by Murima's boldness.

'Is this true?' Bulu asked.

'What woman in her right mind would lay claim to his name?' Murima demanded. 'Who would choose to draw the wrath of the Sol-ket down upon their head? What I tell you is true. My father was the spirit of revolt in this land. The long night of oppression is coming to an end. I and my companions seek to stir the Helati once more.'

At that, several mothers hurried away with their children, as if mere words could put them in harm's way.

Bulu's eyes settled on Shamana. 'And you?'

Emboldened by Murima's example, Shamana slid from the saddle. Closing her eyes, she took the form of the She-wolf, the avatar she had assumed long ago as Queen of the Tanjurs. 'Do you know me now?'

'Your coming was prophesied,' Bulu said. 'I was at Dullah. As a young man, I fought for Shinar. I saw you ride by with him. Forgive me for not recognising you.'

Shamana smiled. 'Many years have passed since those days. Long servitude has withered me. My hair is grown grey. How has life treated you, Bulu?'

He raised the stump that had once been his right hand. 'This was my punishment at the hands of the Sol-ket. They let me keep the left so I could still work. I was one of the lucky ones.'

He caught Cusha's eye. Instantly, his face seemed to glow. He stepped forward and inspected her features. Then, very deliberately, he approached Vishtar.

'There is a resemblance here,' he said. 'Are they brother and sister?'

'You know them,' Shamana said. 'Any Helat who survived the horror of Dullah and the privations of the intervening years will recognise the Holy Children. Look at their eyes. Do you study the Book of Scales, Bulu?'

In the absence of his right hand, the elder raised his left to denote the symbol of the Scales. Some among the crowd gasped.

'I have dreamed of this day,' he said.

'Are there any Sol-ket here?' Shamana asked.

Bulu shook his head. 'The Lost Souls took the slave-master two weeks before the monsoon rains. We were able to hide from the demons in the granary cellars. We were lucky to survive.'

'I am aware that we are putting your lives in jeopardy again,' Murima said, taking over from Shamana, 'but we are hungry and exhausted. Do you have any food?'

Bulu cast his eyes round the expectant crowd. 'We will feed you,' he said.

The decision would have grave consequences. Before nightfall the next day, it would bring the swords of the Sol-ket down on his village.

2

Omar Ebrahin was brushing his fine Selessian mount in the garrison stables when he heard movement behind him. Two Sol-ket were watching him.

'Can I help you?' Omar asked.

'You can take your horse out of this stall,' one said.

Omar stopped brushing. 'I don't understand.'

'Auxiliary troops use those stables,' the second Sol-ket said.

Omar glanced through the open door at the neighbouring stables. 'It is identical to this one,' he said.

'Then there is no problem about moving your horse, desert rat.'

'There isn't room in there,' Omar said, choosing to ignore the insult. 'Every stall is occupied. That's why I brought my mount in here.'

'Well, you can take it out again,' he was told. 'These stables are Sol-ket only.'

'You use Selessian horses, just as we do,' Omar objected. 'All the animals come from the same stock.'

'But the riders don't,' came the answer.

Omar was considering his options when his second-in-command, Mehmet, appeared in the doorway. 'What's this,' he enquired, 'the famous Sol-ket hospitality?'

His arrival gave the Sons of Ra pause for thought. Then two more black-garbed Selessian warriors joined Mehmet.

'Do you still want me to move my horse?' Omar asked. The Sol-ket scowled and brushed past him. Omar addressed their backs. 'I'll keep the beast here then,' he said.

'Were they bothering you?' Mehmet asked.

'What do you think?' Omar said. 'You'd imagine they'd be grateful. It was our fathers and grandfathers who won the Battle of Dullah for them.'

'Gratitude isn't a Sol-ket quality,' Mehmet said. 'When do we ride north?'

'First light,' Omar said. 'I'll be glad to get away from this place.'

'Do you think the Sol-ket will treat us differently anywhere else?' Mehmet asked.

'I doubt it,' Omar said. 'They let us fight their wars. They let us die to protect their way of life. That doesn't mean they treat us as men.'

'Agreed,' Mehmet said. 'It makes you wonder why our ancestors fought for them at all.'

3

The next day, barely a mile from Bulu's village, a patrol was watering their horses. The Sol-ket officer filled his canteen from the stream and hung it from his saddle.

'Have the scouts returned?' he asked.

'Not yet.'

The officer cursed. 'It's like finding a grain of sand in the desert.' He cupped his hands and washed his face. 'Damn this Jingharan dust,' he said.

He was about to make another comment about the hardships of soldiering on the north Jingharan Plain when something caught his eye. A light was flashing.

'Did you see that?' he asked his squire.

'Yes, it's a signal.'

They both read the same message.

'Do you think it's a trick?' the officer said.

'I don't know, Master. Look, there it is again. It's coming from that village.'

'Who's going to know Sol-ket signalling code in a Helat village?'

The message was repeated twice more.

'Should we send scouts, Master?' the squire asked.

The officer shook his head. 'No, if there's any truth in the message, scouts would give the enemy a chance to escape. We will take the whole company.'

The message read: *The rebels are here. Give me time to*

get away. Come at noon. It was followed by a code word.

The officer smiled. 'We can trust the messenger. We will enter the village at the time he says.'

4

The Darkwing wanted some sport. 'You asked me to set you a challenge,' he told Jinghirza. 'Do you remember?'

'Yes, I remember.'

'I am ready to set you your first test.'

The Darkwing gave a gleeful cackle and seized her. As he flew with her over the snow-capped peaks, she looked down. The world seemed to swim around her, the vastness of its empty, fatal spaces menacing her. It would be so easy for the monster to let her fall to her death. She didn't pray for mercy. She hoped he was entertained.

'Where are we going?' she asked, her voice trembling.

'There.' He set her down on an exposed shelf of rock, scoured by ferocious winds.

'What must I do?' Jinghirza asked.

'Look to your left,' the Darkwing said.

Then she understood. There was a curving bridge. The far end of it vanished into mist. It was a fragile structure, carved by some ancient, superhuman craftsmanship from solid rock. It was barely broad enough to set your foot on it and it was covered with a sheen of ice. Jinghirza looked at the treacherous causeway and shuddered. Far beneath the jaws of a vast monster, made of mountain and mist, yawned open.

'Well,' the Darkwing asked, 'do you accept the challenge? If you don't, I will drain your blood here and now. I will make it quick.'

But Jinghirza shook her head. 'I will walk the bridge,'

she said. 'What is my reward for succeeding?'

'You get to live another day,' the Darkwing said.

'I want food for myself and the other prisoners,' Jinghirza said. 'I want you to promise not to feed on them.'

The Darkwing seemed fascinated by her defiance. 'Granted,' he said.

Biting her lip, Jinghirza took her first step. To either side of the narrow walkway there was a dizzy precipice. It looked impossible to negotiate the bridge. The thin ribbon of rock shrank almost to nothingness. But Jinghirza was a maiden of the Khut nation. Hers was a fierce, rugged people, stubborn as the most obstinate mule. In her soft, goatskin shoes, she made steady progress, always aware of the crags and faces thousands of feet below. On she walked, feeling out every inch of the icy surface with her feet, gasping when she slid. Already she was reaching the highest point of the bridge's arc; forcing herself to climb though it was like trying to grip on glass. The rock underfoot was more slippery than ever. Fear clawed at her with each uncertain step, with each heart-stopping slip.

'Please,' she said, her words flying up to her gods, 'don't let me fall. Don't give the monster the pleasure of seeing me fail.'

There was a wobble here, a half-slip there, but eventually she succeeded in reaching the far side. Taking a few rubbery steps away from the edge, she sucked in mouthfuls of air, grateful to be alive.

'You did well,' the Darkwing said, appearing out of the mist. But praise was followed by menace. 'Soon we will have better sport,' he said. 'The next trial will be more difficult.'

The prisoners ate that night. Grateful eyes turned towards Jinghirza. She didn't return the looks. Dread had her by the throat. She was already thinking about the next ordeal.

5

Murak was growing stronger by the day. He took the bowl of chickpeas spiced with garlic from one of the village women and thanked her. He was wiping the bowl with a piece of flatbread when Shamana appeared at the door to the mean hut in which he was sitting.

'You are recovered,' she said.

'The pain is easing,' Murak agreed.

'I came to thank you for what you did at the Demon Wall,' Shamana said. 'You saved my life.'

Murak shrugged. 'You and your comrades saved mine. It's a fair trade.'

Shamana offered her hand. 'Welcome to our fight for freedom, Murak.'

Murak took her hand. 'Will we tarry long in this village?'

'Why do you ask?'

'We are vulnerable here. It is only a matter of time before the Sol-ket follow.'

'You're right,' Shamana said. 'I have come to the same conclusion. We must not put this village in danger by our continued presence. We are about to leave.'

This seemed to satisfy Murak. They would be gone by noon. 'How have you kept your faith all these years, Shamana?' he asked.

'It is the nature of our cause,' Shamana answered. 'Throughout all the generations of mankind, kingdoms and empires have sought to conquer in the name of this or that tyrant. Udmanesh was the first man to claim the world for all mankind. Our long struggle is not to place the Helati or the Tanjurs above other mortal men, but to permit all men and women to hold the wealth of the land in common. All humanity will be free and equal before the Four Winds.'

'It is a great dream,' Murak said. 'Will we live to see it come true, do you think?'

'By the grace of Destiny, yes.'

Hearing footsteps, Shamana turned. 'Oh, it's you Oled.'

The giant seemed happy to see his mother and his friend talking together. 'The horses are ready,' he said. 'The villagers have given us provisions for our journey.'

'Then it is time to depart.'

Oled and Shamana left the hut. Murak followed a few moments later. The whole village gathered to bid farewell.

'May the Four Winds watch over you,' Bulu said.

'And you,' Shamana answered.

They exchanged the symbol of the Scales. Then, sending Aaliya to scout ahead, Shamana led the rebels north east out of the village.

6

A second signalled message had warned the Sol-ket patrol to expect a shape-shifter to go looking for them. The Warriors of Ra duly concealed themselves in a coppice half a mile to the west of the village.

'Do you think that's one of them?' the squire said, watching a hawk fluttering overhead.

'It's possible,' the officer said. 'We will remain out of sight for another few minutes.'

The time seemed to crawl by.

'Did you have any luck contacting the other patrols?' the officer said.

'Only one,' the squire said. 'They are going to teach the village a lesson for harbouring the rebels.'

'Good. We will have the glory of capturing the Holy Children.'

He was excited at the prospect of such an important mission. Only one thing troubled him. Why had their agent in the enemy camp asked them to wait until noon? Still, his orders were to follow the agent's instructions. He watched the sky. It was clear. He gave his men their battle orders.

'Our rules of engagement have been changed,' he told them, 'on the instructions of His Imperial Highness, Lord Muzal. The Holy Children we take prisoner.' He smiled, relishing the task ahead. 'The rest we kill.'

7

Shamana was concerned by Aaliya's report. She had discovered evidence of two Sol-ket patrols but she had only been able to locate one of them.

'Where?'

'South of the village.'

'We took care to leave nothing to implicate the villagers,' Oled said. 'They'll be quite safe. Bulu's a shrewd fellow. He'll know what to say.'

Shamana should have found her son's words reassuring. Nevertheless, she couldn't drive a nagging worry from her mind. Where was the missing patrol? She had trained her apprentice well. Aaliya was a meticulous scout, unlikely to miss a score of armed men. No, there was something wrong. Other forces were at work.

'I want you all to be quiet,' she said.

Glances were exchanged.

'What is it?' Murak asked.

Shamana pressed a finger to her lips and listened.

Untroubled by conversation, she allowed the sounds of Jinghara to float into her mind. At first there was nothing, then she heard something like the flutter of a tiny bird. The faint throbbing became clearer, a pulse, a repetitive drumming rhythm. Hoof beats.

'Prepare for battle!' Shamana yelled.

Murak drew his sword like the others. Nobody saw his puzzled expression. Why was the patrol attacking them when they should be punishing the villagers who had harboured the rebels? Why had they put him in such a difficult situation so early? He had no time to ponder further. The Warriors of the Sun came at the gallop, swords drawn. The scarlet tassels on their helmets rippled in the breeze. Gardep assessed the balance of forces.

'We need to break their charge,' he said. 'Can you do something, Shamana?'

Shamana winked. 'Elephants!' she roared.

Aaliya transformed, following her teacher's example. Two elephants thundered towards the advancing cavalry. They were followed by a rhinoceros, Oled's more modest contribution to the counter-charge. He noticed his mother's look of disgust. Would her son never master the fine points of metamorphosis? The three beasts broke the Sol-ket offensive, throwing the fine Selessian horses into panic. Racing in behind them, Gardep led the remaining fighters forward, falling upon the enemy with sword and bow, piercing flesh, cracking bones. His leadership inspired everyone. Even the youngest members of the group, Harad and Qintu, played their part, jabbing and parrying, covering the more seasoned fighters' backs. Hand to hand fighting followed. The three Tanjurs returned to human form and concentrated their attention on breaking the Sol-ket's formation. The Imperial charge stalled. The Sol-ket wavered.

'Bows!' Gardep ordered. 'Murima, Cusha, Qintu, Harad. You too, Murak. You've proved yourself a good shot.'

The five drew up a line, their shafts whispering through the air and thumping into the Warriors of Ra. Horses screamed and men fell. With the four remaining rebels returning to the fray, swords and battle-axes drawn, the Sol-ket officer broke off the attack. Just as he had done once before, Gardep set about destroying the remnants of the enemy force. His knight, the Lion of Inbacus, Rishal ax-Sol, had taught him well. Ruthlessness was the key to final victory. This time, however, Shamana prevented him embarking on a systematic extermination of the enemy.

'No, Gardep,' she cried. 'There is no time.'

She shouted to the archers. 'Gather as many arrows as you can. At this very moment a second patrol is approaching the village. I fear for our friends.'

8

The second company of Sol-ket swept into the village in battle formation, hurling lighted torches onto the thatched roofs to their right and left. They didn't care whether there was anyone inside the makeshift houses at the time. They too followed Rishal's code of total war. Terror-stricken by the onslaught, mothers, fathers, children spilled screaming from their homes, only to be cut down by the marauding Sol-ket. Half a dozen bodies littered the street in the first charge. Carrying on down the single dirt track between the blazing buildings, the Sol-ket wheeled round, ready to charge again.

'Defend yourselves!' Bulu roared.

The villagers stared at him in disbelief. Most of them

had lived their lives in fear of the Masters, never daring to even make eye contact. Now their elder was ordering resistance. Even as the Sol-ket swung their horses, nobody moved.

'Gather forks, hoes, spades, anything,' Bulu cried.

For the first time, some of the young men and women started running to the tool stores. Then, from Bulu's throat, there sprang an ancient war cry. With his surviving left hand, he swung a sledgehammer above his head and planted himself in the middle of the dirt road. 'Freedom or death!'

The Sol-ket came again, harness jangling, faces taut. Bulu stood his ground, the hammer in his left hand, leading by example. Armed with their hastily gathered implements, the young and the able-bodied ran to join him. In the mêlée that ensued ten of them fell, three dead, the rest wounded by sword cuts. But the slaves didn't run. More importantly, two of the Warriors of Ra fell too. One died, impaled on a pitchfork. Another writhed in the dust until a middle-aged matron finished him with a hoe.

'I never thought this day would come,' she howled with delight. 'We are a risen people once more. The Helati are fighting back, imagine that!'

The Sol-ket started their third pass through the village. This time the resistance was fierce. Where houses still stood, the young men and women clambered onto the roofs, hurling all manner of projectiles. More Imperial soldiers succumbed to the withering hail. A single act of courage had swung the skirmish in the villagers' favour. Bulu's grandson, Nikesh, gathered his friends and hauled a cart across the road, blocking the Sol-ket's escape. Inspired by his example, some of the women started to assemble an impromptu barricade. Within this cauldron of revolt, the wide-eyed Sol-ket stalled, met defeat, died.

9

The Ten entered the village some thirty minutes later. They found the buildings still blazing, the villagers massing around the funeral pyre of the dead. Shamana surveyed the scene with a practised eye. For long moments there was silence. The Ten gazed into the eyes of the villagers and the villagers looked back. Nothing in their expressions gave a clue to what they were thinking. Then Shamana did something that sent a murmur eddying around the crowd. Sliding from her saddle, she walked towards Bulu and fell on her knees before him.

'Forgive me,' she said. 'It was I who brought this catastrophe down on your heads. The blood of your murdered innocents stains my hands.'

Head bowed, she awaited Bulu's answer.

'Stand, Shamana,' he said. 'You should not apologise. You have our gratitude. Forty years we have grovelled in the dirt, abasing ourselves before the Muzals' assassins. This day we have won back our pride.'

'But what of your dead, your wounded?' Murima asked.

'We will mourn,' Bulu answered. 'Of course we will. But know this, bending the knee to the Sol-ket has not saved a single soul. All these years the Masters have killed and tortured to make us work harder, to ensure our obedience, sometimes simply for sport.'

The matron who had helped turn the battle stepped forward.

'One of my sons died in the fighting today,' she said, eyes welling with tears. 'Nobody has more right than I to speak on this matter.' She beat her chest with both fists. 'Though my heart breaks, I have no regrets. I would rather have my son enter the House of the Dead with a weapon in his hand, defending his people, than cowed and servile, regretting his wretched existence.'

Some of the other mothers nodded.

'This is the first day of our freedom,' one said.

'The long night of oppression is over,' her neighbour agreed.

Shamana looked around the massed villagers. 'Do you all feel this way?'

There was a powerful shout of agreement.

'And you realise what this means?'

Bulu answered for the whole village. 'We have made our choice, She-wolf. We will follow you. We will follow the daughter of Shinar and the Holy Children. The Masters have beaten our sons and daughters. They have sold them away from their families. They have tortured and killed our men and taken our women for their pleasure. Even if we die in this great undertaking, we will do so reaching for our freedom.'

The villagers brandished weapons, the hoes and spades with which they had fought, the swords and spears they had stripped from the bodies of the dead Sol-ket.

Oled looked at the two hundred or so Helati and murmured to Gardep. 'This is what we have been waiting for.'

Gardep nodded. 'Yes, it's Shamana's sign. The Four Winds have just given her their answer. What we have before us is the first company of the Army of the Free.'

CHAPTER 5

Fire and Ice

1

Rishal and Kulmat picked their way through the detritus of battle. The Helati had burned the dead of friend and foe alike on a single common pyre, something the Children of Ra found abhorrent. Whatever the villagers could use, they had taken: food supplies, weapons, horses.

'Two companies wiped out,' Rishal said, his eyes sweeping the charred remains of Bulu's village. 'The rebels have stripped our men of everything they could use. They now have weapons, horses, even Lyrian fire. By their idiocy, our own troops are turning the enemy into an army. By the holy face of Ra, is there no end to our troubles? The world is like a candle burning at both ends.'

'Surely the Darkwing is the greater danger, Master,'

Kulmat said. 'This is not the first slave revolt the Empire has faced. It won't be the last. It is in the nature of the Helati to resist their enslavement from time to time. It is a perennial danger, but one we can contain. Were the demon lord to prevail however, the whole world would perish.'

The squire chose his words carefully. Somewhere, somehow, he prayed there might be a happy outcome. If the Sol-ket were to capture the Holy Children, at least they would have to keep them alive. Dead, they were no use against the Darkwing. Kulmat tried to imagine a future in which he and Gardep could be friends, Gardep and his Cusha united. He was shocked at his own thoughts. Born and raised as a Sol-ket, he had started to think like a Helat. Though it was heresy to any Child of the Sun, he had even begun to conjure a world in which there was no struggle, no division between slave and slave-holder. Is it possible, he wondered, or will it be yet another broken dream?

Rishal sighed. 'You're right, you're right. But, if we move against the Darkwing, how can we ignore the fire at our back? No, there is a chance we could save the world only to hand it to the servile masses. We must fight on two fronts, Kulmat. There will be a council of war. Take a company of men. Tell Barath what has happened.'

Kulmat nodded and gave his bugler an order. At the signal, a score of horsemen climbed into the saddle.

'And Kulmat,' Rishal shouted, 'don't try to hide the gravity of the situation. You must let Barath know what we are dealing with here. There are fifty villages within a day's ride. News of a Helat victory will spread like fire in a tinder-dry forest.'

2

'It is beginning,' the Darkwing gloated. 'My scheme unfolds. Cruel winter begins to grip the land.' He had not intended the words to be heard. That didn't prevent Jinghirza interrupting him.

'Is this your doing, Lord?'

The creature's head snapped round. For a moment terror pinned her to the wall as his black eyes seared her mind. His jaws parted, exposing a mouthful of needle-sharp fangs. Then, to Jinghirza's relief, a sly smile spread over the demon lord's inhuman features. 'Do you wish to understand my intentions, Jinghirza?'

'As you see fit, my Lord,' Jinghirza answered, careful not to antagonise him.

The Darkwing released her from her chains. 'Come.'

Heart full of foreboding, Jinghirza followed him to the monastery's colonnaded entrance.

'What do you see?' he asked.

Jinghirza wondered what he was showing her. 'Snow. I see a world of snow.'

'Exactly,' the demon lord said, delighted by her answer. He seized her and flew south, settling on the lower slopes from which they could see the ancestral lands of the Khuts and the Obirs. 'Now tell me what you see.'

Jinghirza stared. Snowstorms were howling across the northern plains, blanketing the Khut villages and driving across the pastures of the Obirs.

'I don't understand,' she said. 'By now our crops should be sprouting. What has happened to the good light of the sun?'

Her answer made the Darkwing's eyes blaze with an intense joy. 'This is my great work, Jinghirza. At last, after all my setbacks, I will have my revenge. This world has taken everything from me: my youth, my lost love Kewara, my humanity. Now I am repaying it in full. You ask what has happened to the good light of the sun, Jinghirza? It is fading. The winter you see spreading across the north land will presently sweep south. The grasslands will wither and die. The cities will shiver. The southern ocean will ice over. Just imagine it. Karangpur will become a snowy confection. Golden Rinaghar will be coated in thick, silvery frost. Even humid Parcep will succumb, its palm-fringed boulevards covered with a sheen of ice. This is the end of things, my child. The age of reckoning is upon us.'

'No,' Jinghirza protested.

'Can you not feel it?' the Darkwing asked. 'Do you not sense the glacial fingers of eternal winter stealing through the marrow of your bones?'

'I don't believe it,' Jinghirza cried. 'I refuse to swallow your lies.'

'You believe it,' the Darkwing said. 'You just won't admit it yet.'

Turning away from her tormentor, Jinghirza watched the snow flurries scouring her native land. Tears stood in her eyes, slowly freezing to her lashes.

3

In the next four weeks, countless villages and hamlets followed the example of Bulu's community. Bulu's grandson Nikesh was the boldest and most respected of the younger generation. Once, when a Sol-ket insulted his sister, he had waited a week before tracking the offender down and killing him. He had made it look like an accident to prevent reprisals. The act had given him almost legendary status in the village. It came as no surprise when he was put in charge of a group of young men. They were given fast horses and told to raise Jinghara against the oppressors. The villages, bled dry for so long by demon and Master alike, feted the riders with garlands and songs. Everywhere they went, uprisings followed. The villagers looted stores, fired Sol-ket villas and dispossessed slave masters. Imperial patrols that had been hunting the Holy Children found themselves tangled in the complications of a string of riots.

Appointed Commander-in-Chief of the Army of the Free, Gardep set about training the thousands of raw recruits that Nikesh brought flocking to his banner. He did his work well. He organised his warriors into companies, platoons, regiments. He interviewed hundreds of eager fighters, selecting the most able and giving them command. All this was done with astonishing speed. The talents Rishal had once recognised were now being turned against the Empire. On a broad front across northern Jinghara, Gardep launched numerous attacks. There was nothing random about them, as he explained one night to an assembly of thirty of its leaders.

'We were nine,' he told them. 'At first recruiting a single man seemed beyond us. Now we are thousands. We are still too weak to meet the Grand Army in the field. As a result, we have had to turn our lack of training and equipment to our advantage. By constantly moving, by striking and running, we've got the enemy chasing us across hundreds of miles of empty grassland. Now is the time to make our move.'

'Meaning?' Murak asked.

'Oled Lonetread will take command of the Jingharan front,' Gardep explained. 'I will lead a northern expedition.

The aim of this force will be to reach Sangra Peak. There, the Holy Children will use their powers to destroy the Darkwing and restore the warmth of the sun.'

Atrakon was taken aback. 'You mean to divide our resources? This is madness.'

Oled found himself in agreement with the Selessian he distrusted so much. He stared at Shamana. 'Did you know anything about this?'

Shamana shook her head. 'You are Commander of the Army of the Free, Gardep. We can't spare you. Atrakon is right. We have had a few successes. That doesn't mean we can go splitting the army in half.'

'You entrusted me with command,' Gardep retorted. 'These are my orders.'

'I understand why you are doing this,' Murima said, trying to find a compromise. 'You want to be by Cusha's side. But Gardep, you mustn't let your personal feelings cloud your judgement. I was at Dullah. I know what division and intrigue can do. This plan of yours is a mistake for which we will pay with blood.'

Cusha and Vishtar watched the exchange of angry words in silence. Gardep's project was as much of a surprise to them as it was to any of the other leaders of the revolt.

'We are not the Sol-ket,' Oled growled. 'We have no absolute leaders to order us about. Our ways are set down in the Book of Scales. We seek a Republic of the Free where all have a voice and none are elevated to untrammelled power. Everyone here has been chosen by the casting of lots. No one man can take decisions for an entire people.'

'So why did you make me general?' Gardep demanded.

'You are a military man,' Shamana said. 'You know the way our enemy thinks. In battle, you are without compare.

But you must heed the advice of your brothers and sisters assembled here. Listen to Oled. This is the way of the Scales.'

'Then set out an alternative to what I propose,' Gardep said, eyes hard with anger.

'There is a way,' Vishtar said. All eyes turned in his direction. 'There is no need to divide our forces,' he said. 'Cusha and I need no protection from the Sol-ket. What are they going to do? We have their captured reports. They know the Darkwing's design. If the sun grows cold in the sky, they will die just as we will. Even if they were to capture us, they would not dare harm us. They need our powers to thwart the demon lord.'

Averting her eyes from Gardep, Cusha spoke in support of her brother. 'What Vishtar says is true. It is not an army we need, nor even a regiment. We will go alone. The Book of Scales prophesied this. It did not speak of an army, but of one heart. All we need is a single resourceful scout to accompany us.'

Atrakon seized on Cusha's words. 'The Holy Child is right. Three people can move quickly. They are more likely to evade our enemies. I volunteer to act as guide.'

'You?' Oled said with a scowl. 'Do you think we are complete fools? You fight with us now, Ebrahin, but there was a time you sold your soul to the priesthood. Do you think we have forgotten the years you spent in the service of the Hotec-Ra?' He shook his head. 'No, there has to be another candidate.'

'I have one,' Shamana said.

Oled looked around. 'Who? Who has the skills? Who can find their way north? Do you want me to go?'

'No, Oled,' Shamana said. 'Your talents are better suited to the battlefield. I mean my apprentice, Aaliya. She has perfected the arts of metamorphosis. She is a skilled swordswoman and archer. She can read the lie of the land as expertly as anyone I have ever known.'

Suddenly the thought of being parted from Aaliya made Oled's heart ache with loss. For all that, he raised no protest against Shamana. The same could not be said of Gardep.

'I will not permit it!' Gardep shouted. 'Do you really intend to send three against all the dangers in their way? They must cross the lands of the Khuts and the Obirs. Who knows what they will face when they reach the Mountains of the Moon?'

'The quest for the Black Tower began with five travellers,' Cusha said gently. 'Who travelled the road from Parcep to the Black Tower? I remember those who were with me then: Shamana and Murima, Harad and Qintu. We were women and boys. You took a different path from me then, Gardep. Sometimes the actions of a few single-minded pilgrims can change the face of the world.'

Her intervention cut the ground from under Gardep's feet. He could find no answer to her.

'Let's put it to the vote,' Bulu said, speaking for the villages that made up the vast majority of the army.

It was carried with only one vote against.

4

By the time Omar Ebrahin and his Selessians reached the Grand Army, the Imperial engineers had rebuilt the fortress of Zindhar. The new construction dwarfed the original. It had been extended to house many thousands of warriors. It was into this growing complex of buildings that the black-garbed desert warriors rode, their cloaks wrapped round them against the biting cold.

'By the Almighty,' Mehmet said. 'I had heard the north Jingharan Plain was windy. But this!'

Omar too wondered about the unnatural cold. Hostile eyes followed the Selessians. The words 'desert rat' were murmured more than once. Omar chose to ignore the insults of the surrounding Sol-ket. There was little choice. If his men threw the abuse back in the faces of the Imperial Army, what then? What could a few thousand do against an entire expeditionary force?

'You, Selessian,' a Sol-ket officer barked. 'Report to General Rishal's quarters.'

Omar looked around. All the buildings looked the same.

'Turn right at the canteen,' the officer said, pointing the building out. 'Carry on straight. You can't miss it. You'll see the sun standards.'

Omar nodded. 'Where are my soldiers' quarters?'

The officer chuckled. 'You're in those tents,' he said, 'outside the main stockade.'

'Tents,' Mehmet said, disgust in his voice, 'in this cold!'

'Get the men settled in,' Omar said. 'I'll see what the general wants.'

He found Rishal's quarters and explained his presence to the guards. After waiting outside for a few minutes, he was escorted to an ante-room. There was a strong smell of freshly hewn timbers. For the second time he was left waiting. Finally, the door swung open and he was brought before the Army Command. There were two-dozen men present. Most were senior officers. There was a single saffron-robed priest.

'You are five days late, Omar Ebrahin,' Rishal complained.

'We were delayed by frequent storms,' Omar answered.

He had expected Rishal to dismiss his explanation as an

excuse. Instead, Rishal introduced the members of the High Command.

'You are probably wondering why you have been transferred from Karangpur, Omar,' Rishal said.

Omar stood impassively. It was the Selessian way.

'The men of the desert kingdom have a reputation as expert trackers,' Rishal continued. 'We have need of your talents. I will allow Lord Timu of the Hotec-Ra to explain the mission.

Omar listened to Timu. Even his impassive features registered shock when the priest revealed the cause of the turbulent storms that were assaulting the northern plains.

'We believe the so-called Holy Children have already set off towards the Mountains of the Moon,' Timu concluded. 'Commander Rishal will suppress the Helat uprising and protect the Imperial heartland. General Barath and I will lead the pursuit of these infernal twins. We will make sure they reach the Darkwing and use their powers to overcome him.'

'Then?' Omar asked, already knowing the likely answer.

'Then they become expendable, of course.' Timu gave the inevitable humourless smile. 'By way of reward, we will sacrifice them to Holy Ra.'

When Omar reached the hundreds of tents raised to house his men, he took Mehmet aside and explained the situation.

'The Sol-ket have been swigging too much kinthi,' Mehmet said. 'It's driven them all mad.'

He was laughing at Omar's crazy story. Then he saw his leader's eyes and the good humour drained from his face. 'You're serious, aren't you?'

'Yes,' Omar replied. 'Insane as all this sounds, I could smell the reek of fear in that room. The Hell-fiend has the entire world by the throat, Mehmet.'

Mehmet looked at the sleet that was slanting across the usually sunlit grasslands. 'We're a long way from home, Omar, such a long way.'

Omar laid out his prayer mat. 'Which way is Juttah, Mehmet?'

Mehmet consulted his compass. 'The needle points that way.'

Omar removed his boots and knelt facing the Selessian holy city. When he had finished his prayers, he gave Mehmet an order to pass on to the men.

'There will be extra worship today,' he said. 'Instruct the men in their devotions. They will pray for the sun's golden light to return.'

5

Gardep and Cusha talked late into the night.

'You must not be afraid,' she told Gardep. 'I will return. I promise.'

Gardep took her hand and held it to his lips. She felt his tears on her skin. 'How can you possibly know?'

Cusha leaned her forehead against his and murmured her reply. 'I trust my brother.'

Gardep frowned. 'Vishtar? What do you mean?'

'We will not be alone in our quest,' Cusha said, earnestness oozing from every pore. 'He has communicated with the Lost Souls.'

Gardep stared at her. 'You trust the undead?'

'I trust Vishtar.'

'You say the Lost Souls speak to your brother?'

'The Book of Scales talks of *an innocent and generous heart*. It's Vishtar, I know it.'

'Lost Souls, redemption, prophecy . . . I am sick of such

talk,' Gardep said. 'I hate it all, the plotting, the sorcery, the endless shifting sands of Fate. I was born with a sword in my hand. I am a soldier, Cusha. I crave the simplicity of open battle. I want an enemy I can fight.'

'That is your strength and your weakness, my love,' Cusha said. 'That is why you need the wisdom of Shamana and the steadiness of Oled. We all fight the enemy in our own way.'

Gardep was stubborn. 'I should be with you.'

Cusha shook her head. 'The people need you. Your sword will lead them to victory against the Children of the Sun. This is the last time we will be apart, I promise.'

'Swear it,' Gardep said. 'Swear it by the Four Winds.'

Cusha put her arms round his neck and kissed him on the lips. 'I have sworn it a thousand times. What can I do to ease your torment?'

'Consent to betrothal,' he said.

By way of an answer, tears spilled from Cusha's eyes. A shaft of moonlight made them glisten on her cheeks. So it came to pass that, the following morning, the day of her departure, Cusha ul-Parcep stood before the Army of the Free to be betrothed to Gardep na-Vassyrian. Shamana conducted the ceremony.

'Take her hands,' she told Gardep.

When their hands were linked, she bound them with prayer scrolls, printed with verses from the Book of Scales. Finally, she poured water over their hands, symbolising their coming union.

'Are you ready to let me go?' Cusha asked.

'So long as you swear to return to be my wife,' Gardep said.

'Nothing,' Cusha said, 'not the demon lord, not the legions of the Sol-ket, not even the fires of hell will keep us apart.'

They embraced. Gardep whispered his love one last

time. Then Cusha said her farewells. She hugged Shamana then Harad and Qintu. She murmured something under her breath, first to Atrakon, then to Oled. She wondered if either of them would take notice. Finally, she threw her arms round Murima's neck and kissed her on the cheek.

'I will miss you so much, Mama-li,' she said.

'And I you, my dearest child,' Murima replied.

Within the hour Cusha had ridden out of the camp with Vishtar and Aaliya at her side.

6

Nobody noticed Murak's absence from the gathering. He slipped into the tent Shamana shared with Aaliya. Casting furtive looks through the flap now and then, he searched for the ingredients he needed. Soon he had them. Taking only the smallest quantities, so as not to be discovered, he left with the precious herbs and spices. He stole out of the camp as the Army of the Free gathered to witness Cusha and Gardep exchange their vows. Heart pounding, fearing discovery at every moment, he made his way to a venerable banyan tree. Under its spreading branches, he put together his mixture and lit it. Easing a thread from his tunic, he dropped it into the fire. The thread was taken from his sacred robes. The tiny flame danced for a moment then turned the saffron colour of the Hotec-Ra. Timu's face appeared.

'Murak,' Timu said, 'what has taken you so long? I was beginning to think you were dead.'

Murak scowled. You'd like that, wouldn't you? he thought. But, for now, the two priests were united in their search for the Holy Children.

'The rebels have been watching me every moment of

every day,' Murak said. 'It has taken me weeks to begin to gain their trust. I once managed to signal a patrol but only for a few moments. This is the first time I have been alone for any time.'

'Do you have any news?'

'Events are shifting in our favour,' Murak said. 'The Holy Children go north alone. They will have a single shape-shifter as their guide.'

Timu anticipated the name. 'The She-wolf?'

Murak shook his head. 'Not even the son, Lonetread. They have chosen the She-wolf's apprentice, Aaliya.'

'As you say,' Timu said, 'the wind has shifted in our direction. This is a less formidable opponent. We will assume the role of guide to Nandraghiri. That way, we will be in control of events. What is your present position?'

Murak gave Timu what information he could.

'I will take your news to General Rishal,' Timu said. 'The Imperial Army will throw a ring of steel around the Helat cockroaches.'

'I will do everything I can to make Rishal's task easier,' Murak said. 'It is time to annihilate them. With the rebel threat removed, we can concentrate on the Darkwing.'

'Consider this uprising strangled at birth,' Timu said. 'Rishal will kill them all.'

7

Cusha, Vishtar and Aaliya were riding towards the unrelenting storms.

'What day is it?' Cusha asked.

'Tomorrow is the first day of Buradish,' Aaliya said. 'I have brought incense. We will celebrate the birth of the scholar Udmanesh.'

Vishtar, always the gloomier of the twins, wondered whether they had anything to celebrate. They had one short month, just sixty days, to reach Nandraghiri and defeat the demon lord. Yes, one Jingharan lunar cycle, sixty fragile, all-too-fleeting days, to save their world from cold, darkness and oblivion.

'The horses are suffering,' Cusha said.

Aaliya nodded. 'I know. By the time we reach the Khut lands, we may have to go on without them.'

'Then how will we reach our destination?' Vishtar demanded.

'You forget,' Aaliya said, 'I am a shape-shifter.'

To prove her point, she transformed into a great snow bear. 'For now I need to preserve my strength. When the time comes I will take this form. Trust me. You will reach Nandraghiri.'

They pressed forward, bowing before the north wind like penitents. They could hear the howl of wolves, scavenging for food in the icy wastes that had only recently been fertile plains.

'I thought I despised the demon lord already,' Vishtar said. 'After all those years of imprisonment, I thought I couldn't loathe him any more. I was wrong.'

'I don't hate him,' Cusha said. 'I pity him. I have Gardep and I have you, Vishtar. After all the years when I had no memory, no knowledge of my previous life, I have something to fight for. What does the Darkwing have? He is consumed by hatred and despair.'

Vishtar was incredulous. 'You think you can persuade him to abandon this fatal scheme, don't you?'

'I think I can reach him, yes.'

'You are too soft-hearted, Cusha,' Vishtar told her. 'Do you still imagine you can find some fragment of humanity inside the creature? Don't you understand the depths of his depravity? Sometimes the madness of hatred can fester so long, torture a soul so deeply that nothing is left.'

Cusha didn't answer. Still, she could not forget the Darkwing's story. He had been in love, just as she was with Gardep. It was love that had saved her. Could it not do the same for the demon lord?

'We can ride another ten miles before nightfall,' Aaliya said.

'It's hard to know day from night,' Vishtar grumbled. 'All we ever see is snow.'

'And it will get worse,' Aaliya said.

Much worse.

8

It was the first day of Buradish. At Zindhar, snowflakes drifted lazily on the icy gusts from the north. The fort was quiet under its light dusting of snow. There was only a skeleton garrison manning the now enormous military complex. A few days before, General Barath had ridden north-east at the head of a considerable force of Sol-ket and Selessian auxiliaries, in pursuit of the Holy Children. He was accompanied by Timu.

Commander Rishal was also on the move. Frustrated by weeks of fruitless skirmishing, he had decided to take the fight to the enemy and force them to fight in the open. With him, he took Linem's priests. They carried pots of red dust, promising to use it to make him a great weapon.

As they rode, Rishal glanced at Kulmat. He was suspicious of the cadet. Before leaving for the Mountains of the Moon, Timu had carried out an examination of the keep at the Demon Wall. It had revealed the cellar in which the rebels had concealed themselves to avoid detection.

But why hadn't Kulmat, a product of eight years of training in the Military Academy, discovered the hatch? It was time to put the boy to the test.

At sunrise, Kulmat was waiting outside General Rishal's tent, wondering why he had been summoned so early. The moment the commander appeared, Kulmat hurried towards him. 'Rishal-Ra, I have just received your message.'

'We have captured a Helat unit. We are going to interrogate them.'

Kulmat wondered why the Commander had taken control of such a minor operation.

'Come on, Kulmat,' Rishal said. 'You want to fight the enemy, don't you?'

'Yes, Rishal-Ra, more than anything.'

He climbed into the saddle and they rode west. By noon, they were approaching a village. Scrawny dogs fought over scraps with malnourished children. Kulmat became ever more concerned. After a few minutes they reached a stockade. Kulmat gave Rishal a questioning look.

'Bring them out,' Rishal commanded.

The gates swung open. From inside the stockade, a few dozen men appeared, some of them little more than boys. They were ill-kempt and many were bruised. They looked as if they hadn't eaten in days. Kulmat's sense of apprehension was growing. The blood was roaring in his ears.

'This is your mission.'

Kulmat surveyed the hungry, listless men. 'I don't understand, Rishal-Ra. You said we were going to interrogate them. They have already been beaten. Why are we here?'

One of the Helati seized on his words. 'It's true, my Lord, your men have beaten us and asked us many questions. We don't know anything. The people you see here are the ones who stayed. When the fighters left to join the daughter of Shinar, we would not go with them. We were afraid of the consequences. Have mercy, Masters, we are not rebels.'

'You are their kinsmen,' Rishal said. 'They will feel your pain.'

The Helat's eyes widened in horror.

Rishal nodded to the stockade guards. 'We are going to make an example of you.'

The Helati were forced to their knees.

'Bring some of your Fire Dust,' Rishal told the Hotec-Ra.

'Do you mean to butcher them in cold blood?' Kulmat asked. 'You're going to kill them, aren't you, Rishal-Ra?'

'No,' Rishal said, 'you are.'

9

The first day of Buradish dawned crisp and cold in the rebel camp. Though many had shivered in their blankets, the Army of the Free was in high spirits. The insurgents' numbers were growing and they now controlled a swathe of Jinghara. Word of the rebellion had travelled south to the towns and villages surrounding the fort of Karangpur and to the coastal settlements north of Rinaghar itself. In some districts they had turned the tables on the Sol-ket. In these pockets, where the resistance was at its strongest, the Warriors of the Sun no longer hunted the rebels. It was the risen Helati who pursued their former oppressors. They had no illusions that they were safe, of course. At Zindhar and in golden Rinaghar, great armies opposed them. But, for now, they were being held at bay.

There was music from veena, flute and tambourine.

Village girls in brightly-coloured costumes were going through their dance steps. For the first time in two generations the birth of great Udmanesh, prophet of the Scales was going to be celebrated in public. Though food was hardly plentiful, the Helati ate well that morning. Meat and vegetables sizzled in Balti dishes. Piles of flat-breads were heaped on plates. There were side orders of spiced onions and tomatoes, potatoes coated with yoghurt and various chutneys. Once they had eaten, they danced and sang. Plays were performed, telling tales of long ago, when the Helati were a free people. Towards evening, Shamana addressed the gathering.

'On this day we celebrate the birth of the scholar Udmanesh,' she said. 'When the Sol-ket sing of great men, it is warriors and priests they celebrate, men who have conquered cities or amassed great fortunes. Our holy man was born a poor flower-seller's son in the city of Inbacus. His greatness lay in his thirst for knowledge and his charitable heart. He left us the Book of Scales to guide us through our lives.'

She seemed to meet the eye of every man, woman and child. 'Most of all, he left us a light to show us the way to freedom. He predicted that two would come, twins, a girl and a boy, representing light and dark, the balance of all things. Even now, the Holy Children go north. This is the month of Buradish, the time of reckoning. By the time of its end, we will have entered a new golden age of peace and freedom or the world will have perished in darkness and chaos.' She lit incense and raised her arms, palms outstretched. 'I now call on the Four Winds to bless those who travel north, to give them wisdom and courage.'

She caught Gardep's eyes. 'Our new Army of the Free has had its first successes,' she said. 'For that we must thank our commanders: Oled, Murima, Atrakon, Bulu and Nikesh.'

'And you, Shamana,' one man shouted.

Shamana smiled. 'Yes, and the She-wolf. But, most of all, we should thank our General, great Gardep. With a heavy heart, he gave his blessing to Cusha. He confirmed what all the oppressed peoples of the land know only too well: great good will not come without great sacrifice.'

Even as her voice faded, rows of dancers burst upon the scene, finger cymbals tinkling as they weaved through the crowd. Shamana watched the bright eyes and smiling mouths of the multitude and her heart sang. There were many miles to go and formidable obstacles to overcome, but her soul throbbed with a rhythm of hope as powerful as the beat of the drums. She approached Murima and the boys Harad and Qintu.

'I sometimes wondered if a day such as this would ever come,' she said.

'I know what you mean,' Murima said. 'All those years I laboured in Rishal's kitchens, putting up with Mistress Serala's scolding, I thought I would die a slave.'

'Cusha will find Nandraghiri, won't she?' Harad asked.

'Of course she will,' Qintu said.

'She reached the Black Tower against much greater odds,' Shamana said. 'I believe in her.'

'I raised that wonderful child as a daughter,' Murima said. 'I know she will have the strength.' She was about to continue when she became aware of a hubbub over to her left. 'What's going on over there?'

Harad saw a horseman surrounded by crowds of people. 'It's Nikesh.' They hurried towards him.

'What is it?' Shamana asked.

The crowd parted to let her through.

'There's been a massacre,' Nikesh cried, eyes wide with

shock and outrage. 'I sent one of my men to persuade a village that had refused to join us. They found nothing but charred bodies. One lived, despite horrific burns. Just before he died, he told my rider what had happened.'

The jostling crowd listened to the news.

'How many?' Murima asked.

Nikesh lowered his eyes. 'Fifty, maybe sixty.'

Tears of rage and pity welled in Murima's eyes. 'There's more to tell, isn't there?'

'Yes,' Nikesh said. 'Some were no older than Harad or Qintu. These Sol-ket, they're killing boys.'

Some of the people turned to Gardep. Raised a Sol-ket himself, he became the object of their rage.

'You were one of them once,' Qintu accused him. 'Explain this outrage . . . if you can.'

But before Gardep could answer, Nikesh spoke again. 'I have the names of the men who commanded this mission. One was the commander-in-chief, Rishal himself.'

'And the other?' Murima asked.

'The officer in charge of the killing party was Kulmat na-Zamir.'

'Kulmat!' Gardep gasped. 'He would never do such a thing.'

'He is Sol-ket,' Qintu cried, 'as you are.'

It was as if he had struck Gardep in the face. 'Are you blaming me for this?' he asked.

'The butcher is your friend. What does that say about you?' Every ounce of good will Qintu had ever felt for Gardep had vanished in an instant. 'Once a Sol-ket, always a Sol-ket.'

Gardep's eyes welled with tears. 'I fought alongside you at the Black Tower. I have been with you every step of the way since. Does that count for nothing?'

Recovering from the shock of the news, Shamana shoved her way to the front of the crowd. Oled too had arrived.

'This is the work of Rishal,' Shamana said.

'The cadet Kulmat carried out the executions,' Qintu retorted, beside himself with anger and bitter humiliation. 'That's right, Gardep's friend ordered the massacre, the blood brother of whom he is so proud. Yet you make him general of the Army of the Free, Shamana. Oled should lead us, not this Sol-ket.'

Qintu's speech set off a chorus of agreement.

'Enough!' Oled roared. 'Cusha would tear out your tongues if she were here. Why do you insult our brother and comrade in arms? You were at the Black Tower, Qintu. You witnessed Gardep's courage. Without him, we would never have prevailed against the demon lord. I have fought alongside Gardep, as have you. He gave up everything to join our cause. His coming was prophesied. Who here will deny what is written in the Book of Scales?'

The giant looked at each of Gardep's accusers in turn. One by one, they lowered their eyes.

Shamana spoke more softly. 'We must not let our hearts be poisoned. By the Four Winds, have we learned nothing on our journey? Thus far we have marched together, united in our dream of freedom. Look at us: we are Helat and Tanjur.' She pointed out Gardep and Murak. 'These two were once Sol-ket. Now they are our brothers. We fight so that the world can have done with master and slave.' She threw out her arms in a gesture of disappointment and exasperation. 'Why do you think Rishal ordered this massacre? Do you not understand his intention? He wants to spread terror in the villages and despair in our hearts. Just imagine how happy he would be to see us at each other's throats. Rishal seeks to divide us in order to conquer us. This is the cruelty against which we fight.'

Her voice soared. 'I was at Dullah,' she cried, 'as were you, Murima. We have witnessed greater horrors than this brutal massacre. My people were hunted down and killed like rabbits. They were very nearly wiped off the face of the Earth. Did I turn against my own kind? Did I turn away from the cause of the Scales? You should be ashamed, my brothers and sisters. By blaming Gardep, you betray our cause and do the enemy's work for them.'

She drew her sword. 'We have no choice but to meet Sol-ket steel with burnished blades of our own,' she cried. 'But what do we fight for? To be like them, to find a people to enslave ourselves? Do you want to maim and torture the innocent? Can we achieve freedom through such actions? Have you learned nothing?' Her green eyes flashed. 'I don't fight the Sol-ket so I can rule over them as they have ruled over us. I want there to be no Sol-ket or Helat, no divisions between us, just women and men living side by side in peace. How, if the moment something goes wrong we seek scapegoats, will we ever achieve our freedom?'

Shaking her head in despair, she turned to Oled. 'Send these people away, my son. There will be no more recriminations.'

CHAPTER 6

North and South

1

From that day, the Sol-ket always maintained the upper hand. Rishal's army, now fully recovered from the mauling they had suffered at the hands of the Darkwing's demon army, swung south and east, pushing the rebels back into the endless grasslands of Jinghara. Time and time again, Nikesh discovered that his raiding parties had been intercepted and defeated. It was as if the Sol-ket now knew the Army of the Free's every move. Every time Gardep met with his commanders, he found the meetings ill-tempered affairs.

'We have lost twenty fighters today,' Nikesh reported. 'Two of our patrols were ambushed this morning alone. The Sol-ket anticipate our attacks. How can that be?'

'Isn't it obvious?' Oled said. 'There is a traitor in our midst. I say we expel the Selessian from this council.'

'Are you blind?' Atrakon retorted. 'Did you hear nothing Cusha said on my behalf? I hate the Empire and everything it stands for. If there is treachery, it doesn't come from me.'

'What about Murak?' Bulu asked. 'He was Sol-ket. Who vouches for him?'

Gardep shook his head. 'I too was Sol-ket, Bulu.'

'That's different, Gardep,' Bulu said. 'You have proved yourself. You crossed the land to protect the Holy Child. What do any of us know about you, Murak?'

Murak didn't speak. But Oled did.

'This man is my brother,' he growled. 'He was at my side at the siege of Karangpur. By the Four Winds, did he not save my mother's life in the skirmish at the Demon Wall?' He jabbed a finger at Atrakon. 'Just look at this desert rat. He was *an assassin*. Murak saved my mother's life. Atrakon tried to kill her. Your people were traitors at Dullah. I say you are traitors still.'

Oled's accusation was too much for Atrakon. Drawing his curved sabre, he leapt to his feet. Equally quickly, Oled drew his battle-axe. Before anyone could stop them, they were engaged in mortal combat, sword blade striking axe head.

'Enough!'

Shamana sprang between them, dashing their drawn weapons away with a spear. 'Are you mad, both of you?' she cried. 'We are meant to lead our people to freedom. Look at us. We have suffered setbacks, that is true. Is that any reason to go tearing out each other's throats?'

Atrakon and Oled faced each other, panting. At any moment the fight might break out again.

'I have a solution,' Shamana said. 'Suspicion has fallen

upon two of our brothers. Though I hold nothing against either of them, we cannot allow this contagion to poison our entire leadership. We must be even-handed. I say we relieve Murak and Atrakon of their posts as commanders and return them to the ranks. One day the truth will emerge. One or both of them will be cleared. Then they will return to the council.'

'This is a wise course of action,' Bulu said. 'I support Shamana.'

Atrakon sheathed his sword. 'The mother is wiser than the son,' he said, scowling at Oled. 'I too support Shamana. I am innocent. I have nothing to fear. When the accusations against me are proven false, I will rejoin this council and do my part in the fight for freedom. Until then, I am proud to be a common soldier.'

Murak wanted to argue against Shamana's proposal but Atrakon had made that impossible. 'I too will gladly return to the ranks,' he said.

'Does anyone oppose this decision?' Bulu asked.

Nobody did. Without another word, Atrakon and Murak withdrew.

'There is one more item on the agenda,' Shamana said. 'I call Nikesh again.'

'Not everything is bleak,' Nikesh said. He cast a glance in Gardep's direction.

'Go on,' Gardep said.

'With their superior numbers,' Nikesh said, 'the Sol-ket have us on the run here in the north. But to the south, in the Jingharan heartland, our Helat comrades are ready to rise in tens of thousands. Already Rinaghar has had to reinforce the garrisons at Durbai and Karangpur. There are even rumours of clashes in Parcep province though our lines of communication don't stretch that far south. We can't confirm the gossip.'

'You are talking of a general rising,' Murima said. 'Are you sure of this?'

'I can only go on the stories my riders bring back,' Nikesh said. 'But I trust the warriors under my command. They are not prone to exaggeration.'

'Nothing is certain in war,' Shamana said. 'There is only one way to test the resolve of the people. That is to march south.' She walked over to Gardep and took the seat next to him. 'I know this is a difficult decision for you to make,' she told him. 'You want to be as close to Cusha as you can. This will feel like a betrayal.'

Gardep had his elbows on his knees, his face buried in his hands. For long moments he said nothing. Finally, he raised his head. 'A hundred miles,' he said, 'five hundred miles, what does it matter now? There is nothing I can do for her. We must strike at the heart of the Empire and pray she succeeds in her quest. If we make our stand here, hungry and outnumbered, we will perish. There will be nothing for Cusha to return to. No, though it breaks my heart to say so, we must do what Nikesh asks. Give the order. Tomorrow, we march south.'

2

Only Vishtar was awake. Huddled in half a dozen thick blankets, he was still cold. Maybe it was all those years imprisoned in the Black Tower. He had never learned to cope with a biting wind. But it wasn't the cold that kept him from sleeping. It was the memories. The Darkwing seemed to fill his every waking moment. Vishtar remembered all those nights the fiend had appeared, as if from thin air, and drained him of his lifeblood. Would he have the courage to face the monster again? He looked at Cusha sleeping peacefully. In spite of his love for her, he actually thought of slipping away into the storm. He dismissed the idea just as quickly. No, he would face the demon lord once more, on a day that might be the end of time. He was still tossing and turning when, through the side of the tent, he saw a shadowy figure. He reached over to wake Aaliya, then stopped. He sat up and whispered a question.

'It's you, isn't it, Jackal?'

Scrambling into his boots, Vishtar slipped out into the bellowing wind. There before him stood Jackal, the night-strider with the blackened bones.

'Is it done?' Vishtar asked.

'Not yet,' the night-strider said.

'Then why did you come?'

Jackal looked south. 'The Sol-ket follow,' he said.

'We expected as much.'

'They won't kill you now,' Jackal said. 'They depend on your powers to defeat the demon lord. But they will slaughter you the moment you free them from the menace of the Darkwing.'

'Yes,' Vishtar said. 'I know.'

'There is terror to the north,' Jackal said. 'The Khuts are frightened. That makes them dangerous. There is no order in the north land.'

'Thank you for your warning,' Vishtar said.

'This is not a warning,'

'Then what?'

'I think I can solve both your problems in one fell swoop.'

Before Jackal could say a word there was the hiss of a sword leaving a scabbard.

'Step back from him,' Aaliya ordered.

'No, Aaliya,' Vishtar told her. 'It's not what you think. This is Jackal.'

He hesitated. 'A friend.'

Behind Aaliya, Cusha opened the tent flap. 'Invite him inside.'

Jackal shook his head. 'No mortal soul invites a night-strider into his home.'

'This isn't our home,' Cusha said brightly. 'That's one problem solved.'

Jackal found himself invited into a human dwelling for the first time in forty years. 'Tell me I am closer to the hour of my redemption,' he said. 'Tell me I will soon have peace.'

'You can trust me,' Vishtar said. 'Now tell me your plan.'

3

Gardep sat brooding for a long time, his back against a boulder, watching a stream rippling over a bed of small, polished stones. Faces floated through his mind, three more than any others. Cusha was foremost in his thoughts, of course. She was to be his bride. For a brief moment her image came to him so vividly, he thought he might be able to hold her, kiss her, smell the scent of her hair. Then she was gone. Kulmat appeared next.

'It's not true, is it?' Gardep murmured. 'You didn't kill those people, not in cold blood?'

An instant later, the face of his former knight Rishal appeared, giving him his answer. 'You were testing Kulmat, weren't you? You suspect him.'

Gardep pulled his fingers down over his face. He found himself looking back over his life. Much of it seemed to be lost in the mists of time. Sometimes he thought his life really began the day he met Rishal, a decade before. Rishal had carried the young Gardep out of the burning city of Inbacus, an orphan discovered wandering alone. Gardep wondered about his parents. But all this time he served as a squire to the great conqueror of Vassyria, Gardep had learned nothing of his past. *Forget what you were*, Rishal always said, *think only of what you will be, a Sol-ket master.* Sometimes spectral images of his family would steal into the depths of his mind. Just as he had done so many times before, he tried to recall them. He failed.

Before he could bring them into sharp focus they crumbled. His training had been thorough, making him more Sol-ket than Vassyrian, yet still there was some small part of him that yearned to know what he had been all those years ago, before the Warriors of the Sun fell like wolves on his home city. After a few moments, he remembered the tattoo Cusha had pointed out. Slipping off his jacket, he examined it, the lion with a bull's head. What did it mean? He shook his head. Here it was, the only direct link with his early years in Vassyria, and it was a mystery to him. He was still staring into the babbling water, remembering the past, when Oled found him.

'It's time to go, Gardep,' he said.

Instinctively, Gardep looked northwards.

'You will see her again,' Oled said.

Gardep smiled. 'Do you think of Aaliya?'

'I think of her all the time. Man's destiny is cruel.'

'Then we must make a new destiny,' Gardep said.

'There is only one problem,' Oled said. 'We have little more than fifty days to do it.'

They climbed the muddy embankment and joined the Army. It numbered many thousands now. Sleet was dancing in the clear blue sky. They knew the strange, all-covering winter was creeping southwards at an alarming rate. Some said even Rinaghar had had a light sprinkling of snow. If it were to come to Parcep then the whole Empire would understand what was happening. In a hundred generations, snow had never fallen on its terracotta-coloured walls and houses. Gardep and Oled joined Shamana, Murima, Nikesh and Parvin at the front of the column and the horses thudded towards central Jinghara. Within weeks they would face the fury of the Muzals.

4

Barath drove his men hard. In just ten days they crossed the Land of Four Rivers and entered Khut territory. They travelled on dirt tracks and logging paths, all now covered with drifting snow. He ordered his Selessians to make ever wider sweeps to the east in search of three travellers, two females and a male. They were under orders to take them alive if they found them. On the eleventh day they were taking their rest by a frozen waterfall, its normally gushing torrent suspended in midair, the ice hanging like inverted spears.

'This is madness,' Mehmet said. 'Any fool could pick up their trails in snow. What are we doing here?'

'I don't think they were expecting these blizzards when they summoned us,' Omar said. 'Could any of us have imagined the power of this Hotec-Ra spell? Besides, if they send us out to do their dirty work, we're the ones who will end up with our skulls split by some Khut hammer-warrior.'

They were turning the matter over when Mehmet's brother Uhmet appeared over the pure white horizon. He gave his report to Omar.

'Barath-Ra,' Omar called, 'Uhmet has some news of your quarry.'

Barath's eyes glinted eagerly.

'I picked up their trail due west of here,' Uhmet told the general.

'How far?'

'It will take us no more than two hours,' Uhmet said.

Barath ordered the men to saddle up.

'There is one other thing,' Uhmet said. 'I was told to look for three sets of tracks.'

'That's right.'

'For a short time they were joined by a fourth person. He walked with them a while and then left.' Uhmet scratched his scalp through the black headdress. 'There was something odd about the fourth set of tracks,' he said.

'Go on.'

'I will draw the print this one made in the snow.' Uhmet used the hilt of his sabre to draw what he had seen.

'It looks like it was made by bare bones, a skeleton,' Omar said.

'It's a night-strider,' Barath said. 'Take no notice. The things are wandering aimlessly across the land. Nobody knows why. We will escort them to their destiny.'

'Then you will kill them?' Omar asked.

Barath smiled. 'Of course.'

5

While Cusha, Vishtar and Aaliya trekked north, pursued by Barath, the Army of the Free went south. They had Rishal's army on their tail. When they reached the plateau of Dhurkhand, they gratefully plunged into its dense sal forests. The great timber-yielding tree gave them sumptuous cover. After many days journeying south, remaining in the saddle throughout the hours of daylight, their rough riders fighting a series of savage rearguard actions to slow the Sol-ket, the Army of the Free finally took a proper rest. From the plateau, a huge shelf rising abruptly from the plain, they would be able to see Rishal's approach.

'The flow of intelligence to the Sol-ket has dried up,' Gardep observed.

'Yes,' Shamana said, 'it looks like we removed our traitor when we asked Murak and Atrakon to leave the war council.'

'I'd have thought that was obvious,' Oled snarled. 'I don't know why you don't let me kill the assassin.'

'Under our laws,' Shamana reminded her son, 'all women and men are innocent until proven guilty by an assembly of their peers. Or do you forget the rule of law in your eagerness to prove yourself right?'

'Nikesh has news,' Murima said, joining the council.

'Is it good or bad?' Gardep asked.

'Ask him yourself,' Murima said.

Nikesh appeared in the clearing, coated with the dust of a day's ride.

'There's no snow to the south then?' Gardep asked.

'It's cold,' Nikesh answered, 'but the storms haven't started there yet.'

'That's good,' Oled said. 'We will make better time than the Grand Army. So what's this news of yours?'

'Inspired by our example,' Nikesh announced, 'a second rising has occurred.'

'Where?'

Nikesh glanced at Murima. 'They chose Gussorah to make their stand.'

Murima rose to her feet. 'Gussorah!'

'It seems they decided to emulate great Shinar,' Nikesh continued. 'As you, his daughter, know only too well,

126

Gussorah is where he lit the beacon of rebellion forty years ago. They thought it would bring the villages flocking to their standard.'

'Did it work?' Oled asked, leaning forward.

'After a fashion,' Nikesh said. 'Unfortunately, they were confronted by a substantial army sent from Rinaghar. Lacking armour, weapons and experienced leaders, they decided to retreat to the Dragon Mountains.'

'We have the weapons they need,' Bulu said, speaking for the first time. 'We have ransacked every store for hundreds of miles. We've got swords, shields, arrows, Lyrian fire.'

'Yes,' Nikesh said, 'and we have experienced leaders.'

'We are thinking along the same lines,' Gardep said. 'Can you get a message to them, Nikesh?'

Nikesh nodded. 'I think my scouts can find them.'

'Is it agreed?' Gardep said, looking round the council.

He saw the approving nods. 'Good. Tell them we will meet them in the Dragon Mountains.'

Shamana counted the days remaining in the month of Buradish. 'I just pray Aaliya and the Holy Children are close to Nandraghiri.'

6

'There they are!' Barath roared.

At the far end of a carpet of pure white snow, broken by just three sets of hoof prints, the troops could see three riders.

'Selessians to the rear,' Barath ordered. 'This moment belongs to the Sons of Ra. Let's collect the Holy Children.'

'Selessians to the rear, indeed!' Mehmet snorted. 'We find them. They take the credit.'

The Sol-ket galloped eagerly.

'What's the hurry?' Omar wondered out loud. 'There are three of them, and two are children.'

But there were far more than three of them. As the Sol-ket thundered over the blanket of snow, hundreds of macabre figures exploded from beneath, creating a barrier between the Warriors of the Sun and their Selessian auxiliaries. At the sound, he swung his horse round.

'Night-striders!'

Omar stared at the triple row of skeletal figures, every one of them armed with a spear, a sword, a battle-axe.

'I thought Barath said these creatures were wandering aimlessly,' Uhmet said. 'This looks pretty purposeful to me.'

'What do we do?' Mehmet asked.

'You do nothing,' one of the night-striders said, stunning the Selessians. It was Jackal. 'This is not your fight, men of the desert.'

Even as the black-garbed warriors were recovering from the surprise of a Lost Soul who spoke, the night-striders engaged the Sol-ket in battle.

'Kill the barbarians!' Barath shouted. 'Selessians, charge!'

'*Now* he wants us with him,' Omar said.

'What are your orders?' Mehmet asked.

'I told you,' Jackal said. 'This is not your fight. The Warriors of the Sun abuse you. They call you desert rats. When are you going to stop doing their dirty work?'

'I didn't think I would ever say this, Omar,' Mehmet said, 'but that pile of bones is talking good sense.'

Omar made his decision. 'Stand down,' he ordered. 'Sheathe your weapons. The creature is right. This is not our fight.'

Seeing his auxiliary stepping away from the fight, Barath led his beleaguered troops in a brave but despairing charge. The Sol-ket fell in their tens, their scores, staining the snow red with their blood. Jackal met Barath in single combat. The first blow crushed Barath's shoulder. The general screamed but he would not surrender. The second blow was decisive. It split Barath's skull.

'Listen to me, Sol-ket,' Jackal roared into the faces of the surviving Warriors of the Sun. 'I know your intentions. You would have accompanied the Holy Children to Nandraghiri, allowed them to exterminate the monster for you, then casually cut their throats. Nobody dies, who doesn't have to. Do you understand?'

Some of the Sol-ket nodded.

'I give you a choice,' Jackal concluded. 'Ride away now and you can return to your quarters. If you choose to make a stand, you will die here.'

Reluctantly, the Sol-ket turned their horses and rode away. The Selessians were about to do the same when the night-strider spoke again.

'Come and meet the Holy Children,' he said. 'You may be interested by what they have to tell you.'

7

At the summit of Sangra Peak, the Darkwing was growing bored. At his approach, Jinghirza spat her defiance. 'Get away from me, monster.'

He looked more inhuman than ever. Serpent heads burst like boils from his flesh. Blue, venomous breath hung round his leathery lips.

'I do like your spirit,' the demon lord drawled. 'You remind me of the Holy Child.' That made Jinghirza stop. 'Ah, so you have heard of Cusha?'

'Of course,' Jinghirza said. 'Her name is written in the scriptures of great Udmanesh.'

'How interesting,' the Darkwing said. 'This Udmanesh certainly got around. Why, he seems to have infected half the world with the virus of rebellion. What would you say if I told you your Holy Child was coming here, to Nandraghiri?'

'I'd tell her to stay well away.'

'Now that would be rather stupid, wouldn't it? Of all the creatures of the Earth only two, Cusha and her snivelling brother Vishtar, have ever defeated me. They are coming to try again.'

Jinghirza stared at him. 'I hope they kill you!'

'Now is that any way to talk to your master?' the Darkwing said. 'I am about to set you a second challenge.'

At this, Jinghirza's heart stopped for a split second.

'You offered, remember?'

Her senses swam as she remembered the walk along the narrow stone bridge. 'What is my ordeal?'

The Darkwing leered. 'I will show you.'

Soon they were standing on an icy mountain path, in swirling snow.

'You look strong, yes, strong and quick.'

Jinghirza could feel the pulse throbbing in her throat. Her lungs were heaving. Terror seemed to be clawing at her insides.

'There is your test.'

Jinghirza stared into the white, howling void.

'The first time, I asked you to walk a narrow path to safety. This time you must jump.'

Jinghirza squinted against the driving snow.

'You will see the other side if you look carefully. It is there somewhere.'

At last Jinghirza saw it, a bare spur of rock on the far

side of a deep chasm. She looked at the narrow path. She would have to get every stride right. One slip, one stumble against the jagged rocks that bordered the path and she would lose momentum and miss the jump. Even so, even if she made the jump, she might miss her handhold and tumble to her death. Success seemed impossible.

'Of course, you can refuse,' the Darkwing said. 'But I would have to kill all your companions and drain every drop of your blood.'

'I will do it,' Jinghirza said, trying to disguise the shudder in her voice.

She walked to the edge of the precipice and waited for the snow to clear a little. For the second time, she glimpsed the spur. Retracing her steps, she crouched, testing the purchase her thin, goatskin shoes gave her on the icy path. Then, sucking in a deep breath, she ran. All her childhood, she had raced her brothers. But she had never tried anything like this.

Sure-footed, she caught the edge of the path, where it fell away, exposing the rocky abyss thousands of feet below. Her arms windmilled. Her legs pedalled. Finally, she thudded against the spur, gratefully grasping the cold granite. Blood trickled from a gashed knee and her upper arms were badly bruised. For all that, she was alive.

'Very impressive,' the Darkwing observed. 'Tonight, you and your friends will have a fire and two kinds of cooked meat. You never know, you may live to see the day the world ends.'

8

Jackal ushered Omar and Mehmet into his yurt. Cusha, Vishtar and Aaliya were already waiting for them.

'You are Omar Ebrahin,' Cusha said.

'How do you know my name?'

'Let me explain,' Vishtar said. 'Jackal here is our eyes and ears.'

Omar thought it would be impolite to mention that the creature had no ears so he said nothing.

'Your clan name is Ebrahin?'

'It is.'

'Where are you from, Omar Ebrahin?' Cusha asked.

'I am from Sahud, about fifty miles from our capital Juttah.'

Cusha and Vishtar exchanged knowing looks. 'Have you ever heard of a man called Atrakon Ebrahin?' Cusha asked.

'Of course I have,' Omar said. 'He was my uncle.'

'Tell me about him.'

Omar was agitated. 'Why do you ask about Atrakon?'

'Just tell the tale.'

'Atrakon was a kinsman,' Omar began.

'Please go on,' Cusha said.

Omar frowned and continued his story. 'A warlord took a fancy to Atrakon's wife, Leila. When Leila resisted him, the warlord killed her. Leila's unborn child died with her.'

'What did Atrakon do?' Cusha asked.

'I have a feeling you know,' Omar said.

'What did he do?'

'Atrakon took his revenge,' Omar concluded. 'But there was a heavy price. He sold himself to the governor and entered his service as an assassin. The Hotec-Ra hired him next and took him across the ocean to Parcep. Nobody has heard of Atrakon from that day to this.'

'Atrakon is an officer in the Army of the Free,' Cusha told them.

'I don't believe you!'

'There is proof.'

'What proof can there be?' Omar asked. 'We are in the middle of an icy wasteland. How can you possibly convince me that what you are saying is true?'

Cusha bowed her head. When she raised it again her face was transformed. In place of the pupils, the irises, the whites, her eyes were the purest black.

'By the Almighty!' cried Omar.

'Come forth, Leila Ebrahin,' Cusha intoned. 'Rise from the House of the Dead. Give witness that what I have told these men is true.'

Within seconds, the ghost of Leila Ebrahin was floating before their eyes.

CHAPTER 7

Attack

I

Sunrise brought terrifying news to the Army of the Free. They had been climbing into the Dragon Mountains for two days, searching for the masses who had marched from Gussorah to meet them. But the Dragon Mountains were a vast system of peaks and passes, valleys and ravines. For many centuries it had been a refuge for the fugitive and the hermit. At sunrise, Nikesh made a discovery.

'Look,' he cried from his vantage point at the edge of the camp. 'There in the foothills. I see scarlet banners.'

Shamana ran to his side. She could see the banners, like rivulets of flame, climbing through the dawn light. 'By the Four Winds!' she cried. 'It's true. Why were we not alerted before? Where are our scouts?'

'Dead,' Nikesh said, surveying the scene. 'If the Imperial troops have come this far unnoticed then you can be sure our outriders are already dead. To find them all, they must have had information from within the camp.'

Gardep joined the gathering crowd as they stood gazing through the mist at the ribbons of scarlet and gold. As yet they could not make out any soldiers, only distant splashes of colour. But they were all the proof the Army of the Free needed that an offensive was well underway. There were cries of dismay as the news spread. Mothers scooped up children and looked in vain for a hiding place. The elderly simply shook their heads and remembered other dawns like this, other beleaguered rebellions.

'It is not just the Sol-ket,' Murak said, running to join them. 'See the white standards. That's a Vassyrian regiment, probably sent from Parcep. There, to the left, you can see the Lukshmiris.'

He went on to point out Khuts, Obirs, Miridans and Ottoviths. Oled marvelled at his friend's composure. It was as if, in spite of his recent torture, the Imperial advance held no terrors for him.

'Sound the alarm,' Gardep ordered. 'Move those who can't fight up towards the snow line. Three valleys lead up to our position. They are narrow and the sides are sheer. We should be able to defend them for quite some time even with our inferior forces.' He called for his horse. 'We have to block the approaches. If they get through the passes, we have nowhere to run.'

Oled nodded. 'You're right, Gardep, but how do we spread our thin resources across three fronts?'

'Four,' Shamana said. 'We will need a reserve looking east in case they launch an attack from the rear. It would be hard to move a force over the mountains, but not impossible.'

Gardep considered the options. 'I will take the northern pass,' he said. 'That's where the Sol-ket are concentrated. I know the way they fight. Shamana, it is best if you take command of the central approach. It is the hardest to defend. I know you will find a way.'

The She-wolf nodded and took her leave immediately. Gardep continued with his battle orders. 'Oled, you hold the southern side. It suits your style of fighting best. You will be able to mount a charge down the gentler slope.'

Gardep ordered that the horns be sounded. It was time to fight.

2

Rishal oversaw the Imperial advance. 'Send forward the Vassyrians, the Miridans and the Khuts,' he ordered.

Kulmat issued the order. Horns sounded and drums beat.

'Climb quickly,' Rishal ordered. 'A rapid advance is the key to success.'

He permitted himself a smile. He had driven his troops hard, sometimes marching night and day to close the gap with the fleeing Helati. But it had been worth it. He had them in a trap and the jaws were closing. This time there would be no mistakes. The offensive had been many weeks in preparation. He had summoned reserves from Karangpur, Durbai and Parcep, leaving the army based in Rinaghar to pursue the Gussorah rebels. From the scraps of intelligence Murak had been able to smuggle out, he knew that the rebels were half-starved and squabbling among themselves. He marvelled that they weren't more disunited. Only the quality of the enemy leadership had prevented desertion and surrender on an enormous scale.

One man in Rishal's company was not of good heart, however. His squire Kulmat was staring up into the morning sun, searching for some sign of his blood brother, Gardep.

'May Ra keep us apart this day,' he prayed silently. 'May the Sun God preserve us both from harm.'

'My spear,' Rishal barked, breaking in on Kulmat's thoughts. 'Wake up, Kulmat. I want to watch the advance.'

'When do we go forward, Rishal-Ra?' Kulmat asked, his flesh crawling with dread.

'The Sol-ket will be the third wave,' Rishal said. 'Auxiliaries first and second to draw the enemy fire. Then, when the rebel arrows have been expended on barbarian flesh, the Warriors of the Sun will squash the cockroaches with their boots.' He slapped Kulmat's back. 'Why so stern, Kulmat? Is it battle hunger? Do you want some action?'

Kulmat forced a smile. It was only with the greatest difficulty that he uttered his reply. 'Yes, my lord, I am eager to cover myself with glory.'

3

The Vassyrians were thrown against the northern approaches. With their chequered scarves and open-faced helmets, they stood out on the battlefield. Gardep watched them advancing under their white banners and could not help but reflect on his own Vassyrian roots. What if Rishal had never come to Inbacus? What if he had never conquered great Vassyria? What course would Gardep's life have taken then?

'String your bows,' Gardep ordered, driving the uncomfortable thoughts to the back of his mind. 'Choose your targets well and show no mercy.'

He reviewed his archers. They held the high ground and were sheltering behind formidable defences. He rode along the line. He remembered the long evenings spent with Rishal, as squire to his master's knight. He recalled every principle the Lion of Inbacus had instilled in him: show no fear, lead by example, take firm decisions and never, ever reveal a single doubt to the troops under your command. They would be his watchwords. Yet nothing stopped the slamming of his heart and the twist of apprehension in his stomach. These were Vassyrians, his countrymen, not Sol-ket. He gave his order. 'Nock your arrows.'

He listened to the creak of the bows. Oled had taken on the role of armourer. He had done a good job, selecting some of the finest fletchers and steel-smiths from the surrounding villages and convincing them to join the Army of the Free. But, for all Oled's powers of persuasion, they remained few in number. The defenders were still poorly equipped compared with the professional regiments that faced them.

'Steady,' Gardep said, his sword raised. 'Don't shoot until I give the order.'

The Vassyrians were coming on, drums beating and cymbals clashing. The wail of horns echoed across the mountains. From behind the white favours, Vassyrian arrows flew but they clattered uselessly against the sheer walls of the canyon. Specially trained foragers scampered forward to collect the arrows. This was how they had learned to add to their weaponry, by taking from the enemy. The Vassyrians had now reached the narrowest part of the valley and were pressed together, able to proceed five abreast only. That's when Gardep gave the order.

'First cohort,' he shouted, 'loose your arrows. Aim true and choose your target well.'

The defenders emitted a murderous volley. The arrows buzzed as they fell. The deadly hail cut down the first rows of the attacking forces. Sol-ket commanders barked their orders. The second row of soldiers was made to climb over their dead comrades.

'Second cohort,' Gardep commanded, 'aim and shoot.'

The second wave of Vassyrian soldiers found themselves looking into the rain of arrows. Each time one group fell, Gardep would order a halt. Then, the moment fresh troops struggled over the dying and the dead, his sword would fall and a new volley would hiss forth. To his relief, he heard the enemy trumpets sounding the retreat. Though he remembered little of his Vassyrian childhood, his heart ached that he had to fight his own kind and leave so many of them littering the slopes before him.

4

Shamana was being harder pressed in the centre. The climb towards her defensive position was less steep and offered the enemy more cover. The Miridan attackers were able to reduce the effect of the archers with a shield wall. Though less formidable fighters than the Vassyrians in the open field, these spearmen were expert skirmishers. They flitted from boulder to boulder, taking whatever cover they could find, taking care not to expose themselves to the defenders' arrows.

'Lower your bows!' Shamana ordered. They were wasting precious arrows. 'It's time to use our secret weapon.'

Shamana had had her troops working for days filling leather sacks with Lyrian fire. Transforming into an elephant, she braced herself against a wooden stockade packed with the primitively made containers.

'Light the charges,' she barked.

At her command, a dozen Helati set blazing torches to the fuses that were poking from the containers. At the first fizz of the fuses, Shamana put all her weight against the stockade. Balls of Lyrian flame leapt from the mountainside. Black, sulphurous liquid roared into the approaching spearmen, roasting their flesh. Shamana watched as men rolled in agony, turned into living torches by her devices. When she spoke, there was no jubilation in her voice.

'How I curse mankind that we have to wage war.'

But even the hellish resort of Lyrian fire did not end the Miridan offensive. For all the terrible losses the makeshift bombs had inflicted, the Imperial Army had reserves aplenty, ready to return to the attack. The Miridan auxiliaries were set to overwhelm the defenders by sheer force of numbers. Shaman looked around desperately. She was reluctant to commit her ill-equipped and poorly-trained fighters to hand-to-hand fighting at this stage. A sudden reverse and the way would be open to the upper slopes, then on to the rebel camp itself. That's when she saw hundreds of Helati non-combatants streaming down the ravine from the snow line. At the head of them was Bulu, giving orders by gesturing with his mutilated right arm, and Murima, accompanied by Qintu and Harad.

'It looked like you needed help,' Bulu said.

'You can't fight,' Shamana protested, looking at the stump.

'I represent the northern villages on the war council,' Bulu answered. 'I can't wield a sword or shoot a bow to any great effect, but I can direct those who can.'

The new arrivals, mostly women and boys, were gathering what weapons they could from the fallen.

'Get the bows,' Shamana cried. 'Shoot their soldiers before they can reach you.'

The Miridans were no more than a few hundred yards from the defensive lines. There was no armour for these light infantrymen. They wore trousers tucked into their boots and thick jackets. Instead of helmets, they wore caps or turbans. Their protection lay in their speed and mobility.

'Murima, Bulu,' Shamana said. 'Try to inject some discipline into their bow work. They must choose their targets and shoot straight at them.'

She clenched her fist and repeated the key word. 'Discipline.'

Satisfied that the pair could slow the Miridan attack, Shamana looked around frantically. She surveyed the heights that overlooked the ravine. A plan started to form.

'You,' she shouted, addressing one of the men who had built the stockade for her fire devices. 'How did you get the timbers up here?'

'Ropes,' he said. 'Our elephants dragged the logs all the way from the sal forest.'

'Choose a team of your strongest men,' Shamana cried. 'I want them up there.'

The mahout got her drift. 'You can rely on me.'

The Miridans had almost reached the rebels. Shamana leapt onto her horse and rode between the lines. Standing upright in the stirrups, she emptied her quiver at the Miridans. Her example stiffened the rebel resistance.

'Support the She-wolf,' Murima ordered.

Flanked by Qintu and Harad, the daughter of Shinar showed deadly accuracy. From that moment, the Helati recovered their faith in themselves. Their every arrow seemed to tell. The Miridans wavered and fell back to raucous cheers from the Helati.

'Don't celebrate too soon,' Shamana warned. 'It will take them no more than a few moments to regroup and come again.'

Sure enough the Miridans surged forward once more, closing on the Helati. Long, expertly-honed javelins faced a motley collection of bamboo spears, scythes, hoes and clubs. Only the warriors Gardep had trained possessed swords. Hungry and ill-equipped, the risen slaves waited for the enemy to charge. The Miridans drummed their spears against their ox-hide shields and hurled their battle cries at their stubborn but anxious foes. But just as they were about to launch their assault, they heard a fearful rumble. Hundreds of boulders crashed down from the heights to either side. When the dust cleared from the unexpected avalanche, an impassable barricade blocked their way. High above, the mahout's team danced in wild celebration. This time Shamana didn't try to stop them. The pass was closed.

5

Rishal read the message and dismissed the rider who had delivered it. His face was hard with fury.

'What news, Rishal-Ra?' Kulmat asked.

'The rebels have closed the central approach,' the commander snarled. 'That's where I expected our first success. I sought to break through and outflank the enemy.'

Kulmat forced a show of outrage.

'But how could slaves hold the line against a regiment of Miridans?' he asked. 'It was a wide valley. They had plenty of cover. It was perfect for the spearmen. What went wrong?'

'This is the She-wolf's doing,' Rishal said. 'More of her shape-shifting tricks. She burned the Miridans' tails with Lyrian fire, the same stock they stole from our own troops.

Now a rock-fall has blocked the pass. The Miridans have suffered grievous losses. Where the hell is Murak? What's the point of a spy when he gives us no information?' He reached for his weapons. 'After this fiasco, I must enter the fray myself. I will destroy the traitor cadet and behead this rebellion. Gardep is mine. Sound the muster, Kulmat.'

Kulmat stood rooted to the spot.

'Now!' Rishal roared. 'Do I have to repeat every order twice?'

'No, Rishal-Ra.'

Kulmat's heart was pounding. The moment he had dreaded was at hand.

6

The defence of the southern valley lay in the balance. Their arrows and spears exhausted, Oled's tiny force would have no choice but to engage the Obirs in close combat. The Obirs were fierce tribesmen from the far north east, a land reputed to be without law or civilisation. Eking out a wretched existence on bleak, wind-swept plains almost devoid of plant growth, the Obirs sold themselves to the highest bidder, simply in order to live. The coffers of Rinaghar ensured their survival, hence their loyalty. But the Helati did not break before their wild onrush. When the slave troops got the signal to charge their battle cry was a simple one:

'Freedom!'

Attacking the Obirs head on was a risky undertaking. Should they fail, they would leave the camp vulnerable. Waiting there, less than five hundred armed fighters were available to defend the old, the young and the weak. Oled led his cavalry down the slope on stolen Selessian horses.

Their forward momentum carried them through the front row of the Obir warriors. A roar went up as the Obirs looked to close the line behind them but Oled had trained his horsemen well. When many cavalry units would have thundered on to pillage the enemy baggage train, Oled's riders refused the spoils of war and returned to the fray. Their cause was freedom, not loot. Wheeling about, they cut a swathe through the massing Obirs and prepared to charge again.

'Stay together,' Oled shouted. 'Keep your formation the way I showed you. Remain disciplined and you will triumph.' He looked around. 'Has anybody seen Murak?'

'Over there.'

Murak had his back to Oled. When Oled shouted to him he very nearly leapt out of his skin.

'What's the matter?' Oled laughed. 'Got a guilty secret?'

'No,' Murak answered, 'I was taking a rest. I am not fully recovered from my injuries.'

'Are you strong enough to fight?' Oled asked, concern in his green eyes.

'I'm ready,' Murak said, picking up his bow and sword and climbing into the saddle.

'Ride by my side,' Oled said. 'Good hunting.'

Murak laughed and they charged again. It was too much for the foot soldiers of Obiristan. Cut down in their dozens, the northmen fled back towards the Imperial camp. A triumphant roar rose from several hundred Helat throats. Then, just as quickly, it died.

'By the Four Winds,' Oled groaned, seeing a new threat emerging from the mist. 'That was but the first wave.'

Less than half a mile away he could see the scarlet and gold banners of the Sol-ket. They were marching up the slope on foot, preceded by the remnants of the Miridans that had attacked Shamana.

'They have to number at least five thousand,' Oled said. He could sense the tide of dismay eddying through his men.

'More like eight,' Murak said. 'See the cavalry being drawn up to either side of the infantry.'

Oled called over two of Nikesh's rough riders. 'You, take a message to the She-wolf. Ask if she can spare us any reinforcements. You, take the same message to Gardep.' He rubbed his whiskery jaw. 'It will be some time before reinforcements can reach us. That's if they come at all. Before then, we are in for a bitter fight.'

Murak nodded. 'At this very moment they will be discussing the reward for your head. They always put a price on the enemy commanders' heads.'

'Really?' Oled said. 'How much do you think I will bring?'

'Oh, a thousand dinar at least.'

'A thousand dinar!' Oled said. 'That's the most I've been worth in my whole life.' The giant gripped his battle-axe. 'Well, the dogs will have to earn their coins.'

Kicking his horse up the hill, Oled set about rallying his cavalry.

'We are facing a multitude many times our size,' he said. 'It isn't Obir tribesmen we're facing now. The backbone of the attacking force is made up of a crack Sol-ket regiment.'

A murmur rose from the ranks.

'Yes, you know the reputation of the Sol-ket. Some of you have been involved in skirmishes with their patrols. Well, this is the real thing, a pitched battle with the Imperial elite.' He could see the tension in hundreds of faces. 'But you know what that means,' he shouted above the battle cries of the enemy. 'They have had to send their best against us. Think about it. It means they're afraid of us. That's right, on Jinghara Plain you didn't run. You fought scores of rearguard actions against them. You drew Sol-ket blood. They are not invincible. They're men. They bleed, just like the rest of us. If they are all-powerful, why are they throwing a whole regiment against us?' He leaned forward in the saddle. By now, he was having to fight to be heard over the drums and horns of the Warriors of the Sun. 'Well, let's not disappoint them. Draw your swords and strike them down. Earn their respect with cold steel. We must hold this position until our comrades send reserves. Prevail against these battle-hardened soldiers and you can take the field against any fighters in the land. Have courage, brothers. Have hope, sisters. Fight for your freedom!'

But as Oled led the charge, he did not see a bow being bent and an arrow hissing through the air towards him.

7

On the northern front of the battle, Kulmat was reluctantly accompanying Rishal to the head of his regiment, doing his best to hide his true feelings. The remnants of the Vassyrian charge were limping past.

'It seems my young protégé has learned his lessons well,' Rishal said.

Oblivious to Kulmat's expression of dread, the commander shielded his eyes.

'He still has a lot to learn, however. He has more fighters than weapons. See, they are short of arrows. Let's test them a while longer with the infantry.'

The infantry moved in from the flanks. They formed a shield wall and started the climb towards the rebel lines. The cavalry advanced behind them, ready to begin their gallop.

'You're a lucky man, Kulmat,' Rishal said.

'How's that, Rishal-Ra?' Kulmat asked, feeling anything but lucky.

'Your first great battle was Jinghara Plain,' Rishal explained. 'There you witnessed the defeat of the Lost Souls. Now you will see the end of the servile threat. We are about to ensure further centuries of Imperial rule. How does it feel to be part of such a great undertaking?'

'I am very lucky,' Kulmat answered, trying to hide the flatness in his voice.

'Indeed you are,' Rishal said. 'Why, I must have been almost thirty years old before I participated in such a conflict.' He indicated the retreating Vassyrians. 'I feel sorry for these men. Once they were the proudest warriors on the continent. Now . . .' He sighed. 'Now we use them as pin cushions to exhaust the enemy's arrows.'

One passing Vassyrian overheard Rishal. His head snapped round and savage resentment lit his face.

'What's the matter?' Rishal demanded, noticing the reaction. 'Do my words offend you?'

The Vassyrian lowered his eyes. 'No, my lord.'

'No,' Rishal said. 'I didn't think so.'

Once he was out of Rishal's sight, the Vassyrian wiped a bitter tear away with his chequered scarf. One day, Rishal would have cause to remember the warrior's name. It was Adrius.

8

From his vantage point overlooking the battlefield, Gardep could see Shamana, Murima and Nikesh leading their troops to support Oled. He knew the Army of the Free was staring defeat in the face.

'This is bad,' he murmured, sensing the lonely burden of command.

Then, relegating his worries to the back of his mind, he went to examine the archers' quivers. They were almost empty.

'When there is nothing else to shoot,' Gardep told them, 'arm yourself any way you can and support our charge.'

The faces that looked back at him were grim. They had accepted that they were going to die. Turning his back on the archers, Gardep joined his cavalry. If Rishal could see their equipment, he would be laughing himself sick. The riders had little armour to protect their bodies and there were even fewer helmets to go round. Whereas every Solket rode a thoroughbred Selessian mount, many of Gardep's cavalry had to make do with ponies, even mules. For all that, Gardep was happy to die alongside these fighters. They were defending a cause greater than themselves: the belief that no man should hold another as a chattel. One thing alone gave him cause for regret. He might never see Cusha again. He imagined her trekking through the Khut lands, snowflakes landing on her hair and settling on her face. Closing his eyes, Gardep could imagine the scene. For a moment, in his mind's eye, he was there beside her, sharing the stark beauty of the Mountains of the Moon. But a shout dispersed his daydream.

'Here they come again!'

At the shouted warning, the archers planted their feet and drew their bows. Their contribution to the battle was almost over. Gardep watched the forward march of the Imperial infantry. Their shields were well made and strengthened with a boss that could club a man senseless. Maybe a third of the remaining arrows would bounce off them. It was time to try another tactic.

'Shoot into the air,' Gardep ordered. 'In this terrain,

they will be forced to bunch together as they attack. When they do, shoot over their shields.'

The archers raised their bows and waited. And waited. The Sol-ket heavy infantrymen were patient. The tramp, tramp, tramp of their boots made the ground shake.

'Steady,' Gardep said.

Officers started to bark commands along the line. The Sol-ket infantry began its charge.

'Now!'

Running at full tilt, the Sol-ket did not have time to raise their shields to protect their heads. The arrows fell like murderous, black rain. Half the attackers had breathed their last. Gardep's move had broken the first offensive. But it did not end the conflict. At that moment, Rishal appeared through the mist, followed by Kulmat.

9

Shamana hoisted herself into the saddle of a loose horse.

'What's he doing?' Murima said, noticing a solitary mounted archer. The man had covered his face. For some reason he had dropped back behind the rest of Oled's unit. He was taking aim not at the enemy but at his own general.

Shamana followed the direction of Murima's stare and cried out: 'Oled, my son!'

Hearing the warning shout, the giant of the Tanjurs reacted with great agility. Loosening the reins, he slipped down in the saddle. The archer's arrow whistled past. Reseating himself, Oled continued the charge as if nothing had happened. The Army of the Free, a thinning band barely numerous enough to deserve that grand title, crashed into the enemy throwing their foremost ranks into disarray. Shamana and Nikesh followed Oled's men into battle. In the confusion, the mysterious archer made his escape.

The Sol-ket were shouting their battle cries. 'Destroy the cockroaches. Victory or death!'

The press of the enemy was becoming irresistible. Oled's cavalry was being hemmed in on every side.

'Cover each other's backs,' Oled ordered. 'You are a band of brothers and sisters. Live together or die together. For freedom!'

He looked around for Murak. 'Has anybody seen Murak?' he cried.

'I think I saw him fall,' one warrior said. 'It was back there.'

Oled beat his saddle with his fist. Murak fallen after having the courage to walk away from the Sol-ket . . . it was almost too much to bear. Another brave man lost in combat, and an exceptional one.

'Nobody runs,' he cried, raging at the injustice of conflict. 'Fight to the last man.'

Oled's beleaguered warriors followed their general's example. Though they were outnumbered and with no hope of relief, they fought furiously. Oled's chest swelled with pride to see slaves become heroes. As he swung his battle-axe to right and left, he wondered about the shout he had heard, warning him about a stray arrow. It had sounded like his mother, but how could that be?

The desperate struggle continued. Soon, such was the crush of the Sol-ket cavalry around the rebels that it was almost impossible to swing a weapon. Strangely, this was working to the advantage of the Army of the Free, preventing the Warriors of the Sun making their greater numbers tell. But Oled knew the stalemate would not last long.

'By the Four Winds,' he murmured. 'We need a miracle to come out of this alive.'

The miracle came in the form of a mighty war elephant thundering into the enemy, followed by a regiment of horses under the command of Nikesh. The power of the charge cut a wedge into the heaving, hacking mass and Oled was able to lead his battered cavalry back up the slope.

'Mother,' he said, seeing Shamana return to human form. 'That warning. I thought it was your voice.'

Shamana chuckled. 'Yes, big as you are, you still need your mother to take care of you!'

10

Amid the terrible clamour of battle, Rishal picked out Gardep. Seeing his former cadet just a few hundred yards away, he roared his challenge.

'Face me, Gardep na-Vassyrian,' he shouted.

Gardep forced his way to the front through the closely packed ranks of his warriors. He emerged from the meagre ranks of the defenders, bloodstained and weary from the long struggle.

'Face me, traitor,' Rishal shouted again.

Standing just behind Rishal's right shoulder, Kulmat willed Gardep to hide, to melt back into rebel ranks. You are not ready to face him, he thought. But he knew it was not in Gardep's character to hide.

'Is this your army?' Rishal cried, beating his way towards his former squire. 'All those years I prepared you for glory and renown in the eyes of Ra. But you gave it up . . . for this! Look around, you damned fool. Slaves these people were and slaves they will be again. That can never change. It is in their nature. Don't you understand that this is the immutable law of life, that some are born to rule and others to be ruled?'

The two men were just yards from each other now. The tide of battle was thinning, leaving a mere handful of exhausted warriors between them.

'Do you not have eyes, na-Vassyrian?' Rishal scoffed. 'You are outnumbered and outfought.'

A bold Helat warrior hurled himself at Rishal. He paid the ultimate price for his courage. Rishal cut him down and shoved his lifeless body away. Then he turned his horse to face Gardep.

'It's over,' Rishal declared. 'Here's a bargain. You know the way of the Sol-ket. Every warrior with a sword in his hand will die by sunset. Shinar had many times this number and he could not beat us. Walk away from this miserable rabble you call an army. Do that and I will let you live.'

Gardep's fighters turned to hear his answer. Their general didn't let them down. He hurled Rishal's offer back in his face. 'Even if I did take you at your word, what kind of life would I have? You say you would let me live. Where? How would I spend my days? Tell me that, Lion of Inbacus. You would throw me in some filthy dungeon, wouldn't you? You would make me suffer the way the Muzals made venerable Udmanesh suffer.'

Every warrior under his command was listening, hanging on his every word. The speech wasn't for Rishal. It was for them.

'Better to die with a sword in my hand and the sun on my face than to live in the gloom of a cell, hating myself for my craven surrender. Prepare yourself, Rishal. We, the Army of the Free, may be few in number but I swear, it will cost you dear to win your victory.'

Spurred by the heartened shouts of his fighters, Gardep joined swords with his former master.

11

'There was an assassin,' Murima said. 'At the same moment your mother cried out, I saw him. He wore a mask and concealed himself among the stragglers. It was no chance arrow. You were his target.'

'An assassin,' Oled said.

'Yes,' Murima said. 'He had his face covered, as I have said. One thing is certain. He did not come from enemy lines. This was a soldier in the Army of the Free. He would have shot you in the back.'

Oled's face clouded. 'Has anybody seen Atrakon?' he demanded.

'There you go again,' Shamana scolded, 'jumping to conclusions.'

'Who is more practised in the arts of assassination than the Selessian?' Oled demanded.

Shamana shook her head. 'There is no time to resolve this now. We have a battle to win.'

'It makes me sick at heart to think that we have a traitor in our ranks,' Oled said, 'and that we have allowed him to ride with us, break bread with us, fight alongside us.'

'Don't you think it hurts me too?' Shamana demanded. 'We share a dream, Oled, of a comradeship of the peoples. I heard Shinar's words all those years ago, before we faced the Warriors of the Sun on the field at Dullah. He reminded us of our aim, to create a Republic of the Free, without oppression or division. Now here, in our ranks, we have a man who reminds us of the old, cruel world. I want the traitor found, Oled. Unlike you, I believe in law. I want proof of his identity.'

At this point Nikesh reminded them of the proximity

of the enemy. Already, the Sol-ket were closing on them once more.

'We must retreat,' Shamana said. 'We can still hold the higher ground.'

Oled nodded. 'I will give the order.'

As Shamana turned to remount her horse, she stumbled.

'Are you all right?' Oled asked anxiously.

Shamana brushed him away. 'I'm getting too old for this,' she said. 'The effort of transformation drained me a little, that's all. I shall recover presently.' She wagged her finger under Oled's nose. 'If you'd learned your lessons better, you could take a weight off my shoulders. I remember when the three of us charged, you, Aaliya and me. Tell me the form you took then. Rhinoceros indeed! Now, let's fall back to those rocks. We must not let them pass.'

Oled nodded. Images burst into his mind, reminding him of the cost of defeat. He thought of the thousands of Helati who had left their villages to join the Army of the Free. They had marched across Jinghara in search of a refuge from lives of unremitting hardship. They had come to escape the casual cruelty of the Sol-ket. He saw the young people, the old, the women heavy with child. The sight of their faces, so bright with hope, so trusting, filled him with torment.

'We will protect our people,' he said defiantly. 'Whatever the cost, they will never return to slavery. Never!'

With that, the Tanjurs, mother and son, led their badly mauled cavalry up the slope towards the camp's final defences. What neither of them saw was the lone archer following at a safe distance.

12

Gardep wheeled round, barely escaping Rishal's lunge. The blade slid along his ribs, slicing open the skin. There was pain but it seemed far away, as if the wound belonged to somebody else. He became aware of a curious stillness, here at the heart of the battle. Though fighting continued in the distance, many warriors, both Helat and Sol-ket, had lowered their weapons. They were watching the furious duel between the opposing generals. Sensing his own deep exhaustion and the anxiety of his soldiers, Gardep forced himself to sit tall in the saddle, despite the blood that was oozing down his side. The wound made him groan. He sensed somebody by his side, guiding him away from Rishal. He recognised his rescuer. It was Atrakon Ebrahin.

'Is the hurt grave, my lord?' the Selessian asked.

Gardep stared at him then spoke.

'Listen to me, all of you,' he said. 'Don't ever call me or any other leader of the Army of the Free *lord.*'

Noticing Kulmat standing among the Sol-ket, listening to him, Gardep chose his words carefully.

'In this cause,' he cried, 'we are all brothers and sisters. We are equal before the sky and the Four Winds. Our loyalty to each other is worth all the coin in golden Rinaghar's treasury. There will be no Masters among us.'

Chastened, Atrakon smiled. 'It is a great dream, Gardep. But you are wounded. Let me take your place against Rishal.'

Gardep shook his head. 'I can't let you do that, Atrakon. I am the general of this army. It is my fight.'

Reluctantly, Atrakon stepped back. 'He comes again, brother Gardep.'

Gardep turned to face Rishal. 'No matter what happens to me,' he told the assembled Helati, 'I have been proud to lead you.'

Then he spurred his horse forward. He had an appointment with death.

CHAPTER 8

A Great Heart Stops Beating

1

While Gardep was preparing to face the man who had once been a second father to him, but now wished to destroy him, the Sol-ket were advancing on the southern front. The Army of the Free were fighting a rearguard action. For all their courage, they were being driven out of the valley. The Imperial infantry continued to press and the Sol-ket cavalry were making repeated charges against the rebel flanks, dispersing their opponents.

'If we do not hold them here,' Murima cried, 'Gardep will be caught in a pincer movement. Our fight for freedom will end on these slopes.'

'Yes,' Oled said, 'then the Sol-ket will have us all at their mercy. I have seen them at the point of conquest. They will make an example of every man, woman and child they can find.'

Everybody remembered the village massacre, when the ashes of fifty innocents were left to nourish the fields of Jinghara. It was impossible not to imagine the outrages the Sol-ket would visit on the Helati presently huddled in the camp. In his years at the fort of Zindhar, Oled in particular had witnessed at first hand the ruthlessness of the Warriors of the Sun. They would not care about the condition of their captives or their ability to fight. Be they old and frail, sick or infirm, they would face the same vengeful wrath. Be they women about to give birth or nursing mothers, they would suffer for the resistance of their fighters. The Sol-ket did not distinguish between their victims. They saw only rebels. They had been known to slaughter entire towns, dispatching every living soul to the House of the Dead. Sometimes they even butchered the animals, not for food, but to demonstrate how they dealt with resistance.

'Archers!' Oled shouted. 'To me. Murima, Bulu, I must prepare the cavalry. Take charge here.'

While Oled addressed the fighters on horseback, Murima reorganised them into three lines. She stood at the front, bow in hand, Bulu paced the lines, passing her instructions along.

'When I give the order, row by row you will keep up a steady stream of arrows. As the archers in the first row release their shafts, those in the second row will string theirs. Behind them, the third row will stand ready, waiting for Bulu to give the sign. In this way we will give the Sol-ket no respite. They must be weakened by the time Oled leads his charge.'

She didn't tell them what would happen if their quivers were empty before Oled was ready.

'On my signal,' Murima said.

The Sol-ket came again.

'First row,' Murima said. 'Now!'

She watched the foremost Imperial soldiers crumple to the ground.

'Second row,' Murima said. 'Now!'

Though they lost many men, the Sol-ket marched on, a remorseless line of red and gold. They were nothing if not courageous.

'Third row. Now!'

So it went on until the last arrow had been shot. Seeing the Sol-ket continuing their advance like an implacable juggernaut, Oled took over and roared his final command.

'Charge!'

He led the way back into the fray, battle-axe swinging. It was at this point, unseen by anyone, that the assassin emerged from the crowd. For a second time he bent his bow. Again, Oled was the target. But once more Shamana's keen ear heard the arrow's flight. With a cry she rode forward, using her mount to push her son out of harm's way. In so doing, she exposed herself to the danger. The arrowhead embedded itself in the flesh between throat and shoulder. Gasping for breath, Shamana crashed to the ground.

'Mother, no!' Oled cried, dismounting.

While he knelt to examine the wound, Nikesh stood over them, raising his shield. The assassin shot two more arrows. One missed its target, the other rebounded off the boss of Nikesh's shield. Then the traitor sought the only sanctuary available to him. He vanished into the welcoming ranks of the Sol-ket, who roared their congratulations.

'Is the wound deep?' Oled asked.

Shamana waved him away. Gritting her teeth, she snapped the shaft. 'It will take more than this to bring me down,' she growled. 'It is but a pinprick. Stop fussing, Oled. We have work to do.'

For all her brave words, pain was written into her features. A sheen of sweat covered her face. 'How goes the fight?' she demanded.

'Badly,' Nikesh said. 'When you went down, the cavalry broke off the charge. Our soldiers are wavering.'

Oled clung to Shamana, like the little boy he had once been. 'No,' he protested, 'you are wounded.'

Shamana squeezed his hand. 'Are you so blind?' she said, pointing to the blood that was soaking her tunic. 'I am worse than wounded. Oled, my son, darkness swims before my eyes. I am dying.'

'No,' Oled moaned. 'I refuse to believe it. Let me accompany you to the rear. I will get you medical attention.'

'Stop it, Oled,' Shamana told him. 'Stop deceiving your-self. How can you deny the evidence of your own eyes? At battle's end I will join my ancestors in the House of the Dead. You can read the signs as well as I.'

Oled continued to protest but with little effect. Shamana pushed him away and took her first stumbling steps towards the Sol-ket.

'Our warriors are on the verge of breaking,' she raged. 'I have to fight. I am the She-wolf, queen of the Tanjurs.'

The thunder of hooves made Shamana's mind up. The Imperial heavy cavalry was about to crash into the falter-ing rebel line.

'I have to keep alive the dream of liberation,' Shamana said. 'This is my final test.'

'Mother, no,' Oled protested. 'No heart is greater than yours, but you are old. You have suffered a grievous wound. Let me try.'

Shamana shook her head. 'How many times have I

scolded you for this?' she said. 'You have spent too much time with the Sol-ket. You have almost forgotten the ancient arts of your people. By the Four Winds, I wish Aaliya were here.'

The words wounded Oled, but there was no time to continue the exchange. By now the rebels had been forced so far back that they could see Gardep's regiment in the distance. Strangely, they seemed to be standing watching something. Nikesh wondered why there was no sign of battle.

'I have to break their charge,' Shamana said. 'It's our only chance.'

Oled was beside himself. 'No,' he cried. 'There has to be another way.'

Shamana whispered in her son's ear. 'Find it in your soul to achieve your destiny, and there will be.'

Then she started to run. As she did, her features began to change. A war elephant replaced the woman. But it was not as before. This time there was agony in her eyes. The transformation seemed to eddy across her body between the two states of being. The blood that had at first stained only her shoulder was now spilling down the grey hide of the elephant. Even as she covered the ground between her own lines and those of the Sol-ket, her pace was slowing. Still she fought to complete the transformation. She was part woman, part beast, staggering towards the onrushing horsemen. The elephant trumpeted. Shamana's voice followed. It was a mantra she had repeated many times: 'Damn me for growing old.'

'She can't do it,' Nikesh yelled, cutting down an attacking Sol-ket. 'It's too much for her.'

Oled rode after her, doing his best to shield her from the enemy arrows.

'No more,' he yelled. 'You're killing yourself.'

But there was a greater danger than the metamorphosis. As she fought to stabilise the transformation, the foremost Sol-ket rose in their stirrups intensifying the volleys of arrows into her throat and chest. Oled's efforts at protection were in vain. Shamana screamed in agony. The elephant's trunk rose pitifully then the beast shrank back into the woman. Scarlet blood burst from her mouth.

'Mother!'

A final arrow thudded into her. Oled saw the source of the arrow. His insides turned over as he recognised the bowman.

2

Far away, Cusha screamed at the very moment Shamana fell under the assassin's arrow.

'What is it?' Vishtar asked.

Cusha fell into her brother's arms.

'Is there nothing you can do to help her?' Omar asked.

Vishtar stared at her in horror. 'The pain is not Cusha's,' he said. 'She suffers another's death throes.'

'Whose?'

Vishtar shook his head.

'Traitor,' Cusha groaned, 'why did we not expose the traitor?' She clawed at her face. 'We tended his wounds. We treated him as our brother.'

She shuddered, as if a cold more intense, more numbing than the glacial wind outside, were stealing through the marrow of her bones.

'We obeyed what is written in the Book of Scales,' she whispered. 'We treated our poor suffering brother as we would be treated ourselves.' She seized Vishtar by the collar. 'Were we wrong?' she asked him. 'Should we have rejected him? In this barbarous world, is pity a crime?'

She released her brother. 'We have condemned the greatest of us to an agonising end,' she sobbed. 'Is there no justice in this land? Is there no goodness?'

She gave another shriek of misery and collapsed back into Vishtar's arms.

3

Gardep was riding towards Rishal. It was the third pass. Both men's armour and shields were dented and spattered with blood. The fight was nearing its end.

'Rishal has the advantage,' Atrakon murmured. 'He is fresh, while Gardep is exhausted from hours in the field.'

As yet, there seemed to be little evidence for this assessment. Master and pupil seemed evenly matched, trading blow for blow in the midst of a lethal struggle. Raising himself high in his stirrups, Gardep braced himself for Rishal's blow. His former master's blows had weakened him more than he cared to admit. When Rishal's sword crashed into the shield, Gardep felt the vibration run right down to the soles of his feet. Sagging back into the saddle, he had a sense of the world spinning around him. Still struggling to clear his head and regain control of his galloping mount, Gardep pointed his sword and gave the battle cry he had learned as a cadet: 'Victory or death!'

Swaying and rocking in the saddle, Gardep managed to gather the reins and turn his horse. Such was the speed of the fourth pass, the world seemed to blur as he swept towards Rishal. When the clash of steel against steel came again, with redoubled force, the shock of impact travelled through Gardep, rocking him backwards. His arm was on fire. His spine shuddered like a young sapling under the blow of the sword. But he was not unhorsed. Desperately twisting his hands through the reins, he clung on.

'This is it,' Atrakon said, 'Rishal is going to kill him.'

Hauling himself upright with his reins, a shaken Gardep struggled to wheel about. But he had no control over his panic-stricken mount. Before he could turn, Rishal was thundering towards him again, sword raised above his head. Gardep knew what that meant. He had thrown caution to the wind and was about to deliver the lethal blow. He had decided his former squire was in no state to defend himself. Pulling frantically at the reins, Gardep tried to steady himself. There was no time. With a roar, Rishal was upon him. This time the Sol-ket general's forward momentum was unstoppable. With a cry, Gardep crashed painfully to the ground. It was through sheer will power that he staggered to his feet. Even as he reeled, blinking sticky gobbets of blood out of his eyes, he saw Rishal striding towards him, confident and strong.

'So this is how it ends, na-Vassyrian. The master teaches the pupil. Then he kills him.'

He didn't waste another word. He scythed down at Gardep. These were not the subtle thrusts and parries Rishal had taught his squire at the Academy. They were brutal, clubbing blows, born out of pure fury. Under the force of one such blow, Gardep sank to the earth. Rishal grabbed his hair and displayed his weary opponent to the ranks of the Helati.

'Do you see, slaves?' Rishal bellowed. 'Do you witness this, you Helat dogs? This is the best man you have. But what is he now? Look at him; he is a boy to be beaten and whipped. I made him and I will destroy him.'

The insult put new strength into Gardep. Seeing his soldiers starting to bow their heads like the slaves they had always been, he tore himself free of Rishal. Incensed and determined to reignite the fire of revolt in their hearts, he summoned every ounce of strength into one last show of defiance.

'Raise your heads,' Gardep cried. 'Be proud, Warriors of the Free. Death will not conquer me. I will be avenged. My blood will nourish new revolts. I will be millions.'

Tossing his shield aside, he took his sword in a two-handed grip and drove at Rishal, rocking him back on his heels.

'You gloat too early, ax-Sol,' he panted.

For a moment, Rishal was himself being forced to retreat. Both men were exhausted and gasping for breath. Finally, Rishal recovered enough to speak. 'Well done, pupil. You're the first man to evade my death-thrust.' He searched for Kulmat in the crowd. 'Do you see, squire Kulmat?' he asked. 'Do you see the man I made? He learns his lessons well.'

Gardep followed the direction of Rishal's stare. He saw that Kulmat had his hand on the hilt of his sword. Was he about to intervene, taking a stand against his own knight? Gardep gave a brief shake of the head and his boyhood friend reluctantly slid the blade back into its scabbard. Straightening his back, Gardep hurled himself at Rishal. But the Lion of Inbacus deflected the blow with disconcerting ease.

'You have great courage,' Rishal told Gardep, 'but that does not make you my equal, Gardep. You will always be the pupil and I the master.'

With that, he swung his sword with such force it brushed Gardep's blade aside. Rishal slashed the younger man's side. Grunting with pain, Gardep clamped a hand to his ribs. He couldn't stop the blood oozing through his fingers. It was soon soaking his uniform. A roar went up from the Sol-ket lines. It was the decisive blow.

'First blood to Rishal-ax-Sol, Lion of Inbacus.'

But it was the last blood he would spill that day. Rishal would be the next to suffer. The wound would come from an unexpected quarter.

4

The Sol-ket fell upon Shamana like vultures, desperate to deliver the deathblow. Half a dozen men jostled to claim a coveted title that would earn him renown across the Empire. They all wanted to be known as the She-wolf's conqueror. Kicking and spitting at her tormentors, Shamana roared her defiance.

'Not one of you is worthy of striking the blow,' she told them. 'Rally, you Warriors of the Free. Don't be downhearted. What do these dogs fight for but to spread misery and fear, to fill their villas with precious things? What kind of cause is that?'

The nearest warrior lunged at her but a blade crossed his. It belonged to the traitor, Murak. 'A pretty speech, witch,' he said. 'I'm going to make sure it's your last. You have found the man worthy of striking the deathblow. I outwitted you. I outwitted your fool of a son.'

'Kill me, then,' Shamana retorted. 'You will not kill my cause. It is written in the Book of Scales that to fight for one tortured and enslaved soul is to fight for all mankind.'

She twisted to call to the Helati. 'Don't give up. Throw them back into the valleys.'

Murak shook his head, almost in pity. But the triumphant smile was short-lived, erased by the vast shadow that had fallen over him. A bull elephant, covered in glittering armour, reared on its hind legs and trumpeted its war rage. Then, with earth-shattering force, it

166

dropped its front legs on two of the soldiers who had encircled Shamana, stamping the life from them.

'Oled!' Pride shone through the She-wolf's pain. 'I prayed for this day to come,' she said. 'You have proven yourself a true son of the Tanjurs. Now destroy the oppressors and defend our people.'

Just as Oled dwarfed all mortal men, so the beast that he had become dwarfed any elephant the Sol-ket had ever seen. Some stood in helpless fascination. Others, with unsteady hands, tried to launch their spears. Still others threw down their weapons and ran. While Nikesh and his men formed a protective cordon, Murima, Qintu and Harad bore Shamana away to safety, and the war elephant drove its tusks through two Sol-ket before tossing them into their comrades.

'Kill him!' Murak howled as he turned to flee.

But the galloping horses of the Sol-ket had been thrown into panic and confusion by the beast's titanic onslaught. They unseated their riders and fled, crashing into the ranks behind them.

'For Ra's sake,' the warrior-priest shrieked at the awestruck Sol-ket, 'stop gawping and fight.'

But the forward rush of the Warriors of the Sun had been halted. Maddened by despair, the war-elephant rampaged through the screaming horses and their horrified riders. Only Murak seemed capable of rational thought. He stopped running and tried to rally the fleeing men. Even as Oled, in the form of the vengeance-intoxicated beast, sought him out, the infiltrator demanded a javelin.

'Javelin, damn you!' he bawled into the face of one wide-eyed young soldier. 'The creature has a heart. It is mortal. We can kill it.'

Spinning round, Murak prepared to hurl his weapon. But the war elephant was upon him, thrusting its mighty tusks at him and snatching the javelin away with its trunk. Disarmed, Murak could only flee, springing into the saddle of a riderless horse and vanishing into the confused maelstrom that was the disintegrating Sol-ket regiment.

5

Seeing Gardep tumble backwards, bleeding heavily, Atrakon ran to his aid, blocking Rishal's way.

'Do you have no sense of honour?' Rishal shouted, outraged that the Selessian had intervened. 'I am the victor. You have no right to intervene.'

'You dare talk of honour!' Atrakon snarled. 'Your infernal Hotec-Ra stole *my* honour. They made me hate myself. Back there in Jinghara, you butchered unarmed boys. You used the sorcery of the Hotec-Ra to burn them alive. Where is the honour in that? No, Rishal, I am a Selessian by birth and by every beat of my heart. Unlike Gardep, I am not bound by your criminal traditions. I will not obey your wretched Sol-ket code.'

'I have triumphed in single combat,' Rishal insisted. 'I demand that you hand over the boy.'

Atrakon drew his sabre. 'Demand all you like, ax-Sol,' he said. 'If you want to get to Gardep, you will have to go through me.' He laughed. 'That's right. War isn't a game. I have only one rule. I will do anything I can to protect my comrades and end the tyrants' rule.' He turned and shouted a new battle cry to the Helat ranks. 'Death to the Muzals!'

Rishal's eyes narrowed. 'You will pay for that, desert rat,' he said. 'I will cut you down and claim my kill.'

Atrakon could sense Gardep trying to get his attention.

'Rishal is right, Atrakon,' Gardep croaked. 'This is between him and me.'

Atrakon shook his head. 'You've got a lot to learn, Gardep. This isn't about two men. It isn't about individual pride or honour, or whatever fool idea drives you. It is about the cause of freedom.'

Rishal listened to the exchange then addressed Atrakon. 'I will make you grovel at my feet, Selessian,' he spat. He half-turned. 'Kulmat,' he said, 'give me a new sword.'

Even as Kulmat hesitated, a spear penetrated the general's thigh. Spinning round, Rishal fixed Atrakon with an accusing stare. 'Coward!' he yelled.

But it was not Atrakon who had thrown the spear. It was a young Vassyrian by the name of Adrius.

He taunted Rishal. 'Now who's a pin cushion, general?'

While the Vassyrians turned on their former masters, the Sol-ket carried Rishal to safety.

6

Sunset brought an uneasy peace to the Dragon Mountains. There was no sense of victory in either camp. In the foothills, Rishal was undergoing surgery. He refused the preparations that would dull the pain.

'Just tell me how long it will be before I can fight again,' he snapped.

The surgeon looked startled. 'Rishal-Ra, I have not even removed the spearhead. How can you think of battle?'

Rishal cursed him. 'You said there was no major damage. I will heal, won't I?'

'That is my best guess, yes.'

'So get the infernal thing out. I will be back in the saddle within weeks.'

He didn't tell the surgeon the reason. The sixty-day month of Buradish was half over. The world was dying.

'Well,' Rishal grumbled, 'what are you waiting for?'

The surgeon gave the general a leather strap to bite on. When he pulled the spearhead from Rishal's thigh, the scream could be heard in the rebel camp. There, Shamana was also receiving medical attention. But there would be no helping the She-wolf. 'What's that noise?' she asked, her voice no more than a frail whisper.

Outside the tent there was the sound of hammering and sawing. The Army of the Free were working on their defensive.

'Bulu is building a palisade,' Murima explained.

'That's good,' Shamana said. 'That's very good.'

Nobody shared her confidence. They all knew that, though the final blow had not been struck in the Battle of the Dragon Mountains, as sure as the winds blow, the Imperial Army would attack at dawn. Around the bed were gathered those who knew Shamana best: Murima, Gardep, Qintu, Harad and Atrakon. Recently returned from having his wounds dressed, Gardep was bandaged and propped up on a makeshift litter. Then, finally, there was her grieving son, Oled.

'You have something to say to Atrakon,' Shamana said.

Tears welled in Oled's green eyes. 'I have been a fool, brother Ebrahin,' he said. 'Do you have it in your heart to forgive me?'

'I bear you no ill will,' Atrakon said with a quiet dignity. 'I too bear the burden of my failings. We are mortal men. We make mistakes. Let the matter rest at that.'

'There must be something we can do,' Harad said, staring at Shamana. 'She can't die.'

Murima shook her head. 'The She-wolf is beyond our help.'

There was no consolation for Oled. He knelt at his mother's side, watching her fade from the world.

'Who's there?' she said, fighting back the darkness that had gathered around her.

'It's me, Oled.'

'You found your greatness today,' she said, patting his arm.

'The price was too great, mother.'

'Who else is here? Cusha?'

Oled, Gardep and Murima exchanged sorrowful glances.

'Cusha is at the end of the world, Shamana,' Gardep reminded her in her delirium. 'She goes to destroy the Darkwing.'

'Yes, of course,' Shamana said. 'I'm losing my wits.'

She heard the sound of the boys, Harad and Qintu, weeping.

'Is that you, Qintu?' she asked. 'You were always teasing me, remember. I didn't think you were so sentimental. As for you, Harad, well, you're soft-hearted by nature. That's not a bad thing.' She reached out and touched each of them. 'You must not mourn, any of you. I am happy. My life has not been in vain. I have lived to see our people rise again.'

She squeezed Oled's hand hard. Oled knew she was in terrible pain.

'Can't you give her something?' Oled asked Murima.

'She refuses everything.'

'Why?' Oled demanded. 'Why won't you take something to ease the pain?'

'I must be alert,' Shamana said. 'I want to see them before I die.'

'See them?' Murima asked. 'See who? Do you mean the Holy Children?'

Shamana shook her head. 'Do you not have ears? Can't you hear them? They're coming. It's our people. They gathered at Gussorah, you know.'

She hoisted herself up on one elbow.

'Dry your tears,' she said. 'Save your mourning for those who want it. I can't abide all this moaning, all these fine words. I want a world fit for future generations to live in. Sow my ashes and raise freedom from them. Many months ago I set you on the road to that world. You promised you would not sleep until we had attained it. I hold you to that promise, every one of you. Now, carry me outside.'

'What!'

'I want to see them. I want to see our brothers and sisters.'

Everybody thought the pain must have driven Shamana mad. That's when Nikesh burst into the tent.

'They're here!' he cried, eyes blazing with joy.

'Who?'

'Thousands of them, tens of thousands,' Nikesh cried. 'They've been wandering the mountains, trying to find us. It's the army that gathered at Gussorah.'

'There,' Shamana said. 'Didn't I tell you?' She frowned at Oled. 'You managed your elephant at last, my boy. Now you must perfect the hearing of a dog. Listen.'

At last Oled heard it: the tramp of thousands of feet, the lilt of flutes, the beat of drums, the sound of veena and sitar. They went outside the tent. Banners fluttered over the heads of the arriving masses. There were the symbols of the Four Winds and the Scales.

'The standards of Shinar,' Murima gasped.

There was even one banner inscribed with the dragon motif of the Tanjurs. The Helati remembered the sacrifice of the dragon-people.

'Carry my mother outside,' Oled ordered. 'Let her see the people.'

Shamana watched the procession of the Helat masses for several minutes, smiling as the endless column climbed the valleys towards them.

'Look at them,' she said, 'I told you they would come. Do you see the torches dancing in the night?'

'We see them,' Gardep said.

'That's your army, Gardep,' Shamana told him. 'Learn your lessons. Become the general we all want you to be.'

She gritted her teeth against the pain and forced out one last speech. Weak as she was, it carried across the multitude.

'I will be watching you all from the House of the Dead,' she said. 'Give the people their freedom. Do it, or I will haunt you to your graves.'

Suddenly her entire body was wracked with convulsions. She died without another word.

7

'She's gone.' Cusha sat staring at the yak-skin carpets that kept out the worst of the bitter cold. 'Shamana's dead.'

'And the others?' Vishtar asked.

Cusha shook her head. 'I felt the doors of the House of the Dead groaning open to admit her. Beyond that, I have no knowledge of the Army.'

'There is a terrible possibility,' Vishtar said. 'What if we defeat the Darkwing only to hand the world back to the Muzals?'

Cusha nodded wearily. 'The same thought has occurred to me. Maybe we should let the world die. At least all our suffering will be over.'

Omar rose abruptly to his feet. 'You don't mean that,' he said.

'How do you know?'

'I can see it in your eyes,' the Selessian said. 'You love life. It shines from your every smile. Yes, even from the intensity of your sorrow. Swear to me, Holy Child, you will not give up your quest while there is breath in you.'

Cusha seemed startled by Omar's words. 'Does this mean you have come to a conclusion yourself?'

'Yes, we Selessians will lend our sword arms to the cause of freedom. We will wash away the stain left on our nation's honour by the scoundrel, Ehut Haraddin.'

'Then let's swear a common oath,' Cusha said. 'I will continue to Nandraghiri with Vishtar and Aaliya. You will go south and join the Army of the Free.'

They embraced, kissing each other on both cheeks. Mehmet and Vishtar swore their oaths too.

8

Dawn saw heavy snow come to the Dragon Mountains. The Darkwing's winter was moving south. Gardep had his litter carried to a point high above the Sol-ket camp. He wanted to see the Grand Army's formation.

'If only these snowstorms would clear,' he said, blinking away the swirling flakes. 'What do the scouts report?'

'Visibility is poor,' Nikesh replied.

It was at this moment that a group of scouts galloped up the ravine.

'Infantry,' they reported. 'They're coming this way.'

Gardep seized the armrests of his chair. 'Are they Sol-ket?'

The head scout shook his head.

'To arms!' Gardep said. 'Rishal's sending his auxiliaries into attack first. I want every archer we can muster. Now!'

Within ten minutes hundreds of archers, most fresh from rallying at Gussorah, had their bows trained on the dense blizzard.

'Nock your arrows,' he said, seeing the first shadowy forms emerging from the snows.

Several hundred dark figures were now moving up the hill. Strangely, they did not raise their shields or form ranks. Their weapons were sheathed.

'What are they doing?' Bulu asked. 'Do they want us to mow them down like ears of corn?'

Gardep gave another order. 'Draw.'

But Murima interrupted him before he could tell his archers to shoot. 'Wait,' she said. 'Look. That's a flag of truce.'

'It's a trick,' Nikesh said.

'It's no trick,' Atrakon said. 'You only have to take a look at the way they're walking towards us. Hear them out.'

'Stay where you are,' Gardep ordered. 'You may send one man to talk for you.'

Without hesitation, one of the Vassyrians unbuckled his sword belt and handed his bow and quiver to his neighbour. Under the flag of truce, he approached the Helat lines.

'Who are you?' Gardep asked.

'My name is Adrius. I was the one who threw the spear at Rishal. I just wish I'd hit him in the heart rather than the leg. Did you not see us rise against the Sol-ket? We Vassyrians have come to a decision.'

'What do you want?'

'My men wish to join you.'

'Do you have proof of your intentions?' Gardep asked.

'Traitors have come to join us before. Your actions could be a ruse.'

Just along the line, Oled listened impassively.

'Is this enough proof?' Adrius asked. He raised his arm. Immediately, a score of buffalo lumbered forward, pulling heavy carts laden with weapons. 'All this was thrown away by the fleeing Sol-ket, or taken from their dead.'

'Fleeing?'

'Yes.' Adrius looked at the faces of the Army of the Free. 'By the gods,' he said, 'you don't know, do you? They've gone.'

'Gone?'

'That's right. At this very moment they're marching away from the field of battle. My guess is, they hope to skirt round to the north and link up with the garrison at Rinaghar.'

'I don't believe it,' Gardep said, his suspicions raised by the talk of sudden retreat. 'Rishal would never sanction it.'

'Of course not,' Adrius said. 'The Lion of Inbacus is a fanatic. He would never break off the fight. But he's delirious with a fever. In his absence, his junior generals decided to cut their losses and make an orderly withdrawal. It seems the arrival of tens of thousands of Helat reinforcements made their minds up.' He looked at the tense faces of those before him. 'Don't you understand?' he asked. 'You've earned a reprieve.'

9

The Army of the Free spent one more night in the Dragon Mountains. It was time to complete the valediction to their fallen. They gathered as a crimson sunset stained the snowy slopes. The storm had abated a little so the massed ranks assembled in drifting sleet. Many pyres were lit that night for the dead. Shamana's was the last to be fired. Her body was borne on an ox-cart, down an avenue of torch-bearers. All bowed their heads. All grieved for the She-wolf, the heart and soul of freedom. A funeral party made up of Murima, Qintu, Harad, Atrakon and Oled carried her to the summit of the pyre. Gardep, still recovering from his wounds, watched from his chair. The companions made a circle and hurled blazing torches onto the pyre. The firelight shone across the mountains, illuminating their stillness and their majesty.

'Look,' Nikesh said, pointing into the valleys below. 'It is as if our flames are lighting the whole of Jinghara. Did you ever see anything like it?'

'Give me your spyglass, Gardep,' Bulu said.

He stepped forward to examine the world below. It was true. Not only the valleys but also the foothills of the Dragon Mountains, the barren thorn forests and all the lands beyond seemed to glow in the night. Then he understood why. Everywhere he looked there were campfires. There were more banners bearing the symbols of the Four Winds and the Scales. The entire area was alive with activity.

'Word of what happened here is spreading,' Bulu said. 'The villagers have seen the Sol-ket crawling away with their tails between their legs. They are joining us in their many thousands.'

Even as Bulu spoke, Shamana's ghost rose from the pyre. The She-wolf looked upon the face of her son, Oled Lonetread, and there was joy in her eyes. Her cause was reborn in her son and in all the thousands gathered in and around the Dragon Mountains. As her ghost faded into the night, never to be seen again, a single sound echoed across the mountains, the howl of the wolf.

It was the thirty-second day of Buradish.

CHAPTER 9

Winter Deepens

I

The Darkwing had a new toy. The demon lord's captives shuddered as the creature slid out of the gloom. They saw the flickering tongues of the serpent heads, the floating night-black eyes. Then, wisely, they averted their gaze.

'Squeamish, are you?' the Darkwing gloated, casting a glance round the manacled prisoners. He stalked across the room and seized his new discovery by the throat. 'Do you know what we have here?' he said. He pulled back the newcomer's heavy winter cloak to reveal the saffron robes of the Hotec-Ra. 'That's right,' he chuckled, 'a priest of the Sun. I found him wandering in the storm. It seems he got separated from the Sol-ket. What's your name, priest?'

Timu kept his own counsel.

'You will tell me, you know,' the Darkwing said. 'Even Lord Linem spilled his guts eventually.' He saw the fear creep into Timu's eyes. 'What's this? You know your master's fate, don't you? Then you understand what might happen to you.'

A terrified answer shuddered from his captive's throat. 'My name is Timu.'

The Darkwing nodded slowly. 'I've heard of you. You're one of Linem's apprentices. Maybe you're hoping to step into his shoes. I'm sure I can arrange that, in more ways than one. What brings you to the Khut lands, Timu?'

The priest hesitated.

'Do you want me to take your eyes first,' the Darkwing asked, drawing a lethal-looking talon over Timu's face, 'or your tongue?' The threat was persuasive enough.

'I was to take possession of the Holy Children and guide them safely to your lair,' Timu said, fearing the consequences of his admission.

'To what end?'

Timu lowered his eyes. 'To destroy you and prevent the dying of the sun.'

The Darkwing's black eyes narrowed. Timu was seen to tremble visibly.

Then the demon lord leaned forward and roared into the priest's face. A swarm of flies buzzed from his open mouth.

'Now,' he said, 'what can you do to make amends?' His eyes settled on Jinghirza. 'This young woman is a Khut maiden,' he said. 'From time to time, in moments of boredom as I await the final going down of the sun, I set her various tests to pass the time. Would you like to take part in one?'

Timu stammered a reply. 'Yes, my lord.'

The Darkwing leered. 'I thought you would.'

2

Rishal ax-Sol surfaced from his fever. For some moments he listened. 'Why do I not hear the clamour of battle?' he demanded.

'We have left the Dragon Mountains, Rishal-Ra,' Kulmat said quietly.

Rishal's eyes sparkled greedily. 'A victory?'

Kulmat shook his head. 'A retreat.'

'What!'

'While you were lying ill, the Helat troops were joined by an army several tens of thousands strong. Your commanders thought the balance of forces was in the enemy's favour. They decided on an orderly withdrawal.'

'You mean the curs ran away! I want to see them all in an hour.'

Kulmat nodded. 'I will arrange it.'

As he walked to the tent flap, Rishal remembered something. 'You didn't hand me my sword when I demanded it. Why?'

'I feared that you had been weakened by the fight with Gardep,' Kulmat answered. 'I feared that, by fighting again so quickly, you might succumb to the Selessian.'

'That was the only reason?'

'It was.'

Through the open tent flap, Rishal could see the wide Jingharan Plain. 'Is that snow?'

'Yes, Rishal-Ra,' Kulmat replied. 'The flakes have been in the air since noon. Winter is moving south at a terrific pace. Soon golden Rinaghar and even Tiger-gated Parcep may be shuddering before its glacial blast.'

'That's it, then,' Rishal said. 'The demon's claims are more than idle boasts.'

'Yes, Rishal-Ra, this is the beginning of the Darkwing winter.'

He continued to stare after Kulmat long after the squire had gone. For all his ready answers, Kulmat had not allayed Rishal's suspicions. There was something flowery and evasive in his answers. Rishal vowed not to take his eyes off the boy.

3

Two days later, when Rishal was able to stand with the aid of crutches, he reviewed his troops. He could smell the reek of defeat. The previous afternoon he had raged at his officers, spewing his anger at them for the retreat from the Dragon Mountains. Now it was time to inject some much-needed morale into his dispirited troops.

'Warriors of Ra,' he began, 'since my recovery, I keep hearing the same word. That word is defeat. Let me say this as clearly as I can for you, we were not defeated. I vanquished their general in mortal combat. Is that defeat? But the rebel cockroaches refused to abide by the rules of battle. They have no honour. You all saw how a traitor's spear laid me low. The Vassyrian attacked without warning from our own ranks. It was the act of a coward.' He clenched his fist and roared his conclusion. 'They are craven curs. We are men. We were not defeated on the field of conflict!'

His eyes swept the listening soldiers. 'Then,' he continued, 'while I was incapacitated by a fever, some of your officers decided on an "orderly retreat."'

He let the words sink in. He had loaded them with bitter irony.

'What do these words mean?' he asked, weighing them in his open palms. '*Orderly* and *retreat*. I have a word for this strange idea. I call it cowardice. Some of your senior officers chose to run away.'

The objects of his scorn shuffled their feet.

'They are now standing with you in the ranks. They will fight their next battle as infantrymen. In their place, I have elevated new officers. Any repetition of such craven behaviour and I will kill any man who tries to step back from the cauldron of war.'

He could almost hear the sound of backbones being stiffened.

'But good did come out of the campaign,' he said. 'They have lost their chief sorcerer. Thanks to Murak here, the She-wolf is dead. Who is going to lead them now? Let's examine the candidates. Gardep na-Vassyrian? I whipped him in front of his troops. That's right, I had the fabled boy-warrior at my mercy. Oled Lonetread? He is still snivelling about his mother.' He saved his best joke till last. 'Murima ul-Parcep? She's a fat cook!'

The troops roared with laughter.

'This is our time,' Rishal told them. 'We will draw them onto open ground. Our heavy horse will grind them into the soil. This time we will meet them on the flat Jingharan Plain.'

Propping himself up on one crutch, he raised the other belligerently.

'I have sent envoys to Rinaghar and to Parcep. I have ordered reinforcements on a scale not seen in two genera-tions. We are going to throw the full might of the Sons of Ra against the slaves. We will intercept them and chase them to the field of Dullah.'

A murmur ran through the mass of soldiers.

'That's right, Dullah. There, our forefathers crushed the revolt of the criminal Shinar. We showed them Sol-ket steel. We broke their bones. We broke their hearts too. We whipped them back into servitude. There, forty years on, we will drown the present uprising in blood. They will regret the day they took arms against the mightiest army on Earth!'

The troops had received Rishal politely at first, even sullenly. By the time he had finished speaking they were drumming their feet and bellowing their war cry. On and on it went, like rolling thunder.

'Victory or death!'

When the men had dispersed, Rishal drew Murak aside. Kulmat was the third man in attendance. 'Are you privy to the experiments of your fellow Hotec-Ra?' he asked.

'The Fire Dust?' Murak asked. 'Yes, I know all about it.'

'The priests have at last got the mixture right,' Rishal said, 'but they have not yet perfected a delivery system for the stuff.'

'What's the problem?'

'They've been trying to imitate the projectiles the She-wolf launched at our men during the battle. Unfortunately, Shamana's method would be no use to us. She used leather to enclose her Lyrian fire. This Fire Dust is far more volatile. It ignites when it touches anything made of animal skin. It simply consumes the container.'

'I see.'

'They tried using the pots in which they store it,' Rishal continued.

'More problems?'

Rishal nodded. 'The moment they left the catapult, the pots became uncorked and the dust sprayed everywhere. We lost five soldiers and two priests in the trials. It is very frustrating. We have a weapon that can turn the tide of any battle and we can't find a way to use it.'

Murak nodded. 'I'll give it some thought. We'll find a way to torch the rebels.'

Then general and priest sat down to share a meal. Having heard their plans, Kulmat could only pick at his.

4

By the thirty-eighth day of Buradish, Rishal's intentions were clear to the leaders of the Army of the Free. They met in full council on the slopes above their growing army on the Gussorah road. Atrakon had been reinstated. Gardep summoned Nikesh to address his commanders.

'Tell them what you told me,' he said.

'It's the Sol-ket,' Nikesh said. 'They are on the move, throwing a ring of steel around us. Two armies come from the south. Another is on the road from Karangpur to the north.'

'How many?' Oled asked.

'There are three huge columns. They are approaching in battle formation. They come in full armour, standards flying. Rishal leads one army. A new general, Ghushan, commands the northern divisions.' He hesitated.

'And the final one?' Oled demanded.

'Oled,' Nikesh said, 'prepare yourself. Rishal has made the murderer of your mother General.'

Oled's eyes hardened. So that's how it was. The Empire had rewarded his mother's killer with promotion.

Nikesh continued to break the bad news. 'Murak has at least twenty thousand men under his command.'

'Twenty thousand!' Gardep exclaimed. 'That alone constitutes a Grand Army, and it is but one column. How many do they number altogether?'

'The lowest estimate is fifty thousand.'

'And the highest?'

'Eighty thousand.'

Every listener stared at Nikesh. Their faces registered absolute shock.

'It's true,' Bulu confirmed. 'I witnessed it with my own eyes. I only saw the armies commanded by Rishal and Murak. But never did I see such a multitude.'

Murima interjected. 'That's not exactly true, is it, Bulu? You saw such a host once before. It was at Dullah, the most terrible of battles. By all the rivers that run, it is starting again.'

Determined not to give in to the mood of depression that was eddying through the assembly, Gardep chose to be decisive. He laid out a map.

'Come here, Nikesh,' he said. 'Show me how Rishal has set out his forces.'

Nikesh indicated the deployment of the Imperial Army. Three pincers: one from the south-west, one from the south-east and another from the north-west. Rinaghar lay due east, completing the encirclement. Gardep saw the pattern emerge.

'That's their strategy,' he said, tracing the direction of the three columns with his finger. 'They understand the symbolism of Dullah as well as we do. They mean to engage us there.'

'Of course,' Oled said, 'they have chosen the ground where Shinar's rebellion was destroyed. They know that we will be burdened by the nightmare of the past. If they win this second battle, no slave will ever dare fight for freedom again.'

'We're agreed then,' Murima said defiantly. 'We don't let the masters win.'

5

'We have to escape,' Jinghirza said.

Timu stared straight ahead, maintaining a stubborn silence.

'What's this?' Jinghirza demanded. 'Don't you talk to we lesser breeds?'

Still, Timu stared ahead impassively. She noticed that he was clinging tightly to a small object, enclosing it protectively in his palm.

'You think you're better than us, don't you?' Jinghirza asked. 'But we all breathe the same air and walk in the same sunlight. Believe me, when the sun dies, we will all die with it.'

'Don't you think I know that?' Timu said, breaking his silence.

'Then why don't we work together?' Jinghirza whispered.

Timu stared. 'What do you mean?'

'I've seen that package you've been hiding.'

Timu's face betrayed the surge of anxiety her words had caused. 'You won't give me away to him, will you?'

'Why would I?' Jinghirza asked. 'I have resisted the monster all the way. I want to walk away from this terrible place and return to my old life. The Khuts have many faults. Treachery isn't one of them. We don't crawl behind our enemy's backs. We meet them face to face and crack their heads. Well, what have you got in that precious little pouch of yours?'

'Fire Dust.'

Jinghirza was intrigued. 'Explain.'

Timu looked around the other prisoners. They were all either asleep or slumped in a kind of traumatised stupor. 'Kick that piece of meat over here.'

Jinghirza reached out and used her toe to punt the scrap of leftover food to Timu. The priest dropped a single, infinitesimal grain on the wallet-sized piece of meat. It immediately burst into flame. When the strange phosphorescence died, nothing was left but a minuscule cinder.

Jinghirza stared at the priest wide-eyed. 'This could change the face of warfare. How much damage could the whole package do?'

Timu smiled for the first time. 'I am hoping that it will destroy the demon.' Then the smile faded. 'You know what I can bring to our cooperation. What can you do?'

Jinghirza permitted herself a smile. 'I can get us out of these chains.'

Timu leant forward. 'How?' he whispered excitedly.

'You have already seen the reason,' Jinghirza said. 'The Darkwing gives me tests, ordeals. I remind him of someone. He likes to see me fight the terrors he throws against me.'

'I still don't see how this will help us escape.'

Shuddering from the searing cold, Jinghirza explained what she had in mind.

6

The first sighting of Sangra Peak came on the fortieth day of Buradish. For a few hours a day the blizzards would clear and they could see the Mountains of the Moon floating in a silvery haze. Until now, the other mountains in the chain had obscured Sangra Peak.

'That's it,' Aaliya said.

'How long will it take to get there?' Vishtar asked.

'Ten days,' Aaliya said, 'maybe fifteen if the snows get

worse.'

'That's too slow,' Cusha complained. 'The sun dies just twenty-one days from now.'

'It would help to know the Darkwing's whereabouts,' Vishtar said. 'It would help if we could penetrate Nandraghiri without his knowledge. Is there anything you can do, Aaliya?'

'I don't just transform into bears,' she said. 'It is dangerous but I will do it. Just keep going due north. I will find you on my return.'

Without further ado, she adopted the white plumage of the ptarmigan and set off across the grey sky.

'May the Four Winds watch over you,' Cusha murmured. 'Of your entire race, only two now remain.'

7

On the site of Shinar's fabled rising, in the open fields of Gussorah, Gardep addressed the Army of the Free. Oled and Murima, Nikesh and Bulu, Atrakon and Adrius flanked him. As he looked at the multitude, he imagined it as an endless sea. But they were farmers and boat-builders, carpenters and metalworkers, seamstresses and servants. They were not soldiers.

'I stand before you as your general,' he said. 'Some of you look at me and see only a Sol-ket.'

Qintu looked embarrassed and lowered his eyes.

'That was true once,' Gardep continued, 'not any more. This monstrous Empire killed many of our comrades, Shamana included. She was the finest woman I ever knew.'

He raised his voice. 'You are my brothers and sisters. We suffered together in the Dragon Mountains. We fought and died together. If you honour me with your trust, I will lead you. Do I have that trust?'

The question was met with a returning roar of acclamation. Qintu led the shout.

'The Sol-ket are coming,' Gardep continued. 'They are eighty-thousand strong. They think we will run to be hunted down like frightened deer. They're wrong. For good or for ill, we will meet them on the field of battle. They are trying to force us to take our stand at Dullah. They know this fateful spot is burned into the memory of our people. But we will not flinch from our destiny. Forty years ago, a great wrong was done there. We will right it.'

The roar of the crowd swelled once more. But Gardep wasn't finished. 'The Sol-ket think history will repeat itself. There is a difference. Forty years ago Shinar trusted his allies. The Selessian Erut Haraddin betrayed that trust. This time there will be no false friends. We will fight together, side by side, shoulder to shoulder. We will have freedom or we will have death.' He threw out a question to the throng. 'Which will you have: freedom or death?'

The reply came from thousands of throats. 'Freedom! Freedom!'

Gardep smiled. 'I expected no less. I am proud to have known you and led you in battle. Now put aside your fears. Set your faces towards the aim of liberation. On to Dullah!'

8

An hour after his speech, Gardep was wandering alone through the snow. He marvelled at the drifting whiteness. It was strange how the world sounded different in the snow. There was a great stillness about it, hinting at distant echoes. Standing there, he tried to imagine Cusha's face, so dark against all this whiteness. Conjuring her dark eyes, he smiled.

'Are you close to your destination, my love?' he murmured. 'Do you see Nandraghiri?'

But there was no reply. Only the sob of the wind could be heard over the open land.

At this moment, alone in the wind and the snow, Gardep felt weighed down by his destiny. To destroy the Darkwing at one end of the land, and defeat the Imperial Army at the other; was it possible? Kulmat's face swam in the drifting clouds of snow. Gardep remembered how he had drawn his sword, ready to fight his own knight.

'But I stopped you throwing your life away for nothing.'

Love, friendship, they were the only weapons he had against a gargantuan foe. The Sons of Ra possessed terror, cruelty, wealth, betrayal, torture and deceit. It seemed such an uneven struggle. Amid his musings, he heard movement. 'Who's there?'

'It's me, Adrius.'

Gardep turned to look at the Vassyrian. 'We have barely had time to talk. You took a great risk, throwing that javelin at Rishal. Did you know your Vassyrians would follow you?'

'Sometimes,' Adrius said, 'you have to take a gamble. That's how history is made.'

'That makes your action all the braver,' Gardep said. 'Do you have something to say?'

'I have something to ask. I have heard the soldiers call you na-Vassyrian. Why is that?'

'Do you not know the story?'

Adrius shook his head.

'I was born in Inbacus,' Gardep said.

Adrius seemed surprised.

'Rishal found me wandering the streets of Inbacus during the sacking of the city, an orphan of the war,' Gardep explained. 'He brought me back to Parcep to be raised in the Academy.'

'That doesn't sound like an ax-Sol,' Adrius said. 'Of all the orphans of that bitter war, why would he take pity on this particular boy? The Muzals are not known for their charity.'

Gardep stared. Why had he never asked this question himself?

'Do you remember nothing of your childhood?'

'Very little,' Gardep said. 'Oh, I have this.'

In spite of the biting cold, he slipped off his two heavy jackets and showed Adrius the tattoo on his bicep. It was Adrius's turn to look shocked.

'But this is the insignia of the royal family!' he cried, falling to one knee.

'Stand up,' Gardep said. 'What do you mean?'

'This lion with the bull's head,' Adrius answered. 'You are a prince of the royal line at the very least. But it can't be. Nobody survived the sack of the royal palace. Rishal killed them all.'

Suddenly, Gardep knew how Cusha must have felt just before she breathed in the vapours of the memory lamp. He was about to discover where he came from.

CHAPTER 10

A Gathering Storm

I

A pure white bird, perfectly suited to merge with the world of snow, would stand out in the chambers, tunnels and passages of Nandraghiri. Alighting on the thirty stone steps that led to the monastery entrance, Aaliya transformed into a mouse. For a few seconds she rose on her hind legs, staring with tiny, beady eyes at the vertiginous peaks and snow-scoured heights. Then, scurrying gratefully inside to escape the raw, northerly winds, she kept to the wall, fearful that she might be discovered at any moment. Scenting the Darkwing, the mouse's tiny heart beat even faster, an accelerated ripple of fear. Scampering on, she inspected every possible route through the complex. Particularly intriguing were several gloomy walkways that seemed to corkscrew downwards through the heart of the mountain.

Eventually, still wandering about the steep, winding steps, she entered the main sanctum. There she discovered eleven prisoners, one or two more dead than alive. Jinghirza drew her attention. She looked filthy and emaciated but otherwise well. Her resilience emanated from every pore. She was sturdy and brave, a born survivor. Timu too had some fight left in him. Hearing the scrape of steely claws on the stone floor, Aaliya squeezed into a crevice, willing herself to remain unseen and undiscovered.

'I am restless,' the Darkwing said, peering at Jinghirza. 'You are the only creature in this shivering, hostile world who entertains me. I am looking forward to your next trial.'

Jinghirza made her move. 'I have an idea.'

'*You* do!'

'My ordeals have always occurred in conditions of your choosing,' she said, doing her best to suppress her eagerness for the plan. 'I tire of your games.'

The Darkwing was intrigued. 'What do you have in mind?'

'Let me fight the Hotec-Ra,' Jinghirza demanded. 'His people oppress mine. They use us to fight their wars. He made an innocent boy suffer in one of your foul experiments. Is it too much to ask, a fight to the death with a mortal enemy?'

'I will tear you to shreds, girl,' Timu snarled. 'Don't insult me, master Darkwing. I, a senior priest of the Hotec-Ra, pitted against a mere girl? I won't do it.'

The Darkwing looked interested – more than interested, fascinated. 'This Khut maiden is a resourceful individual, Timu. You may have your work cut out.'

'She is beneath my contempt,' Timu said. 'I would

skewer her with the point of my sword. It would not even merit the title *combat*.'

The exchange sounded heartfelt enough. Yet something didn't ring true. Something aroused Aaliya's instincts. She watched Jinghirza's face, then Timu's. There wasn't a shred of doubt in her mind. It was all an act. But to what purpose? Aaliya thought of her companions waiting for news. But surely this took priority. Something was happening here. A spark was about to ignite a flame. She was going to stay.

2

Rishal stirred; his healing thigh wound made him restless and easily woken. Kulmat held his breath for a moment. Ever since the campaign in the Dragon Mountains, they had shared a tent, separated by a thin partition, in case Rishal needed attention during the night. Kulmat thought it was more likely to have something to do with his moment of resistance on the battlefield. He was standing on a splintering glass floor. Feeling vulnerable and exposed, he willed Rishal to slip back into a deep sleep.

After a few moments, he could hear the regular murmur of his master's breathing. Reassured that he was fast asleep, Kulmat slipped out of the tent. In the distance he saw the lights of the rebel camp. For the last few days, as both armies moved at an even pace, each acutely aware of the presence of the other, there had only been a few miles between them, the Sol-ket stalking their slave enemy ever closer to Dullah.

Kulmat stared at the inviting lights. How quickly their numbers had grown. They had been swollen tenfold by the outcome of the bitter struggle in the Dragon Mountains.

There would be no more prevarication. He had to warn them of the awesome weapon Rishal was developing.

Glancing back at the tent, Kulmat looked for the path he had seen earlier. He cursed inwardly that everything looked so different at night, especially now that there was a considerable dusting of snow. He paced up and down for a few moments, wincing at the crunch of his boots on the thickening white layer. Finally, he was able to make out the track. He was about to set off along it towards the Helat lines when he saw Rishal's shadow, silhouetted against the side of the tent by the lamp that hung from the roof. Fearing discovery, he knew he had to do something. Run now and Rishal would hear him. He planted his feet and waited for the general to appear.

'Kulmat, what are you doing?'

'I'm relieving myself, Rishal-Ra.'

Rishal listened for a moment before returning to bed. Resigned to serving him for another day, Kulmat walked back to the tent. Before retiring, he made Gardep a promise. Tomorrow, my brother, I will be with you. Together, we will fight to bring down this evil dynasty.

3

Far across the plain, Gardep was sitting with Oled and Atrakon.

'It seems strange to see you two breaking bread together,' Gardep said.

Atrakon shrugged. 'Oled didn't want to think ill of his friend. I can understand that.'

'There is a friend who is always in my thoughts,' Gardep said. 'In a few days, Kulmat and I could meet on the field of battle.'

'If he is a true friend, this is the time to turn his face from the Sol-ket,' Atrakon said.

'I think he wants to,' Gardep said.

He told them about Kulmat starting to draw his sword against Rishal.

'There is a change in the wind,' Oled said. 'The people don't fear the Sol-ket as they once did. Did any of us foresee Adrius and his Vassyrians coming over to us?'

'No,' Gardep said. 'Nobody did. But don't underestimate our foe.'

He pointed to the sea of lights far off in the night.

'Most of those men have been trained since their eighth year,' he said. 'They are disciplined and brave. Their only objective is to kill and eliminate any threat to the Empire.'

'It sounds as if you still admire them,' Oled said.

'I hate the power they serve,' Gardep said. 'That doesn't stop me respecting the individual fighters and their iron will. Rishal taught me everything I know.'

'Rishal is not your knight,' Oled said. 'You are no longer his squire. Don't think of yourself even as a former Sol-ket. Those days are long gone. You're a free man now, Gardep. Forget your past. Forget Rishal.'

'I wish it were that easy,' Gardep said.

'Very well,' Atrakon said. 'Remember what he taught you. But drive any affection you have left from your heart. Did you not learn from Shamana? To make a new world, you must make yourself anew.'

'As you have?' Oled asked.

'Yes Oled, as I have.'

Murima joined them. 'Are you unable to sleep, too?'

The three men nodded.

'Within days we will fight a battle that could decide our future,' Gardep said. 'So long as Cusha succeeds.'

Murima nodded. 'I think of her all the time.' She

watched the many figures, as sleepless as they, crouched around their campfires. 'It is a night for fears. Everywhere I walk among the people, they are whispering, wondering if we can overcome the Sol-ket, wondering if the Holy Children can prevail against the demon lord.'

'What do you say, Murima?' Oled asked.

Murima watched the campfires winking in the night. 'You may as well ask where the wind is born. I am proud that we have thrown off our oppressors' shackles. But if we were to be defeated again . . .'

'We will not be defeated,' Oled said fiercely. 'I would fight their entire army by myself, if I could avenge my mother's death. I would pursue this Murak into the depths of the House of the Dead. Let the dogs throw every man they have against us. We will overcome them all.'

4

Jinghirza struck the first blow. Timu stepped back, using the mannered, practised moves of the Hotec-Ra. He parried her axe with his sword, then stepped forward and thrust at the Khut maiden, making her skip back. Aaliya watched from her corner, taking in every attack and defence. There was something missing. There was no passion in their exchange, no hatred. Aaliya shot a look in the Darkwing's direction, wondering what he made of it. Surely he must notice that everything was just that tiny bit too slow, too predictable?

'I see no hatred,' the Darkwing yawned, confirming Aaliya's fears. 'Where is your fire, Jinghirza? I thought you wanted to avenge your oppressed people against this infernal priest.'

Jinghirza's eye caught Timu's. Yes, Aaliya thought,

recognising the look, you've got to make it more convincing. The thrusts, the feints, the parrying and slashing grew fiercer, more reckless. Their movements around the room became more rapid and dangerous. This pleased the Darkwing.

'That's more like it. This is a fight to the death, remember.'

He didn't appear to notice that the two fighters were edging ever closer to him, moving within striking distance of their tormentor. Aaliya craned forward. Was this it? Was this their plan, to strike at the monster as they fought? Jinghirza swung her axe at Timu. For once, her judgement failed her. The fabric tore and a small packet fell, unseen by the demon lord, a few paces from where Aaliya had concealed herself. Jinghirza saw the look of panic in Timu's eyes as he realised what had happened. Crashing the stock of the axe into his chest, she sent him sprawling to the floor in the desperate hope that he could recover the packet. To her horror, the Darkwing seized Timu and threw him back into the fray.

'Is this the girl you would cut to shreds, priest?' he chuckled.

Aaliya read the fighters' expressions and knew what they were going to do next. She felt indecision throbbing inside her. Should she join them and risk three deaths or should she bide her time? It was an agonising choice. In the end, she contented herself with dragging the package into a corner with her paws. It seemed important. She sniffed at it. Now she understood why. Her animal senses told her the sulphurous substance was combustible, a thing of fire.

Finally, having lost their weapon, the fighters moved against the demon lord. With a cry of hatred, Jinghirza turned her axe on the Darkwing. He fended off the blow easily, hurling her across the chamber. Timu attacked next. Lacking the same fondness for the priest that he had for the girl, the Darkwing drove his claws through Timu's heart in a single lethal thrust. Timu died with a startled look in his eyes, his life fading in an instant. Having finished with the priest, the Darkwing approached Jinghirza.

'You disappoint me,' he hissed. 'I expected something better than this. I allowed you to take the Holy Child's place in my heart. But the entertainment is over. You bore me now.'

Screaming, Jinghirza flung herself at him. But the Darkwing was too powerful. He raked a single claw across her forearm, causing a fiery pain to blaze through it. Jinghirza dropped the axe.

'I remember the fear in your eyes when I made you jump the mountain peaks,' he said. 'How I enjoyed it. Yes, that's where you will meet your end.'

He dragged Jinghirza away. A tiny mouse followed.

5

Rishal had a visitor. Kulmat saw Murak approaching and felt the first stirrings of unease.

'Well,' Rishal demanded, seeing Murak striding towards him, 'have you found a solution to our problem?'

'I have, Rishal-Ra. Would you like to see it? I have prepared a demonstration.'

Rishal grabbed his crutches, then hesitated and put them aside. Though he was limping, he could keep up with Murak. 'Show me.'

Murak took the knight and his squire to a secluded area, about a quarter of a mile from the camp. There, Murak's

Hotec-Ra had set up three lines of dummies. The straw figures had been made to represent an enemy regiment. In order to simulate human flesh, the dummies had been smeared with animal fat. Two hundred metres away, there was a catapult. Murak produced an object for the general to inspect. There were two pieces of metal, each like a soldier's helmet with a broad, circular brim. The brims clipped together. Holes were drilled through them. Rishal turned the sections of the container over in his hands.

'How does it work?' he asked.

'You fill the pan with the Fire Dust,' Murak explained. 'Next, you clip the brims together, taking care not to spark an explosion. We are trying to design special gloves to prevent the dust coming into contact with the operators' skin. Waxed paper seems to work best, like the first, small packets we made to carry the material. Once there is a good seal, you drive metal pegs through the holes. It can now be thrown by catapult without spilling the dust.'

'This is good, Murak,' Rishal said approvingly. 'Don't you think so, Kulmat?'

'Yes, Rishal-Ra,' Kulmat said. 'It's ingenious.'

'When the projectile hits the ground,' Murak continued, warming to his task, 'the impact drives the pegs from the holes. As a result, the two sections come apart and the Fire Dust spills over the enemy. Are you ready for the demonstration?'

Rishal's features were taut with excitement. 'Yes.'

Murak signalled to the catapult operators. They wound back the lever controlling the tension. Then, releasing the trigger, they sent a single projectile hurtling towards the dummies. They were in three lines of twenty-five each. When the projectile hit the ground in front of them, all seventy-five went up in flames.

'Well,' Murak said, 'what do you think?'

'Magnificent!' Rishal exclaimed. 'Truly magnificent. Within days, we will destroy the enemy.'

'The Helati have no chance,' Kulmat murmured.

Rishal clapped him on the back. 'You could be right, Kulmat. I can't wait to see the weapon in action.'

6

Aaliya followed the Darkwing, wondering what to do. She knew he was armed with an almost impenetrable carapace. He seemed even more powerful than the creature who had haunted the Black Tower. Should she attack now or wait for some unforeseen opportunity? She would have no help from Jinghirza. The girl was weak from loss of blood. Every few steps she would sag to the floor, only to be hauled back to her feet. The creature sniffed at Jinghirza for a moment. Seeing his hungry interest in the Khut maiden, Aaliya quietly transformed back to human form. Slipping her bow from her back, she strung it and eased an arrow from her quiver.

The Darkwing's tongue flickered over Jinghirza's face, his half-human, half-reptilian eyes seeming to savour the taste of her flesh. He lapped briefly at her fresh blood but seemed disappointed. Maybe she was too weak from lack of food to satisfy his appetite. Maybe she was the wrong prey. Jinghirza continued to struggle fitfully, but weakly. The Darkwing lifted her into the air. Then, almost casually, he tossed Jinghirza down the mountainside to die.

Kulmat was determined not to botch his second attempt
at escape. Too much rested on the news he could bring to
the Army of the Free. Even when they reached Dullah,
they must not engage the Sol-ket. Armed with the incen-
diary weapon, the Imperial Army would be invincible.
Giving a last furtive look round, Kulmat slipped out of the
tent and started to run. This time there was no hesitation.
He raced through the ankle-deep snow, keeping his eyes
on the flickering lights of the Army of the Free. His face
glowed. I should have done this long ago, he told himself.
His faith in the Empire and holy Ra had been draining
away from him ever since the Battle of Jinghara Plain. He
should have gone with Gardep then. The memory of what
he had been made to do to the fifty helpless prisoners
haunted him. But soon he and Gardep would be together
again, brothers in arms against the monstrous tyranny that
had made him a cold-blooded killer.

Murak's weapon was the last straw. Armed with my
information, Kulmat thought, we will turn the tables on
the Imperial Army. His mind filled with thoughts of the
future. I will see Gardep married to Cusha. Then I will
find a wife of my own. We will raise a family somewhere
by the sea, a little fishing village near Parcep maybe. But
the usual tendrils of darkness soon coiled around the wonderful images. Was any of this really possible? It could
only happen under certain conditions. If the Army of the
Free vanquished Rishal's disciplined and ruthless force. If
Cusha destroyed the foul demon in the northern mountains. Kulmat ran on, willing both dreams to come true.

But he never reached the rebel camp. Even as he
stumbled through a waist-high drift, he heard the jangle of

harness. Turning, he saw five horsemen. They were Rishal's own handpicked bodyguard. Kulmat felt a blinding pain shoot through his temple. Then all was darkness.

8

On the forty-fourth day of Buradish, a familiar, skeletal figure tramped into view.

'Jackal!' Vishtar shouted.

'I have news,' the night-strider announced.

'Of Aaliya?'

'Yes.'

'She's not dead?' Vishtar cried.

Jackal shook his head. 'Far from it. She is at Bhadra Zhoi. She is in the company of a Khut maiden. My comrades have just alerted me to the fact. I will point the way.'

'Will you come with us?' Vishtar asked.

Jackal shook his head. 'There is much for me to do. But I will not be far.'

The pair reached Bhadra Zhoi as a troubled, grey twilight gathered over the settlement. The snow was banked up to the eaves. Entry into the mean, wooden houses was only possible through the smoke hatches in the roof. In such a small village, it didn't take long to discover Aaliya and Jinghirza. Both were bruised and Jinghirza had her arm bandaged. Other than that, they were well.

'Why were you so long?' Cusha asked. 'How did you escape?'

Aaliya explained how she had discovered Jinghirza and Timu and the plot they had hatched.

'Do you think you could have trusted Timu?' Vishtar asked. 'He was a senior Hotec-Ra.'

Jinghirza shrugged. 'It was an alliance born out of

necessity. Once we had destroyed the Darkwing, we would have been enemies again. Even so, I regret his death.'

'But how did you escape?'

Jinghirza told the tale. 'I was barely conscious. I knew I was falling. As I tumbled through the air, I could feel myself floating away. I think it was dead. I'm not sure I thought about what was going to happen to me. I was in a kind of dream state. Then I saw a bird.' She glanced at Aaliya. 'It was a condor. I felt its talons grip my dress. It slowed my fall, but it could not halt it. Down and down we tumbled, slowing all the time. I wondered what was happening to me. I thought it might even be a predator, about to devour me. We started to spin. I could feel the bird straining to hold me. The wind was buffeting us. Then, as I slowly came to, I could see the snow rushing towards me. It was as if huge fists were pounding me. I rolled over and over, sensing the condor's feathers against my face. We seemed tangled, almost a single creature. The next thing I knew, I was lying beside a woman I had never seen before.'

She gave Aaliya a grateful look. 'I have heard many stories of you shape-shifters. I was raised on them. I always believed you were like the demons, unnatural. Now I know different.'

'You must tell us what you saw at Nandraghiri,' Vishtar said.

Cusha squeezed his hand. 'It will do tomorrow.'

Vishtar started to protest but Cusha shook her head. She said just one word. 'Tomorrow.'

9

'Bring him to me,' Rishal ordered.

He was speaking of Kulmat. Two squires had served him since his return from Inbacus, the scene of his greatest triumphs. Both had committed the basest treachery. Truly, he was cursed among men. Where did this ingratitude come from? Kulmat was brought into the commander's tent in chains. He had already suffered a beating. His face was swollen and his right eye was almost closed.

'Leave us.'

The Sol-ket who had delivered Kulmat exchanged glances.

'What, are you worried about me?' Rishal laughed. 'I may be recovering from a flesh wound but I can handle Kulmat. He has been beaten within an inch of his life and he is in chains. What more reassurance do you think I need?'

The soldiers left.

'Why?' Rishal asked. 'Why do you betray me? You had everything. Why throw your life away? What is it about these wretched Helati that you find so attractive?'

Kulmat remained stubbornly silent. He stood before his knight, having to draw on all his reserves of strength to remain upright; such was the punishment the Sol-ket had inflicted.

'Well, speak up, Kulmat. You have nothing to lose. Tomorrow is the last time you will see the sun. Nothing can alter that. Tell me the truth. It will be your last act in this world.'

It was some time before Kulmat could put his thoughts into words. When he did, they were simple.

'It is about . . . brotherhood.'

'Brotherhood!' Rishal scoffed. 'Do you put this brotherhood of yours before the Sol-ket code? Do you raise your great friend Gardep above your Emperor and your god? He is a mortal man. He could not even best me in arms. Why would you treasure his friendship above all things?'

Kulmat shook his head. 'You do not understand, Rishal-Ra.' His voice fell to a whisper. 'I hardly understand it myself.'

Rishal couldn't disguise his contempt. 'Go on. Let's hear it all. I want every heretic idea in that confused head of yours.'

'It is not just that Gardep is a brother to me,' Kulmat said uncertainly. 'There is a feeling among these slaves . . .'

'You're beginning to sound like one of them,' Rishal sneered, 'with their Book of Scales and their thoughts of heaven on Earth. Maybe you've been reading the forbidden texts of Udmanesh.'

'Maybe I do wish to be like them,' Kulmat retorted. 'Maybe I am not that different from Gardep. Maybe I want to live in a better world than this murderous chaos.'

'I would laugh if you were not such a sorry spectacle,' Rishal said. 'Just look at you, for Ra's sake. You are beaten and bloodied. Your bones ache. You can hardly see. This is where your soft heart and your even softer head have brought you. Tomorrow, we will break you on the sun wheel. It will be an example to the slaves and to any future renegades in the Imperial Army.'

Kulmat flinched at the thought of the sun wheel. It was one of the most terrible punishments man could inflict. He would be beaten until his bones broke. Then, kept from losing consciousness by the Hotec-Ra's potions, he would be bound to a great sun wheel and left to the buzzards and the vultures. He had seen men linger for days before they died.

'Beg for mercy,' Rishal said. 'Renounce Gardep and these ideas of brotherhood and I will spare you the agony of the wheel. I will give you a quick end.'

Kulmat shook his head. 'I am resigned to my punishment, Rishal-Ra. I will not beg.'

'Guards,' Rishal shouted.

'I have one question for you, master,' Kulmat said. 'Why are you afraid?'

'Afraid? Are you mad?'

'The slaves terrify you,' Kulmat said. 'Deny it. You see them in every household and every workshop, digging every canal and road, hoeing and seeding every field. They are the foundation on which Sol-ket power stands. I can see it in your eyes. You think they might do it, don't you? You think they might just topple an Empire.'

Rishal turned his back. 'Take him away,' he said. 'You know what to do.'

10

'Gardep!'

It was Harad's voice. Since before daybreak, he had been sitting at the edge of the camp, maintaining a lonely vigil, wondering where Cusha was now. Harad missed her terribly. Though they were not brother and sister by birth, their bond was every bit as close. In the greyish light of a sickly dawn, he saw the Sol-ket erecting a strange platform in the distance. They had ridden forward from their lines to carry out their gruesome work. It was some moments before he could work out what it was. When he did, he went running for the boy-general.

'Gardep, come quickly.'

Gardep reached Harad's side and cried out in anguish.

'Kulmat! What have they done to you?'

Commander Rishal had carried out his threat. His squire was displayed across a steel frame hoisted high above the Sol-ket lines. The rising sun showed the full horror of the punishment. A few hundred yards away, Kulmat was lying at an awkward angle, his body twisted unnaturally by the breaking of his bones.

'Is he alive?' Qintu asked, appalled by the sight.

'Oh yes,' Gardep said, 'they will have made sure of that. He's alive. That is the whole point of the punishment. They want you to experience a living death. This is the way of the Sol-ket, as it is with the Hotec-Ra. They wish to brand great dread into the minds of the living. They show you what it means to provoke their vengeance. That is how they maintain their rule.'

He was interrupted by Rishal's voice. 'Do you hear me, Gardep na-Vassyrian?'

Gardep shouted his reply. 'I hear you, ax-Sol. You are cursed among men. For this, I will find you on the battle field and I will kill you.'

Rishal gave a forced laugh. 'Do your worst, *boy*. You'll need to make a better job of it this time.'

With that, the Sol-ket rode the few miles back to their lines, leaving a small company to prevent the Helati attempting a rescue.

Oled arrived. 'Don't let him provoke you, Gardep.'

'Provoke me!' Gardep cried. 'Oled, this is my oldest friend. They have broken him on the wheel. How would you have me feel?'

'I would have you *think*,' Oled said, restraining his friend. 'You are our general. You will one day rule our people. You must have the interests of the people at heart. Begin by sparing Kulmat this anguish.'

'What are you asking?'

'Only what Kulmat will be asking himself. End his suffering.'

'Do you mean that I should kill him?'

'He will not recover from these injuries,' Oled said. 'It is the only thing to do.'

'I can't,' Gardep said. 'We were raised together. We learned our lessons together. We stole together. We even took beatings together.'

He took a scrap of bloodied bandage from his tunic. A tear spilled down his cheek.

'Oled, do you realise what you're saying?' Gardep thought for a long time. 'Can you take animal form and speak to Kulmat?'

Oled nodded. 'I managed a war elephant. A bird should be little problem.'

He chose the form of a songbird, tiny enough to escape the notice of the Sol-ket. Soon he was fluttering around Kulmat. The boy's face was caked with blood, his lips blistered, his eyes so swollen he could barely see.

'Kulmat.'

'Who's there?' Kulmat asked, trying to see through the blood and the darkness.

'Gardep sent me,' Oled said. 'He wants to know your wishes,'

Kulmat rocked his head. 'The pain.'

'Find your voice,' Oled said, his heart torn to see such suffering.

At long last, Kulmat summoned the strength, though it wracked his body with pain. 'Gar-dep!' His voice echoed across the snowy plain.

Gardep wept to hear it. 'I hear you, my brother.'

'End it,' Kulmat cried. 'End this agony.'

'Kulmat, how can I? You ask too much.'

But Kulmat's strength came back even more intensely.

'My body is broken. Don't let them break my spirit too. You have it in your power to release me. Do it.' Kulmat turned to the bird that was Oled. 'I have one last message. Listen carefully. It may save many lives.'

Once Kulmat had finished his story, Oled thanked him and returned to the Army of the Free.

'End it, Gardep,' the Tanjur said. 'For pity's sake, you must spare him this terrible agony.'

Gardep nodded grimly. 'I don't know if I have the strength.'

'It is a just act,' Oled said. 'The Four Winds will guide your arm.'

Gardep duly strung his bow and tested the tension. Then he nocked an arrow and bent the bow, looking along the flight of the arrow. Though tears were blurring his vision, he could see Kulmat's tormented form on the wheel.

'You are my brother, Kulmat,' he murmured as he drew the taut string to his eye. 'So you will be for all time.'

Then he let loose the string and watched the arrow on its way. It struck its target and the life went out of Kulmat. His suffering was over.

11

The Army of the Free discussed the threat posed by the Hotec-Ra's new weapon.

'A single projectile,' Gardep said, 'capable of killing seventy-five warriors. It is beyond belief.'

'It is worse than that,' Oled said. 'It was Kulmat's opinion that a single device could kill double that, especially in the press of battle.'

'You have flown over the Sol-ket lines,' Atrakon said. 'How many catapults did you see?'

The answer was disturbing. 'There were at least twenty-five,' Oled said.

'And how many of these projectiles to each catapult?'

'They were covered by tarpaulins,' Oled answered. 'I would guess at a score.'

The eyes of the war council were on him. The carnage would be unimaginable.

'This weapon could destroy an entire army without a sword being drawn,' Murima said.

'This is not warfare,' Gardep said. 'It is annihilation. We would be like animals led to the slaughter.'

Atrakon crashed his fist down on the table. 'We can't sit here and wait for them to burn us alive,' he said. 'We must destroy their artillery.'

'Do you have an idea?' Adrius demanded.

Atrakon nodded.

'How many warriors do you need?' Gardep asked. 'Fifty? One hundred?'

Atrakon shook his head.

'Then how many?'

Atrakon smiled. 'Just two.'

12

In the early hours of a frosty morning, a mongoose scampered across the snow. Oled concealed himself behind the catapults and waited, watching the guards struggling to stay awake. He imagined Atrakon, using his assassin's skills, moving through the encampment like a black ghost. For the plan to work, the Selessian would have to pick his way undetected through half the enemy camp. If there was a man who could do it, it was Atrakon.

'May the Four Winds protect you.'

His words came out as a tiny squeak. Nobody heard him. Satisfied that the guards were paying no attention to the small animal, Oled scurried over to the first pile of projectiles. Gripping the pegs with his paws, he eased them out. Having loosened two, he moved on. In this way, after three hours' painstaking labour, he had opened two or three projectiles in each heap. Finally, as he crouched, watching the guards, he saw one of them crumple to the ground. Within two minutes, three more had fallen to the unseen killer who had emerged from the darkness.

'You're good at your trade,' Oled observed.

'I am not proud of the fact,' Atrakon whispered. 'Let's get this done.'

Oled transformed and the two men gingerly ran trails of the red powder from pile to pile. Then, shrinking back into the gloom, Atrakon dipped the tip of an arrow into a sample of the Fire Dust.

'Do you think it is everything Kulmat said?' he asked.

Oled smiled. 'We are about to find out.'

Atrakon drew his bow and shot his arrow. The moment the arrowhead hit the canisters, a sheet of fire fifty metres tall exploded through the night, firing the catapults, their attendants and ten metres of earth to either side of the artillery positions. Its heat seared the faces of the two men, scorching their eyebrows.

'By the Almighty!' Atrakon gasped, watching the lurid flames licking the night sky.

'Don't just stand there gaping,' Oled said. 'They will be after us any moment.'

He transformed into a Selessian thoroughbred. 'We've got to go.'

Atrakon leapt into the saddle. In the confusion of the continuing explosions, the two men escaped. So ended the forty-fifth day of Buradish.

13

At dawn, Rishal and Murak inspected the damage to the artillery.

'A thousand men dead, all our catapults destroyed, virtually the entire stock of Fire Dust wasted,' Rishal groaned. 'How did this happen?'

'Do you have the names of the men who were attending Kulmat when he died?' Murak asked.

'I can find out,' Rishal said.

Half an hour later five anxious Sol-ket were standing before the commander and the lord-priest of the Hotec-Ra.

'Did anything unusual happen before Kulmat died?' Murak asked.

'We broke his bones,' one of the guards said.

'Are you trying to be funny?' Murak demanded angrily.

'No, Your Holiness.'

'I will repeat the question: was there anything unusual?'

'He cried out with great force,' another guard said. 'We were shocked. Where did he get the strength from?'

'Did he mention the Fire Dust?' Rishal asked.

All five shook their heads.

'No, Rishal-Ra.'

'So how did the rebels know of its existence?'

Murak thought for a few moments. 'Are you sure there was nothing else? Think, even the tiniest detail may be important.'

One man's face lit with understanding.

'What is it?' Rishal cried.

'I didn't think it was important at the time,' the guard said, 'but there was a tiny bird fluttering around him. He seemed to be talking to it. We were laughing at him, saying he had gone mad.'

Murak sighed. 'The She-wolf has had the last laugh on us. This is her son, Oled's work. Perhaps, Rishal, he is not quite the gullible fool I took him to be. It seems the mother's mantle has passed to the son.'

'He must suffer for what he has done,' Rishal said, looking at the plumes of smoke still hovering over the camp.

'Oh, he will,' Murak said. 'I will make sure of that.'

CHAPTER 11

Cat and Mouse

I

'The monster knows that you're coming,' Jinghirza said.

'I'm aware of that,' Cusha answered. 'I think he's looking forward to it.'

'When he watched me,' Jinghirza said, 'he saw you. In you he feels the life he has lost.'

Cusha said nothing.

'What are you thinking?' Jinghirza said, seeing the hooded expression in Cusha's face.

Their eyes met.

'No, tell me I'm wrong,' Jinghirza cried. 'You can't believe he is worth saving.'

'All the creatures of the Earth are worth saving,' Cusha said. 'So it is written in the Book of Scales. I have seen into his soul. I know his story. He loved a woman. He was loved in return.'

'I have heard this story,' Jinghirza said, wondering what bearing it could have.

'Then you know,' Cusha said. 'Once he was Sabray. He fought Lord Muzal, his father. Is there no way you can admit the possibility that there is something of the boy he was, some trace of goodness and humanity?'

'In all my days of captivity,' Jinghirza retorted, frustrated by Cusha's words, 'I was denied food. I was made to undergo terrifying ordeals. I was frightened and lonely and he mocked me in my misery.' Her eyes flashed with disbelief that Cusha could expect humanity from the Darkwing. 'You faced him, Cusha. He would have killed you. How can you think that he is anything but evil?'

'I have seen an assassin redeemed,' Cusha said, remembering Atrakon, 'and he was a man dedicated to killing. Is this so very different?'

'Yes,' Jinghirza insisted, 'an assassin is a mortal man. The Darkwing is the accumulation of all the world's despair and pain. Oh, Cusha, how can you be so blind? He is death!'

'Maybe you should return to your people,' Cusha said, stung by Jinghirza's words. 'Your family will be waiting for you.'

Jinghirza shook her head. 'You don't get rid of me so easily. First I will see the monster dead, then I will return home. It is a question of honour.'

They heard boots crunch through the snow. It was Vishtar and Aaliya. They sensed the tension between Cusha and Jinghirza.

'Cusha thinks she can reach the demon,' Jinghirza said. 'She thinks she can find some human quality in him and make him change his mind.'

'Is it not worth trying?' Cusha asked.

Neither Vishtar nor Aaliya spoke.

'Well,' Cusha said, 'will you not answer me?' She was to discover that, where it concerned the Darkwing, she was in a minority of one.

'I saw the monster,' Aaliya said. 'He must be destroyed.'

'I know him better than any other living being,' Vishtar said. 'I was his captive for eight summers and eight winters. Can you imagine how many times I tried to appeal to him? There is no power in heaven or in hell that will heal the wounds he has suffered. The fog of madness drifts through his mind. His entire being is ablaze with hatred. Pity him, sister, and he will destroy you.'

Cusha turned her back. The conversation was at an end. Riding off in silence, the three companions and their Khut ally continued north.

2

'I think you were impressed by the Holy Children, Omar,' Mehmet said, 'the girl especially.'

'I never dreamed that I would meet somebody with such powers,' Omar said. 'You saw the shade of Leila Ebrahin with your own eyes. Cusha raised her from the remotest regions of the House of the Dead. How is such a thing possible?'

Mehmet shrugged. He was a practical man, not given to easy enthusiasm.

'Sometimes,' Omar said, answering his own question, 'once in several generations, there comes a special person who changes the world. I swear, this Cusha is one such person.'

'But can a child really overcome such evil?' Mehmet asked.

'She did once.'

Mehmet was not convinced. 'For all the efforts of these Holy Children, the monster still lives. The girl won a battle. She did not win the war. The world is in greater peril than ever. There was no victory, Omar.'

The Selessians plodded on through the swirling snow, many wondering how they had come so far from the desert. Finally, they saw the towers and turrets of Karangpur in the distance.

'The Sol-ket gave us a hostile reception the last time we were here,' Mehmet said with a scowl.

Omar smiled. 'I wonder if their hospitality has improved.'

'Not if they know what we did when the night-striders attacked their column,' Mehmet reminded him.

Omar saw a Sol-ket patrol in the distance. 'We need fresh horses,' he said. 'Let's test the water.'

'What if they've had news from the north?' Mehmet asked.

'Then we fight.'

This satisfied Mehmet. Omar rode towards the Sol-ket and hailed their officer. There was no hint of suspicion. That was a good sign.

'We were reassigned to Karangpur,' Omar said. 'Our business is done in the north. Is General Ghushan still commanding the garrison here?'

'You've been gone a long time,' the officer said. 'Ghushan-Ra is now commanding a third of the Grand Army. He is leading his forces to Dullah. Our troops are about to destroy the Helat rising.'

'Is that right?' Mehmet said, encouraged by the news. 'So what's happening to the garrison here at Karangpur in the meantime?'

'There isn't much of it left,' the officer said. 'Just a

couple of hundred cadets. We're throwing all our efforts against the rebel cockroaches.'

'Really?' Omar said. He winked at Mehmet. They were going to get their fresh horses.

3

The Darkwing came after nightfall. Cusha was lying awake, going over her disagreement with Jinghirza, when she noticed Aaliya stiffen.

'What is it?' she whispered.

Aaliya pressed a finger to her lips and nodded at the wall of the tent. In the dying firelight a familiar silhouette had appeared: the unfurled wings, the reptilian form. Aaliya drew her bow and shot at the demon lord through the canvas. The arrow pinged off his carapace. A split-second after, his sinister head exploded through the material. Eyes blazed, fangs glistened, razor-sharp claws slashed.

'Raise the alarm!' Aaliya yelled, fending him off with her sword and axe.

While she struggled with the inhuman assailant, Cusha scrambled through the tent flap to summon Vishtar and Jinghirza.

'Help,' she screamed. 'We're under attack!'

Aaliya was barely holding the monstrous invader at bay. Then, as quickly as he had appeared out of the night, he shrank back into it. Vishtar and Jinghirza joined the panting Aaliya.

'I'm surprised we put him to flight so easily,' she said.

The words alerted Vishtar to a terrifying possibility. 'Where's Cusha?' he demanded.

'I don't know,' Aaliya said. 'She went to raise the alarm. I thought she'd be with you.'

Vishtar caught her eye.

'The Darkwing!' they said in unison.

They raced outside. There, just a few metres away, they saw the demon lord. He had his claws hooked through Cusha's cloak. In spite of her desperate struggles, he had succeeded in lifting her a couple of metres off the ground.

'Get away from her!' Vishtar shouted, hurling his sword at the demon lord.

'Ah,' the Darkwing said, 'there you are, Vishtar, the cup from which I drank all those years. What makes you hurry to face me, Vishtar? Are you so eager for me to feed on you again?'

Seeing Aaliya preparing fire arrows, the Darkwing rose rapidly into the sky. Cusha was trapped in his razor-sharp talons. She was kicking and screaming, her legs pedalling frantically in an attempt to break loose. The creature gave her a gloating look. But the eyes that met his were as dark as his own.

'Look into your past, demon,' Cusha cried, fixing him with a stare.

For a moment the shade of Princess Kewara of Banshu hovered round her features.

Mesmerised by the long-lost voice, the Darkwing flew lower. Encouraged, Cusha called on Kewara.

'Rise, sister,' she cried. 'Look into this creature's heart. Find Sabray the man.'

But before the ghost of Kewara could take form, the Darkwing dashed Cusha's hopes. 'You will not fool me with your party tricks,' he snarled. 'I know how you turned Atrakon's head. The Selessian is a sentimental fool. You will find me infinitely more difficult to hoodwink, Holy Child.'

He glanced at Jinghirza looking up from the earth below. 'I fed on her, you know,' he said. 'In your absence,

I made her my handmaiden, but she was almost tasteless. You're the one who will nourish me, Holy Child.'

At that moment, a sigh of dismay left Cusha's lips only to be followed, an instant later, by an agonised shriek from her abductor. With his attention held by Cusha, the demon lord had allowed himself to drift into range of Aaliya's fire arrows. Two tore through his wings. When a third hissed into his side, the monster released Cusha and started tearing the arrows from his flesh. A leaping tiger broke Cusha's fall. She fell with Aaliya into a snowdrift.

'You did well,' Aaliya said.

Cusha grinned. 'You did better.'

'I will see you all again soon,' the Darkwing said, snapping the final arrow in two. 'I will remember the pain you have just caused me. Believe me, it will be repaid in full. I will have you watch the black dawn of a new world, lightless and without the presence of mankind to sour the air. You should know, I have taken new captives. I now have fourteen, one for every day left of the sun's life. I will keep them alive until the day of my final victory. Then I will sacrifice them to celebrate the onset of eternal night. Remember me in your dreams . . . or your nightmares.'

With that, he was gone.

Jinghirza turned to a still-shaken Cusha. 'Do you still think you can find some conscience in this monster?'

Cusha did not evade the question. 'I will still try,' she said.

4

Mehmet found Omar in the Sol-ket stables, staring at the empty stalls as if each one held a memory.

'The men are ready,' he said.

'The Sons of Ra wouldn't let me stable my horse here,' Omar said. 'Do you remember?'

'I remember.'

'What did you do with the garrison?' Omar asked.

'The intelligent ones are locked in the dungeons with a two-week supply of food,' Mehmet told him. 'The stupid ones are dead.'

'You know your trade, Mehmet,' Omar said. 'You're a fine soldier.'

'When we get to Dullah, young master,' Mehmet replied, 'I'll show you what soldiering is.'

Omar strode out to review his warriors. They had eaten well, bathed and rested. They had fresh horses and supplies to last them on the journey. They were in high spirits.

'We ride on Dullah,' Omar shouted.

The Selessians roared their battle cries.

'By the time we get there,' Mehmet said, 'there had better be someone left to fight.'

Omar laughed. 'Who would deny a band of brothers such as this?' he said. 'You'll have your battle, Mehmet.' As he spurred his horse forward, he shouted, 'Men of Selessia, we have a hard ride ahead of us and a great battle at the end of it. Are you ready?' He listened to the cheers of his men. 'I never doubted it,' he said. 'On to Dullah!'

5

Buoyed by the success of the raid on the Sol-ket artillery, the Army of the Free were approaching Dullah. For days the pursuing Imperial Army seemed to have been preparing itself for imminent attack.

'They aren't chasing us at the same pace,' Nikesh reported.

'That's because we destroyed Rishal's fire weapon,' Gardep told the war council. 'I know the way the man thinks. If he still possessed it, he wouldn't have waited until we reached the sacred ground of Dullah. He would have exterminated us earlier. Now he will bide his time. He covets the symbolism a second battle of Dullah will have. He sees the coming conflict as a decisive moment. An Imperial victory would crush the spirit of rebellion for generations, maybe for ever.'

'We will arrive first,' Oled said. 'That will give us the high ground. We will have that advantage, at least.'

'It is an advantage,' Atrakon said. 'It will not be decisive.'

'Then what will?' Adrius asked, worried by the comment.

'The determination of the combatants,' Atrakon answered. 'Which of the two armies wants victory most. In the end, it always comes down to that.'

'Then we are bound to win,' Gardep said. 'Just rage fills our hearts. The Sol-ket cheat and deceive. They slaughter innocents. Our cause is righteous. We must sweep them from the field.'

He leaned on his battle-axe. 'There will be no mercy,' he said. 'I spoke of reconciliation once. I even befriended one of them, the murderer Murak. I was gullible, a soft-hearted fool. My actions led directly to my mother's death. I'm finished with foolish notions like forgiveness. It is time to break the enemy's power forever, even if it means slitting the throat of every Sol-ket in the land!'

His words were met with a deafening roar.

6

It was the morning after the war council in the rebel camp. The Helat masses would now be able to see Dullah on the horizon. Linem was gone and Timu lost, possibly also dead, far to the north. All the obstacles to Murak's power were falling one by one. On the morrow another, the slave rebellion, would go the way of the senior priests. Murak was now lord-priest of the Hotec-Ra and third man in the Empire behind Muzal and Rishal. With a resounding victory to point to, he would be within touching distance of the Sun Throne.

For all that, he felt hollow inside. Envisage the moment, he told himself. Picture yourself climbing the many steps of the Ziggurat of Ra. There you will stand before the exultant crowds of golden Rinaghar, master of the greatest Empire the world has seen. Still, the thought held no pleasure for him. It was not just that the fate of the world was in the balance. He was no longer sure that absolute power was what he wanted.

Instead, he kept thinking about the Army of the Free. Most of all, he thought about his friendship with Oled. Madness, Murak told himself. I betrayed Lonetread. I killed his mother. And what do I feel? Yes, I am jealous. He has the one thing I don't. There is comradeship among the enemy, whereas we Children of Ra cheat and deceive. We even turn our knives on one another in a desperate struggle for dominance. I am without friends or confidants. In my loneliness, I envy my foe. Utter madness.

'Murak.'

Hearing Rishal's voice, he looked up. 'What is it, Rishal-Ra?'

'I have just received a communication from General

Ghushan,' Rishal said. 'His troops have been held up by deep snowdrifts on the road from Karangpur. He will not arrive for two or three days. He suggests that we delay the attack until he is in place.'

Murak nodded. It suited his mood. 'That would make it the fiftieth day of Buradish.'

'Yes, a good round number,' Rishal said. 'A memorable date. If we are to write our names in the annals of glory, the fiftieth day of Buradish seems an auspicious date, don't you think?'

Murak smiled. 'Yes, Rishal-Ra.'

'That's settled then,' Rishal said. 'I will convene a meeting of the senior officers.'

Murak watched him go. The fiftieth day of Buradish, that's when it was all going to be decided. Strangely, only one word stuck in Murak's mind. It wasn't glory or victory. It was the word he had conjured earlier.

Madness.

7

'Look!'

Vishtar was pointing excitedly through the white veil that now cloaked the entire northland. At first, nobody could make out what he was showing them. Then Cusha saw, a hundred immobile forms etched against the blizzard. It was the Lost Souls.

'A hundred,' Vishtar said. 'Is this all you could muster?'

'It is all you need,' Jackal said. 'An army could not climb Sangra Peak. The rest of our doleful throng are needed elsewhere.'

'But where are the others?' Vishtar cried. 'Where are the thousands?'

'The servile masses need them more than you do,' Jackal said simply. 'On the morrow, the fiftieth day of Buradish, two colossal armies will collide and the future of mankind will be decided.' A thought lit his lidless, usually expressionless eyes. 'If, by the grace of the Four Winds, we succeed here at Nandraghiri and bequeath mankind a future.'

Jinghirza gazed at the foothills of Sangra Peak. 'At this time of year, the lower slopes are usually verdant and warm. How will we ever reach the top in just ten days?'

Jackal listened to the question in his usual emotionless fashion. 'There is a second route,' he said. He saw the light of recognition in Aaliya's face. 'You know something of this?'

'I have entered the demon's lair. I saw the passageways and wondered where they led.'

Jackal nodded. 'Come with me.'

He led them to a frozen waterfall. Immediately behind the jagged sheet of ice that now replaced the tumbling waters, there was a hidden cave mouth.

'Tens of thousands of steps climb within the mountain,' Jackal said. 'Sangra Peak is honeycombed with them. I have spent hours exploring the various passageways.'

'So that's why you had to leave us,' Vishtar said.

'It was one reason,' Jackal said. 'If we are to prevail, we need the element of surprise. You mortals will take this path. You will have a greater chance of success this way. Meanwhile, my people will follow the more arduous route up the mountain. The Darkwing will be expecting his enemy to approach from there.'

Jinghirza shielded her eyes and squinted against the dazzling whiteness. 'How can anyone, even the undead, climb such heights in these conditions?'

Jackal touched his chin with a bony finger.

'Many of us will fall,' he said, 'but some will get

226

through. All Commanders endure the suffering of those they lead.'

Vishtar heard something in Jackal's voice, a deep, abiding pain.

'You must lend us some of your clothing,' Jackal said. 'We will hide our true identities from the Darkwing for as long as possible. No matter what it costs to conduct the Holy Children to Nandraghiri, it must be done.'

Jinghirza shrugged off her outer robes. 'I would make any sacrifice to destroy the demon.'

'Cusha, Vishtar,' Jackal said, 'we need your cloaks most of all. This way we may distract the monster.'

8

Hearts slamming with the effort of climbing the snow-heaped slope that led to Dullah, the Army of the Free fell gratefully to their knees on the white-carpeted ground. Within the hour, they would set about clearing spaces for their tents and lighting fires. For the time being, they would gather their breath.

'So this is where our forefathers fell,' Nikesh said.

Dullah was a raised plateau, overlooking the rest of the plain.

'This is where they died,' Murima said. 'I was here, watching. My father led the final charge down that slope. You could see the enemy wavering.' A tear spilled down her cheek. 'That's when the Selessians came.'

She turned to point. 'Ehut Haraddin had his reserves lined up along that ridge,' she said. 'When the black-garbed horsemen streamed towards Shinar's fighters, we all cheered. That's when we saw the Selessians crash into the rearmost ranks of the Army of the Free. We had fed them. We had given them gold. It was the cruellest betrayal.' She fell on all fours and dug her fingers through the snow into the ochre dust of Dullah. 'I never thought the people would rise again after such a defeat. I did not dream that I would see this place again.'

It was Atrakon, bitterly aware of his Selessian identity, who helped her to her feet. 'It will be different this time,' he said. Then he made a joke of it. 'It will be colder, for a start.'

Gardep watched clouds of snow, like the crests of a tidal wave, approaching from the south-east. 'That's Rishal,' he said.

Oled saw similar patterns rising in the grey sky to the north-west. 'That is Ghushan, freshly arrived from Karangpur. Tomorrow we fight.' He looked around the others. 'It may be for the last time.'

Minute after long, silent minute the rebels stood or sat in the falling snow, letting it settle on them. Soon, the entire army resembled a mass of petrified, white statues. Then, without an order from anyone, the multitude stirred itself as one and started pitching their tents and preparing their battle lines.

9

Few slept that final night before the second Battle of Dullah. Tormented by the Darkwing winter, they huddled in their tents. But a deeper cold had them in its grip. Master and slave, Sol-ket and Helat, Hotec-Ra and Tanjur, the assembled thousands shivered at the icy touch of impending doom. Nobody, no matter how brave or carefree by nature, could keep the brush of mortal terror at bay. All felt the same foreboding. They might win the battle and still succumb to endless night.

Men like Atrakon and Adrius thought of their home-lands and wondered if they would ever see them again. Harad and Qintu feared that they might never reach man-hood. Nikesh trembled at the thought that he might give in to cowardice before his men. Bulu prayed that he had not been wrong to raise his people against the oppressor that day when the riders had fallen upon his village. Even Rishal stared bleak destiny in the face. What if, this time, Gardep were to turn the tables on him? What would happen to the Empire's golden cities? What would happen to his wife Serala and his daughter Julmira, the most precious gemstones in the treasury of his heart?

Murima thought of her great father Shinar, so long in his grave, and her adopted daughter Cusha all those miles away, facing who knows what dangers. Cusha was at the forefront of Gardep's mind too. Even now, it felt as if he barely knew her. Their lips had barely touched to celebrate their love before events had torn them apart once more. The boy-general dwelt too on the fate of his dear friend Kulmat and he set his heart on vengeance. Vengeance, finally, was the emotion that stirred Oled to action. He saw Murak every waking moment of every day. He saw the assassin's arrow sink into his mother's throat and he beat his fists against his head in a vain attempt to drive the memory from his mind.

'Murak!' he bellowed into the snapping wind.

By some turn of chance or destiny, the Tanjur giant's cry was borne across the blizzard-swept plain. Murak heard its guilt-ridden accusation and bowed his head. Though he was afraid of no man, with every moment that passed, he dreaded Oled more. It wasn't that he feared his prowess in battle, though that was great. What he had begun to fear was having to explain a simple question. Why had he immersed himself so readily in the subterfuges of the Hotec-Ra? Why had he been so keen to stain his hands with blood?

Why?

CHAPTER 12

Dullah

I

Rishal was the first to send his men into battle.

'Today is the fiftieth day of Buradish,' he told them, his voice strong and confident. 'Let this date be seared into the mind of every living soul in the Empire. This is the day we finally, and for all time, crush the Helat threat.' He looked around his men. 'Some of your officers failed you in the Dragon Mountains. You will not find your general lacking in courage or leadership. The traitor Gardep is mine. None shall touch him but me. Warriors, we have unfinished business.'

His speech was greeted with deafening roars. Then, with pounding drums and braying horns, the Sol-ket quickened the pace.

'Javelins,' Rishal ordered.

The Sol-ket weighed their heavy spears, steadying themselves for the throw. Rishal had chosen spears above arrows. They were getting in close and the heavy steel spear points caused more carnage than any arrow head, as he knew from personal experience.

'Throw!' he ordered.

But Gardep had prepared for just this moment. His fighters broke their line briefly, then once the shafts had passed without inflicting serious damage, they closed the gaps once more.

'It is as I expected,' Gardep said. 'The battle will begin with an exchange of arrows and spears. Whoever has the strongest right arm will inflict the greater casualties. Then the auxiliaries will come at us. Rishal will use them to make us tire. But the real fighting will be done by the Sol-ket. When they charge, the earth will shake at their coming.'

'You still admire them, don't you?' Murima said. 'In spite of everything.'

'No,' Gardep answered, 'admiration is the wrong word for what I feel. I was raised to make war. I respect their prowess. It's different.'

For a while he did not speak again, only to speak a name. He felt the beat of another's heart, a mortal soul who had become his other half. Far from the beat of the drums and the shrill chorus of the horns, she was fighting a battle every bit as vital to the future of mankind.

'Cusha,' Gardep murmured.

Then, as he had predicted, the exchange of arrows started, a swarm of shafts that soon blackened the sky. The Army of the Free held the higher ground so their volleys told while those of the enemy fell short. In the short time he had had to train his regiments, Gardep had instilled an iron discipline in his fighters, drilling them to stand impassively while the juggernaut of the Imperial Army drove forward. Murima and Bulu commanded the archers. Again and again the urgent hiss of their arrows was heard. Each time many Imperial troops fell, reddening the snow with their blood.

The spearmen of Miridan and Lyria came next, rushing forward to hurl their shafts. But Gardep had selected his position well. In the lea of the hill on which the rebel fighters stood, there were several frozen streams and some boulder-strewn terrain. With the additional difficulty of thick snow, the spearmen were slow and vulnerable. The archers treated them to a withering hail of missiles. When the spearmen retreated, Rishal brought up what war engines he had left after the raid that had destroyed his catapults. The ballistae hurled immense bolts hundreds of yards. But Gardep had prepared for the enemy artillery. His regiments were mobile and responded with speed to every command, opening their ranks the moment a projectile arced through the air. In this way, though the Imperial officers had got their range, the Army of the Free avoided major losses.

'They'll try to get us down off this plateau,' Murima said. 'They will feign retreat to draw us out.'

'We don't move until I say,' Gardep answered.

He was no longer the boy who had wavered between love and duty. He was the general Rishal had trained him to be, the hero of the oppressed Shamana had foreseen. Rishal did as he had expected, launching his Obirs at the rebel lines. Forced to clamber over ramparts and palisades, they fell in their scores to the murderous hail of arrows from the Helat bows. Rishal had no regard for his auxiliary troops. By throwing them carelessly against the rebel defences, he was probing for a weak spot. It hardly mattered that the ground was littered with the dead and the dying.

'Selessians,' Nikesh reported, seeing a new danger.

The men in black belonged to the Haraddin clan, descendants of the notorious Ehut and for decades the ruling order in the desert kingdom. They duly thundered up the hill on their magnificent stallions, horses of such quality that the Sol-ket now bred thousands every year for their own cavalry.

'Light the ditches,' Gardep ordered.

Three ditches filled with Lyrian fire were soon blazing, forcing the cavalry to retreat. But the burning pitch wasn't the obstacle he had hoped. Hundreds of Obir infantry rushed forward. Wild and undisciplined they may have been, but they attacked with extraordinary boldness and courage. They carried wooden bridges to span the blazing trenches. Still the Helat archers shot their volleys but they were starting to run ominously short of arrows. The tribesmen had established a way over the ditches and the Selessians came again, thundering over the makeshift bridges.

'They were expecting us to use fire ditches,' Nikesh said, watching the Selessian tide sweeping towards them.

'Rishal taught me everything I know,' Gardep said. 'Is it any wonder we anticipate each other?' Then, raising his sword, he addressed his fighters. 'On my order.'

His ranks waited, and waited. On came the Selessians leaping over obstacles and evading arrows and spears. 'Now!'

Gardep signalled to Oled and the giant spurred his horse, leading his cavalry in a headlong gallop down the hill. With the advantage of the high ground, Oled's charge drove the attackers back. There was no wild pursuit of the retreating Selessians. Oled ordered his warriors to wheel around and return to the heights. The Selessians would come again, and behind them the mass of the Sol-ket. Battle was about to be joined in earnest.

2

It was at this point that Rishal played his hand. He sent an envoy to Murak, asking him to go forward. The moment Oled saw Murak's Hotec-Ra standard he was filled with rage. Giving a roar of hatred, he led his horsemen in a second charge. The sight sent a shudder through Gardep.

'This is a ruse,' he said. 'Rishal knew Oled would take the bait.'

He watched in horror as Oled's cavalry thundered forward, ignoring his express orders. Even as they engaged Murak's front rank, Rishal threw some of his own horsemen into the mêlée, threatening to surround Oled.

'Why didn't he wait for my orders?' Gardep groaned.

'He saw his mother's killer,' Atrakon said. 'How did you expect him to react?'

Gardep shook his head. 'He is a leader of men. He must transcend his instinct for revenge.' He watched in an agony of indecision.

'What are you waiting for?' Murima demanded. 'Are you going to let the Sol-ket surround him?'

'If we leave the high ground,' Gardep said, 'we will lose our advantage.'

'And if we stay here,' Atrakon protested, 'Oled will lose his life.'

Gardep watched the furious struggle unfolding before him.

'Gardep,' Atrakon said, 'you must make a decision.'

Gardep sensed his dilemma keenly. If he attacked without a strategy, defeat was inevitable. If he left Oled's troops to be massacred, he would have betrayed every ideal Shamana had taught him. In the end, he let his heart triumph over his head.

'Nikesh, Atrakon, Adrius,' he cried, 'go to his aid.'

With Nikesh's rough riders to his right and Adrius' Vassyrians to his left, Atrakon spurred his horse forward. Thousands followed on horseback and on foot. The hastily assembled force crashed into the enemy. But soon came a sight that would steady the beleaguered Imperial troops. Tens of thousands of heavy Sol-ket infantry, held in reserve for just such a moment, were running towards them. It was Oled, cheered by the arrival of reinforcements, who rallied his troops. For all his recklessness, he was indeed a leader.

'Just look at them,' he laughed, brushing aside the murmurs of dismay that rose from his warriors, 'they rush onto our sword points.'

He swung his battle-axe and killed one of the foremost attackers. 'See, they bleed like any man. Their skulls split under a blade. What are you waiting for? Make them bleed some more.'

The Sol-ket were beating their shields and shouting their battle cries. But, heartened by Oled's example, the alliance of Tanjur general and Helat ranks did not waver. The battle song of blade and bow resounded loudly. There were curses, screams, shouts of rage, all the elemental fury of warfare. That's when Oled saw Murak's personal standard fluttering nearby.

'Murderer!' he bellowed, seeking out the enemy.

Even before Oled's eyes found him, Murak caught sight of the giant hurtling towards him, wild in his battle-rage, carving a path through the thinning ranks that separated them.

'Where are you, Murak?' Oled yelled.

Through all the swirling confusion of combat, there was only one face he wanted to see, that of the assassin who had killed Shamana. It seemed to hover in a scarlet mist, just like the Blood Moon. But by the time Oled had hacked his way through to Murak's battle-standard, the priest-general had gone.

3

It was at this point that Rishal's standard was seen for the first time. A long line of foot soldiers raced across the battlefield in front of the Sol-ket centre. These were the drummers, over a thousand strong, trained to beat fear into the hearts of the enemy. In perfect time, they began to climb the slope, hammering out the rhythm of war.

'Will you listen to that?' Harad said, his gaunt face tense with apprehension.

'I can feel the beat of those drums in the marrow of my bones,' Qintu said.

'Ignore it,' Gardep said. 'What is it but stick against hide? They will have as much effect on the outcome as waiting vultures.'

But his words did little to reassure those around him. The martial cannonade of the drums was unnerving many.

'Stand steady,' Gardep roared.

His command was passed down the line. Already however, many looked panic-stricken. There wasn't a soul present who was not haunted by the folk memory of past defeat. Seeing the effect of the drummers on the Helat ranks, Murima snatched up Shinar's ancient standard and set off at the gallop, riding the length of the rebel defences.

'Be scared if you want,' she told the Army of the Free, 'but don't take a single step back. Tremble if you want, but don't drop your weapons. Quake if you want, but don't forget to strike down your foe. We have not come here to retreat before mere drummers. What next? Are you going to falter before trumpeters?' She laughed out loud. 'And what would you do if they blew a whistle at you?'

At last the grim faces relaxed.

'We have come here to win our freedom,' Murima reminded them. 'So fight, damn you, fight!'

By the time she had ridden back to Gardep's side, the panic had subsided, replaced once more by battle-readiness.

'You truly are Shinar's daughter,' Gardep said, greeting her on her return.

'True enough,' Murima whispered, 'but, for all my brave words, I'm as scared as anyone here.'

Halfway up the slope, the drummers fell into a hundred lines of single file, allowing Rishal's cavalry to pass between them. The Sol-ket were now advancing at the trot.

'This is it,' Gardep said. 'Send the spear fighters forward.' The Sol-ket were beginning to canter. 'Throw your javelins,' he ordered.

The Sol-ket charged, galloping through the spears as if they were made of paper.

'Slingers,' Gardep ordered.

Replacing their bows with slingshots, Murima's archers took up slingshots. Soon the hum of stones and clay pellets filled the air and many riders fell. For all that, the Sol-ket charge had not been broken. Rishal had issued his riders with long shields and most had survived the rain of slingshot.

'They frustrate our efforts at every turn,' Gardep complained.

But worse was yet to come.

'Look!' Harad gasped.

Thousands of Sol-ket infantry had worked their way

round the hill and were racing forward to encircle the Helat army.

'Not again,' Murima murmured under her breath, crushed by the sight of the new menace. 'Please, not again.'

'Courage,' Gardep said. 'Remember your own words to the Army.' Then he raised his own voice to address his fighters. 'Listen to me, Oled has galloped into the heart of the foe. Brothers, sisters, will we do any less?'

He prepared to throw his own cavalry into the fight. They were his last reserves. He glanced at Harad and Qintu, then finally at Murima. 'Stay with me,' he told them. 'We live together or die together.'

As he led the charge, he appraised the situation. Everywhere slave and master were embroiled in hand-to-hand combat. The Army of the Free had lost the high ground and its warriors had been drawn into close fighting. In his heart of hearts, Gardep knew there could only be one outcome.

'We've lost, haven't we?' Murima whispered.

Gardep didn't answer. He couldn't. All around him, the Sol-ket were steadily driving forward. They were disciplined, ruthless, implacable.

'Rally!' Oled cried, beside himself with rage that the Army of the Free were starting to fall back.

'Fight for your freedom!' Murima shouted.

But the Helati were wavering. One more decisive blow and the Sol-ket would have them on the run. Then, just as all seemed lost, a shudder ran through the enemy ranks. There were cries of horror.

'What's happening there?' Gardep demanded, pointing to his right.

Nobody could furnish him with an explanation. That's when he saw with his own eyes what had thrown the enemy into such confusion. Everywhere, fleshless hands were breaking through the earth. Gardep looked around. Everyone was equally bewildered.

'This has got something to do with Cusha and Vishtar,' Murima said. 'It's got to be them. They talk to the undead.'

Even as she spoke, the soil exploded, showering the advancing Sol-ket. Horses reared and men tumbled as thousands of skeletal figures erupted from the swelling ground. Still the macabre beings poured from the fractured land, like so many insects swarming from a crack in the wall. Then their battle chorus could be heard echoing over and over again.

'Vishtar! Cusha! Shinar!'

'Didn't I tell you?' Murima cried, eyes gleaming to hear her father's name being chanted once again. 'They spoke to the undead. They have assembled an Army of the Lost Souls.'

The Army of the Free took up the chant. 'Vishtar! Cusha! Shinar!'

'The Lost Souls have their redemption,' Murima said.

The night breed, now a regiment of the Army of the Free, swarmed over the Sol-ket, slashing, cutting, beating and bludgeoning. Savage cries rose from them though they had no throats. They raced over the snowy ground like dancing puppets, things of bone and ripped flesh. They cared not whether they were run through or beaten down. They fought in a wild frenzy, abandoning themselves to the sheer exhilaration of engaging their ancient oppressors.

4

Rishal watched mesmerised. At the point of victory, an entire new army had risen against him, more terrible and more self-sacrificing than the first. Full of fury, he cut and cut again with his sword as the creatures threw themselves at him. But each time he severed a head the creature crumpled to the ground laughing in its death-throes. When he ran one through, its bony jaw gaped in gratitude. Each and every one of the Lost Souls relished its self-destruction, perishing as it was in the act of liberation. Rishal remembered the terror of conflict with the demon host. They fought without fear.

'Where is General Ghushan?' he cried.

At that moment, Murak appeared. Remembering the lessons Oled had once taught him he shouted to Rishal.

'We must pull back to stony ground,' he told him. 'That way, at least they won't be able to tunnel under us.'

Reluctantly, Rishal gave the command. The Sol-ket withdrew. Encouraged, the Lost Souls rushed forward in a frenzy of retribution, hurling themselves again and again onto the sword points of the Warriors of the Sun. That's when Murak noticed that the creatures were not attacking the auxiliaries. As a result, the Sol-ket's allies were simply standing and watching.

'Attack the demons!' Rishal cried.

Some of the auxiliaries responded to the appeal. Others remained rooted to the spot.

'You are our allies,' he screamed, lashing out left and right.

Then Rishal heard a sound he never thought to experience in this world. One of the hell-fiends was speaking to him.

'You have no allies,' it said. 'They fight for you because they fear you, or because you pay them. How many of them have you mocked or cursed? How many have you turned against you with your haughty contempt? Ask yourself this, ax-Sol, who will raise a hand to help you now?'

It was true. Rishal's army had broken in half. The auxiliaries, realising they were in no danger from the Lost Souls, simply fell back. Meanwhile the Sol-ket themselves, still many tens of thousands strong, were struggling to beat back the fevered assault of the night-creatures. Finally, with the battle still in the balance, Ghushan's northern army at last appeared on the horizon. Rishal met Murak's stare.

'It's not over,' Rishal yelled. 'We've got to steady the troops. We can still win.'

5

The Army of the Free was experiencing the same wild twisting and turning of emotion. Just as it seemed they had victory in their grasp, Ghushan's twenty-thousand-strong northern army was being thrown into the fray against them. Gardep and Oled rode back and forth across the battlefield, filling gaps in the line with any troops they could find.

'Don't tire now,' Gardep told them. 'Raise your standards. Grip your weapons. You are not slaves. You are free men and women. Fight on!'

The weary Helati stirred themselves and prepared to attack Ghushan's fresh troops. Even as they started to move forward a groan rose from hundreds of throats.

'What now?' Gardep demanded.

'There,' Oled said, 'that's what they've seen.'

Thousands of Selessian riders were pouring over a ridge to the northwest. Like a black tide, they swept down the slope, just as the men of Ehut Haraddin had come forty years before. Black silk banners fluttered at their head. Murima could only stare.

'Let me go to them,' Atrakon cried. 'Maybe there is still a chance to persuade them not to fight.'

'Do what you can,' Gardep said, turning to face Ghushan's advancing army. 'Just do it quickly.'

Atrakon kicked his mount up the hill, riding standing in the stirrups, waving his arms. He was still galloping towards the regiment in this way when he heard their battle cry. It was one word: 'Ebrahin!'

Atrakon stared in disbelief. Now he could read the slogans on the silk banners. Some mentioned him by name, proclaiming him Sultan. Others spoke of washing away the shame of the past. He met the looks of the lead riders.

'That's my name on your banners!' he cried, astonishment written in his eyes. 'I am Atrakon Ebrahin.'

'Then lead us,' Omar told him.

Turning his horse in a single, fluid movement, Atrakon drew his sabre. Aware of the Haraddin watching them across the battlefield, he changed the war cry. It was not the clan name Ebrahin he shouted. Instead he raised the cry of a unified country.

'This is our moment,' he roared. 'We can free our land from the oppressor. Men of the desert, let's wash away the stain of the past. For Selesssia!'

Immediately the Haraddin brandished their swords and added their voices to those of the Ebrahin.

'Selessia!'

The black streams came together in a single dark torrent and struck Ghushan's unsuspecting troops head on.

'Well,' Gardep shouted, 'what are you all waiting for? Charge!'

6

Even then, when it was obvious that the tide of battle had turned, the Sol-ket fought on. Reeling from the shock of the Lost Souls' appearance on the battlefield, demoralised by the intervention of the Selessians, the Warriors of the Sun fought a rearguard action without hope of victory. Oled, in particular, terrified them with his swinging battle-axe as he went looking for Murak. Rishal called his generals together.

'The best we can hope for,' he told Murak and Ghushan, 'is a strategic withdrawal. Rinaghar must be protected. This is my order to you both: retreat in good order. You may yet save the Empire.'

Murak noticed his use of the word *you*. 'Explain yourself, Rishal-Ra,' he said.

'I will hold them,' Rishal said. 'Break off the fight, both of you. My Parcep regiments will hold the line while you retreat towards Rinaghar. Well, don't just stand there gawping. I am Commander-in-Chief of the Grand Army. This is a direct order. No bugles, no horns. Organise it quietly. Just go.'

With that, he rode to the front of his troops and explained that the order to fall back was not meant for them. Their lot was to perish in order to salvage something from the defeat.

'Though we will fall,' he told them, 'the core of the army will withdraw to fight another day. You are my brother Sol-ket. We were together at Inbacus and at the Battle of Jinghara Plain. We have marched through the fires of Hell together. This is our final struggle. Let's acquit ourselves with courage. Victory or death!'

Hearts heavy, the regiments of Parcep waited for the

end. Oled and Atrakon broke in from the left, Murima, Nikesh and Adrius from the right. The end came when Gardep's cavalry outflanked Rishal and completed the encirclement of his troops.

'Give me Murak,' Oled demanded, as he careered through the ocean of humanity. 'Bring him to me.'

But Murak was gone. Rishal's rearguard action had bought the Imperial Army the time they needed. The reckoning would have to wait.

7

For Gardep, the reckoning was imminent. Just before sunset on the fiftieth day of Buradish, he received a messenger from his former mentor and knight, Commander Rishal ax-Sol. Sol-ket resistance was continuing. The battle would last into a second day.

'What does it say?' Murima asked.

'He challenges me to mortal combat,' Gardep said. 'He wants us to conclude our unfinished business.'

'So what are you smiling about?' Murima asked.

'It is the way he sets out his challenge,' Gardep explained, handing the note to her. 'See how he addresses me? He calls me squire Gardep, as if he still expects me to be his servant.'

'Don't do it,' Murima said.

'She's right,' Oled told him. 'You've no need to risk your life. The tide has turned, Gardep. We've got them on the run. Two-thirds of their army has fled towards Rinaghar. There is no need for this fight. Tomorrow we will finish the job here and pursue them along the Rinaghar road.'

Gardep was not to be persuaded. 'It is something I must

do. It is a matter of honour.'

'There is no honour in dying,' Murima retorted. 'Soon, by the grace of the Four Winds, my daughter will return to marry you, Gardep. Remember your promises to her. How could I explain that you had chosen to throw your life away . . . for honour?'

'Don't forget the fight in the Dragon Mountains,' Atrakon said. 'I watched an unequal battle. You are not ready to face him.'

Gardep ignored them all. 'He forced me to slay my own blood brother. This time I will kill him. I owe it to Kulmat.'

Some distance away, just out of earshot, Rishal's messenger was waiting patiently for a reply. Gardep summoned him.

'Tell Commander Rishal that I will meet him in battle on one condition. If I defeat him, his men will lay down their weapons and surrender. I want no further unnecessary bloodshed.'

The messenger returned an hour later. 'The commander agrees to your terms,' he said. 'Because this is a rite of mortal combat, as set down in the code of the Sol-ket, he requests that you wear this armour.'

Gardep looked at the Sol-ket uniform. 'I will not wear it,' he said quietly.

'You refuse! But it is the way of the Sol-ket.'

'That is the point,' Gardep replied. 'I am no longer Sol-ket. The last time we fought, deep in my soul, I think part of me still belonged to Ra. This time I will stand before your master as a free man, general of freed slaves, a servant of the Scales. I will not wear the uniform of the oppressor just to please the murderer of Kulmat. I will come dressed as I am now.'

The messenger scowled. 'You look like a Helat.'

246

'You think the word is an insult,' Gardep said. 'I consider it a great honour. I have surrendered every earthly possession and privilege I had so that my fellow man and woman could gain the world, to be held in common. Now go. Give the commander my answer. I will be waiting for him at first light.'

'You spoke well,' Oled said.

'Let's hope my blade speaks as eloquently tomorrow,' Gardep answered. 'Now leave me, all of you. I need some time alone.'

Gardep watched the light fading from the sky. Just for a moment the sun seemed to regain a little of its own strength, as if gladdened by the events of that day. The last of its rays stained the distant hills scarlet. It was an omen. Blood would stain the morrow.

8

There was a blare of trumpets, announcing General Rishal ax-Sol, commander-in-chief of the Grand Army. He marched between an honour guard of his men, acknowledging their battle cries. Gardep watched him in silence. The Army of the Free followed his example. He had ordered no ceremony, no show of ritual. In his mind, this was a private matter between two men.

'Show no emotion,' Atrakon advised Gardep.

The Selessian was acting as his second.

'You must be as cold as an assassin is cold,' Atrakon continued. 'I know killing.' He gripped Gardep by the wrist. 'Are you listening to me?'

Gardep nodded slowly but his gaze had drifted away to the approaching Rishal.

'Forget that you were once his squire,' Atrakon insisted.

'Forget that he slew Kulmat. Make the kill quick.'

Atrakon watched Gardep set off towards Rishal. Had he listened to a single word?

'Is this how you present yourself?' Rishal demanded. 'You look like a common footsoldier.'

'That is what I am,' Gardep said, breaking his silence. 'I serve a greater cause than myself.'

The words were meant for his troops' consumption as much as for Rishal's.

'What cause is that, in the name of Ra?' Rishal demanded. 'Freedom?' He glared at the Helat ranks. 'What do you think these cockroaches will do with their freedom? They are low born. They have no nobility.'

Gardep retorted immediately. 'And what nobility do you have, Rishal? You ordered your men to break Kulmat's bones. You had fifty innocents burned alive. You are not fit to kiss the feet of a single one of these men and women.'

Rishal scowled. 'We've talked enough,' he snarled, drawing his sword. 'Let's get to the matter in hand.'

Without another word, he stabbed at Gardep, aiming for the heart. Gardep side-stepped the lunge and countered with a sword-thrust of his own. Rishal raised his shield, emblazoned with an image of the rising sun, and parried it effortlessly. After that, steel clashed against steel. Both men sweated and grunted, struggling for purchase on the dry, dusty ground. Soon they were grimed with dirt and tiring. This was no repeat of the fight in the Dragon Mountains. They were evenly matched. Gardep noticed a slowness in his former master's movements, a legacy of Adrius' javelin. He recalled every lesson he had been taught. Don't strain for victory too early, he told himself. War is work, hard work. Victory must be earned. Gardep didn't go for the winning blow. He protected his head and his heart and resolved to use his youth to wear the older man down.

'It seems war has made you a man at last,' Rishal panted.

'Brotherhood did that,' Gardep retorted, remembering Kulmat's broken body displayed on the wheel. 'It is something you will never understand.'

Rishal slashed at his shins but Gardep skipped over the shining blade. His former master was tiring. His ribcage heaved with the effort and sweat dripped from his nose. What's more, blood had started to ooze from his thigh. The exertions of battle had reopened the wound. Gardep took advantage of Rishal's weariness to fire a question at him. 'Who am I?'

Rishal's eyes narrowed, as if trying to make sense of the question.

'I know that I am of royal blood,' Gardep said. 'Who am I? I want the truth.'

Hearing the yearning in Gardep's voice, Rishal unsheathed a new weapon. 'Yes,' he said, 'you used to ask me about Vassyria when you were a boy.'

Gardep waited.

'You want to know about your family, don't you?'

Their swords locked.

'I'll tell you about them,' Rishal hissed. 'I killed them all. That's right, *boy*, the day Inbacus fell I was first to reach the palace. Your father was called Imzal. He was the king's brother, a general who had sworn to protect him. He knew how to fight but I was always the stronger man. I killed him. Do you want to know how?' Rishal chuckled. 'I clubbed him to the ground and stuck him like a pig.'

Gardep's eyes burned with hatred.

'Yes,' Rishal gloated, seeing that he had struck a chord, 'then I watched his blood pool on the tiled floor of the palace. But that's not all.' He wagged the point of his sword under Gardep's nose. 'Do you want to know the rest?' he asked.

'Speak your mind, ax-Sol,' Gardep told him, 'before I kill you.'

Rishal jabbed. Gardep jumped back.

'Your father gave me a tougher fight than any man before or since,' the Commander said. 'While we fought, a project formed in my mind. Being without a male heir myself, I resolved to take his son and raise him to be the inheritor of my office. You came from fighting stock. I would fashion you into the greatest warrior the world had ever seen. There was only one obstacle to my plan. That was your mother, Nuqiba. You were sleeping in a side room. To protect you, she came at me with a knife.' He let this sink in, then continued. 'While you lay slumbering, dreaming sweet infant dreams, I killed her before your sisters' eyes.' He laughed. 'Then I dispatched them too. I was carrying you away to my quarters when you awoke in my arms. I remember the way you cried for your mother.'

He imitated the sound. '"Mummy, mummy," you wailed. Oh, I was so comforting. I told you that she was going to join us soon. In time you forgot my promise, of course, along with the faces of your family. What irony, Gardep! You clung to the man who sent your family to the House of the Dead. That's your story, the past you always wanted me to tell you about.'

It was too much for Gardep. With an animal roar, he set about Rishal. It was just what the commander had been hoping for. Rishal slashed Gardep across the chest. A groan rose from the Helat ranks as Gardep staggered back. His senses were swimming. As if through a fog, he saw Rishal moving in for the kill, slashing and stabbing. He felt another sharp buzz of pain. Then he saw Rishal smile. It cleared his mind. Gardep retreated, crouching, feeling the blood oozing from him. It was only with the greatest effort that he managed to parry Rishal's blows. He could hear the roars of the Sol-ket. Blinking the sour sweat from his eyes, he glimpsed the silent ranks of the Army of the Free. In that moment, like the cold heart of a flame, within Gardep's anger and despair, within the bitter fury he felt for Rishal, a cold, merciless core of determination formed. He went beyond anger, beyond battle-rage, to will. He felt the hands of his murdered ancestors steadying his sword. Rishal must die.

'What's that?' Rishal demanded. 'Speak up, *boy*. I want to hear your voice before I send you to the House of the Dead. At least you'll see Kulmat again.'

It was one jibe too many. Gardep launched himself at Rishal, stabbing through his armour. It was Rishal's turn to groan. His wound was grievous. His eyes dimmed. His heart faltered.

'You've learned your lessons well,' Rishal said, his legs buckling.

Gardep ripped off Rishal's helmet and pressed his sword point to his throat.

'Is it true?' he demanded. 'The story you just told me – is it all true?'

'You know it is,' Rishal said. 'I killed them all then I took you from your homeland. I made you in my image.'

Gardep gripped Rishal's hair just as the commander had once gripped his. 'I will never be like you, ax-Sol.'

Rishal sagged forward and clung to Gardep.

'The House of the Dead is opening to admit me,' Rishal said. 'I'm not going to beg for my life. What's the point? Finish it. Do it quickly.'

But Gardep had no mercy for the man who had killed

his family and had his best friend tortured and left to die. The lethal composure that had defeated Rishal hardened into a terrible alloy of cruelty and vengeance. Gardep sheathed his sword and shoved Rishal away to lie dying in the dust.

'You will have no mercy from me, ax-Sol,' he said. 'I am going to leave you here. You will die slowly, just as you planned for Kulmat. Each beat of your heart will pump your lifeblood into the earth. Spend your dying moments looking into the eyes of my murdered family. I hope you suffer greatly for your crimes.'

Rishal writhed on the ground. 'Do you have no honour?' he whined. 'I was a father to you, Gardep. For Ra's sake, don't leave me here like a dog. Kill me now.'

But Gardep simply walked away. When some of the commander's Sol-ket tried to go to him, the Helati closest to Gardep drew their arrows.

'Stand guard over the butcher,' Gardep ordered. 'Kill anyone who tries to help him.'

With that, he retired to his quarters.

CHAPTER 13

Into the Demon's Jaws

I

Gardep didn't look up when Oled entered his tent. Sitting cross-legged in one corner, he continued to brood on the day's events.

'If you have something to say to me, Oled,' he murmured finally, 'just speak your heart.'

'You have done our cause a great wrong,' Oled said. 'Your treatment of Rishal ax-Sol was an abomination.'

'I met him in mortal combat,' Gardep said. 'I prevailed. That's all there is to it.'

'You left one of nature's creatures dying in agony,' Oled retorted. 'How can you justify it? How can you live with yourself? It was left to me to restore the honour of our cause. Do you know what I did, Gardep? I countermanded your orders. That's right, I told your men to stand down. My battle-axe sang a song of mercy. I gave Rishal his wish.'

Gardep looked up for the first time. 'Are you telling me you delivered the death blow?'

'Exactly that.'

Gardep rose to his feet, trembling with fury. 'You had no right! He murdered my family. He tortured my friend. He deserved nothing.'

'He deserved a dignified end,' Oled answered. 'It is the right of all men. This is the way of the Scales.'

Gardep was beside himself.

'I am proud of my actions,' Oled said. 'Proud! How could I leave him writhing in pain? It would diminish me as a man. I understand your hatred for this Sol-ket but it is wrong to inflict such suffering.'

Gardep's eyes were cold. Still he said nothing.

'Even in war,' Oled said, 'there must be rules. We are not like the Sol-ket. Let them massacre the innocent. Let them torture their victims. Let them use deceit and treachery. We will conduct ourselves differently. How, if we behave just like them, can we make the world anew? When we rose against the Empire of the Sun, we swore to replace despotism with law and justice. What you did today was to inflict unnecessary pain. It was unforgivable.'

Gardep spoke at last. 'I don't need your forgiveness. I don't want it. I'll not have you judge me.'

He drew close to Oled and met his stare.

'What about you?' he demanded. 'I remember what you said on the eve of battle. No forgiveness, you said. Murak killed your mother. You sought him on the battlefield. What will you do when you meet him face to face? Before you stand here berating me, answer this question. Will you show mercy to Shamana's murderer? Well, will you?'

They continued to stare at each other.

'No,' Gardep said. 'I thought not.' He pointed to the tent flap. 'You're a hypocrite, Oled Lonetread. Get out of my sight.'

2

Cusha, Vishtar, Aaliya and Jinghirza had been climbing for hours. Their legs were heavy and their lungs were bursting.

'It is time to take a rest,' Jinghirza said. She used her torch to illuminate the ledge of rock before them. 'This will do.'

There was evidence of human habitation. The floor was littered with buckets and tools. The walls were covered with frescoes. But it was no scene of peace and harmony. Some were defaced and painted over with symbols of the sun.

'The Sol-ket were here,' Vishtar said. 'See, all the images of the god Sangra and the other deities have been chipped away or covered with their graffiti.'

Cusha got up and explored the gloom. 'You're right,' she said. 'The Sol-ket were here.'

Vishtar and Aaliya joined her. In a corner there were skeletons slumped against a wall. A sword blade was still lodged in the ribcage of one of them. A shield boss had smashed the skull of another. A ligature hung from the throat of a third.

'Now we know what happened to the monks of Nandraghiri,' Cusha said. 'The Sol-ket slaughtered them and destroyed the cult of Sangra.'

The deeper they penetrated into the cave, the more reminders there were of the massacre. Evidence of the monks' presence was everywhere. There were jute bags and conical bamboo baskets. In a wooden box, Vishtar discovered a scribe's tools: metal compasses, etching utensils and an ivory stylus. There were more wall paintings. They depicted Sangra and Ra as brothers. There was no sign of the fratricidal hatred between the two avatars as there was in the temples of Parcep and Rinaghar. The monastery had been built in an earlier age when the world was ruled by ideas of peace, not conflict. They were shown living in harmony, twin custodians of the land. But, once again, the images of Sangra had been defaced. The mottos painted underneath the frescoes had mostly been erased. Those that survived expressed a familiar message: *Through difference, unity. All things in balance.*

It was the message of their own faith, the way of the Scales.

3

To the east, in golden Rinaghar, Emperor Muzal ax-Sol, Light of the Sun, Conqueror of Shinar, was receiving the commanders who had survived the battle of Dullah. They had been riding hard for days. Their warriors were following, pursued by the Army of the Free.

'You swore it would never come to this!' he raged, spitting venomous recriminations at the men gathered in his throne room. 'The Empire is torn in half. All Jinghara is in the hands of the cockroaches.'

'Your Imperial Majesty,' Murak said. 'All is not lost. A great army will defend golden Rinaghar.'

Muzal's eyes narrowed. 'Yes, and by the time they get here the rebels' ranks will have swollen to many times their present size.' He waved a sheaf of reports. 'Look at these.

Lord Asun has just put them into my hands. Every province in the Empire reports Helat risings. The Vassyrian legions have risen against us, the Selessians too. The Miridans have deserted us. They have simply walked away from their officers. I have just had another message. The night-striders have crushed General Barath's forces. How do we turn back the tide of revolt?' His accusing stare swept the room. 'Well?'

The officers shifted their feet uneasily.

'We can promise you only this, Your Imperial Majesty,' Murak said. 'We will fight to the last drop of blood to defend the Imperial heartland.'

'I have heard all this before,' Muzal fumed. He jabbed a finger at his general. 'There were women in the Helat army, I hear. Is that true, Ghushan? Did you run from their painted fingernails?'

'Your Imperial Highness,' Ghushan protested, 'you insult my honour!'

'And you insult my intelligence!' Muzal bellowed into his face. 'What are you going to do to defend the city?'

'There is something I can do, Highness,' Murak said.

'Go on.'

'I slew the She-wolf. Her son, Oled Lonetread hates me more than any living man. I will challenge him to mortal combat.'

'Can you defeat him by force of arms?'

'I can try.'

'What if you do vanquish him?' Muzal snarled. 'Do you imagine that two hundred thousand slaves will then meekly walk from our walls?'

Asun intervened at this point. 'Your Imperial Majesty, Murak may have a point, though not the one he was trying to make.'

'Explain.'

'The slaves may appear a mighty throng. But they are new to war. It is only the quality of their leaders that has guaranteed their success thus far.'

For the first time, the Emperor sounded mollified. 'Go on.'

'We will tip Murak's sword with poison,' Asun said, warming to his theme. 'He only needs to scratch the giant and he will win the contest. Our assassins will target Gardep and the other leaders. Without their leaders, the Helat mob will disintegrate.'

'There,' Muzal said, 'at least somebody is talking sense. It is a good plan, Asun.'

Murak saw the delight in Asun's eyes, and the ambition. It begins again, he thought, the jockeying for position, the conspiring.

'Does anyone have an alternative to Asun's plan?' Muzal demanded.

Nobody did.

'Very well,' the Emperor said. 'Issue your challenge, Murak.'

4

The Darkwing attacked in the early hours of the morning, when he expected his human prey to be at their most vulnerable. Swooping down the cliffs, he fell upon the climbers with primal screeches that echoed eerily through the mountains. The clangour of steel reverberated from peak to peak. The Darkwing sent several of the hooded figures tumbling down steep crevasses. As the bitter struggle continued, the demon lord searched for two in particular.

'Where are you, Holy Children?'

Finally, he fastened on them, identifiable by their cloaks. They were several metres away from the others. Throwing himself into the searing winds, he plummeted towards them, only spreading his wings at the last moment as he opened his talons.

'This time,' he hissed, 'there will be no escape.'

He fell on the boy first, rounding on him with a low, phlegmy hiss. His mouth was close to his victim's, belching spite. Pulling back the familiar hood, he leered into the exposed figure's face. But it wasn't the expected Vishtar he saw. Staring back from a fleshless skull were the eyes of Jackal. Reeling from the shock, the Darkwing unmasked the creature beneath Cusha's cloak. For the second time, he felt a long tremor of disappointment. It was another night-strider. With a shriek of temper, the Darkwing broke off the attack.

Jackal watched the demon lord vanish into the darkness. 'He is coming, Holy Children,' he growled. 'May the Four Winds protect you.'

5

On the fifty-eighth day of Buradish, Emperor Muzal ax-Sol was plucked from his sleep by a cacophony of beating drums, alarm bells, gongs and shouts. For a moment, he lay in his bed, soaked in his own sweat. The noise fused with the nightmare he had just had. Millions strong, a slave army swarmed towards him, hands scrabbling at his puckered, ageing flesh while, over the whole scene, vast leathery wings spread outwards blocking the dying sun. Barely conscious, Muzal screamed in terror. His personal slave appeared at the door.

'What is it, Your Imperial Majesty?'

'It's nothing, Sanjay,' Muzal panted, 'just a dream, a stupid nightmare.'

Dismissing his night fears, the Emperor pulled on a gown. He was disgusted with himself for showing fear in front of a Helat.

'What is all the noise?' he asked, hearing a rising cacophony outside.

'Your Imperial Majesty,' Sanjay stammered. 'It is the rebel army. It masses before the city walls.'

Minutes later, Muzal was standing with Murak, Asun and Ghushan on the city walls.

'By the holy face of Ra,' he said. 'This is the sight all my ancestors have dreaded. Even that dog Shinar did not reach golden Rinaghar itself.'

For as far as the eye could see, the risen Helati filled the plain. Not only that, the rearguard were swarming down the hillsides beyond, carpeting the frosty slopes like ants.

'Have you issued your challenge?' Muzal asked Murak.

'A messenger left an hour ago,' Murak said.

'Is the poison prepared?' Muzal demanded.

'It is ready,' Asun said. 'My assassins are on the battlements.'

Minutes later, Murak's envoy returned.

'The barbarian accepts your challenge,' he told Murak.

'One scratch,' Muzal said. 'Don't fail me, Murak. We may yet snatch victory from the jaws of defeat.'

6

It didn't take the Darkwing long to discover his prey. Thrown into frenzy by the smell of human blood, he burst upon the four friends. But his real target was the Holy Children. Within moments, the silent cavern had become a wild maelstrom of sibilant screams. The clotted, predatory voice of the Darkwing reverberated through the winding tunnels. The shadows filled with his macabre form. The swords of the four friends glanced ineffectually off the armoured hide of their hell-born foe. As ever, it was Cusha the Darkwing wanted most.

'Stand back!' Aaliya yelled.

As Cusha, Vishtar and Jinghirza hurled themselves out of harm's way, the shape-shifter loosed her arrow. It embedded itself deep in the creature's throat. But he just laughed. A serpent head poked from a fold in his flesh and bit off the shaft.

'He's stronger than ever,' Vishtar cried. 'We can't hold him.'

Suddenly, everyone was stumbling back, fighting a panicky, stuttering rearguard action against the demon lord's ferocious onslaught. A moment later Cusha alerted her companions to a new horror.

'Look!' she screamed as more of the things welled up from the depths. 'His breath.'

Bluish vapour was spilling from the Darkwing's jaws. It was venom.

7

It was noon on the fifty-eighth day of Buradish when Murak took the poison-tipped sword from Asun.

'One scratch, Murak,' Asun reminded him.

Murak swung the blade, deftly positioning it just inches from Asun's throat. 'I know my business.' There was something playfully murderous about the look in his eye. 'Don't remind me again, Asun. My hand might just slip. The Hotec-Ra are making a habit of losing priests.

Do you want to add to the toll?'

The point wavered under Asun's chin. Seeing a single bead of perspiration work its way down his fellow priest's brow, Murak grinned. 'That's better,' he said.

'Are you ready, Murak?' the captain of guards asked.

'I'm ready.'

Murak looked up at the walls of Rinaghar. Two sets of standards fluttered there, the scarlet and gold flags of the Sol-ket and the saffron-fringed streamers of the Hotec-Ra. Murak waited behind the colossal Gates of Ra. Out of the corner of his eye, he glimpsed Emperor Muzal watching him. He didn't return the look. Instead, he waited for the gates to swing open. It took mere seconds, yet it felt like an age. Finally, the hinges creaked and he saw the Helat masses. The ranks of the Army of the Free were oddly silent, still and determined in the wind and the horizontal sleet. There was no drumming of sword hilt on shield. There were no battle cries. They watched Murak stride through the gates and every pair of eyes flashed an accusation. He was the man who had killed the She-wolf by stealth. He was a murderer. Even as these thoughts rippled through his mind, Murak saw the man he had avoided for so long. It was Oled.

'You fled from me before, Murak,' the giant said, his voice carrying over the silent plain.

'There will be no more running, priest. Face me here. Face me now.'

Murak weighed the sword in his hand, but it was his conscience that spoke. 'I'm ready, Lonetread. I'm weary of warfare. Let's be done with it.'

Two men who had once declared their friendship marched towards one another. Murak bore the great shield of Ra on his left arm and carried his sword in his right hand. Oled was content to use his battle-axe alone. He fought without a shield. He found the thing cumbersome. Oled was the first to attack, his axe striking Murak's sword and shield again and again with downward blows. Murak held his ground but failed to offer an offensive strike. Oled's power had reduced his muscles to water. From the battlements, Muzal watched, willing his man to jab, slash, anything to penetrate the Tanjur's skin and let the venom work.

'The shape-shifter is wide open,' he said. 'All it takes is a pin-prick. Why doesn't he strike?'

Asun said nothing. Instead, he glanced at the bowmen crouched behind the battlements. They nocked their arrows.

Oled continued to advance, crashing his axe repeatedly into Murak's shield.

'Look into my eyes,' he said. 'They are green, like my mother's. Do you remember her eyes, priest?'

He crashed the stock of the axe into Murak's face, forcing him to his knees. Murak was on all fours, spitting out gobbets of blood.

'What do you want me to say, Oled?' he panted.

'Get up, Murak,' Oled growled. 'I won't kill you while you crouch like a beaten animal. Face me.'

On the city walls, Muzal leaned forward.

'Strike now,' the Emperor hissed under his breath. 'Cut him. Stab the foot, the leg, anything.'

He saw Murak tightening his grip on the hilt.

'That's it,' Muzal murmured, 'do it now.'

Anticipating the fatal strike, Asun nodded to the archers. They drew their bows tight, ready to shoot.

'On my order,' he whispered.

Murak finally raised his head and looked into Oled's face. 'What are you waiting for?' he asked. 'You've won. Kill me. I betrayed you. Everything you say is true. By stealth I slew your mother. You have every right to take my life.'

'That's it,' Muzal said, 'get him off guard. Use your wits. Wheedle. Whine. Get him off guard, then strike.' He made an encouraging gesture, as if stabbing with a sword of his own. 'Strike hard.'

Oled raised his axe. Murak crouched in his shadow. One brief jab of his blade and the Tanjur was doomed.

'What's this I see?' he asked, gazing into Oled's eyes. 'Do you plan to deal a wounding blow, the way Gardep did? Do you want me writhing in agony like Commander Rishal?'

Oled gripped the axe with both hands until his muscles bulged and his eyes became like gemstones, hard as emeralds. Then, with a shudder almost like agony, he lowered his weapon and turned his back on Murak.

'I'm not going to kill you,' Oled said. 'Though you deserve to die a thousand times, there is a time to put aside the sword. You are a beaten man. It would be another pointless death.'

At that moment, seeing Oled walking away defenceless, the Emperor could contain himself no longer. He screamed at the top of his voice.

'Now, Murak! Kill him now!'

In response, Murak sprang to his feet. Sensing the movement, Oled spun round. But Murak didn't strike.

'The battlements, Oled,' he shouted. 'They mean treachery.'

Gardep saw the Sol-ket bowmen rising. 'Archers,' he cried. 'Look to the city walls.'

In the exchange of arrows, two shafts passed within a hair's breadth of the boy-general. But Gardep was too fast. Hurling himself to one side, he shot twice with his own bow, killing his would-be assassins. Hundreds of Helat arrows clattered against the city walls, sending the enemy archers scuttling for cover.

'What's this?' Oled demanded, turning to fix Murak with a stare.

'The sword they gave me is tipped with poison,' Murak said. 'Those archers were meant to slay your leaders.'

A frown creased Oled's brow. 'So why didn't you go through with it?'

'You spared me,' Murak croaked, his throat tight with emotion. 'In spite of everything I have done, you spared me. After that, I could not betray you again.'

As Muzal stamped away in disgust, followed by Asun, a murmur rippled through the multitude, Helat and Solket alike. This had never been seen before. Both men, at different moments, had their opponent at their mercy. Neither had had the will to strike. What did it mean? Oled marched past Gardep on his way back to his quarters. Their eyes met and Gardep nodded his understanding of the Tanjur's actions. He stepped forward, standing alone beneath the walls. Five thousand Helat archers trained their bows on the battlements, lest there be more treachery.

'The war is over,' Gardep cried, his voice echoing across the plain. 'This is the meaning of Oled Lonetread's act of mercy. If you want it, the conflict ends this moment. Vengeance is easy. But it solves nothing. Listen to me, fighters on both sides. No man has suffered more than Oled Lonetread. By subterfuge, Murak slew his mother, Queen of Tanjurs. But Oled did not take the priest's life in return.'

He drew his sword. 'There has to be a time,' he said, 'when we put our weapons aside. He thrust the blade into the snow-dusted ground. 'The sword is not the answer to every question. You have until dawn tomorrow to decide.

Will you follow your corrupt and dishonourable Emperor and continue a war that can only end in your deaths?'

His eyes swept the listening Sol-ket. 'Or will you lay down your arms? I give you my word, there will be no reprisals. It is your decision, men of Rinaghar.'

Gardep's voice faded into the chill air. He would wait for the city's answer.

8

'Traitor!' the Emperor cried, storming into his apartments. 'Did you see him, Asun? Did you see what your brother-priest did out there?'

Asun bowed. 'I did, Your Imperial Majesty.'

'All it took was a scratch,' Muzal snarled. 'But what did he do? He threw down his sword. What madness possessed him?'

Asun made a show of bewilderment, though inwardly he was delighted by what his rival had done.

'The dog has gone over to the enemy,' Muzal bawled, sweeping plates and goblets from the table that dominated the room. 'He seeks peace with the cockroaches. It's over, Asun. That was our last chance to destroy their leadership. Even if we survive the Darkwing winter, the Empire will fall.'

Asun's eyes narrowed. 'Maybe not, Majesty.'

Muzal seized on the priest's words. 'What is it, Asun? Is there something you can do to save us yet?'

'I have been talking to Murak's priests,' Asun said. 'The rebels destroyed our artillery before Dullah. They destroyed our entire stock of Fire Dust.'

'I know this, priest!'

'Your Imperial Majesty,' Asun said patiently, 'what they

failed to do was destroy our *knowledge* of its properties. The firing of Commander Rishal's artillery was a setback. It was not the end of our hopes. My brother-priests think they can manufacture enough Fire Dust to defend the city.'

'So why are you standing here, talking to me?' Muzal demanded. 'Set them to work!'

Asun smiled. 'Majesty, I already have.'

9

In the cavernous passages of Sangra Peak, the Darkwing's black eyes fixed his victims.

'You'll not take me again,' Jinghirza cried. 'I would rather take my own life.'

'Then do it,' the Darkwing hissed, 'and good riddance. You were a poor plaything.'

Aaliya kept up a steady volley of arrows but most of the shafts glanced off her target's carapace. Her three comrades cut and slashed at the advancing demon without success. They could feel the paralysing vapours stealing into their lungs. They were weakening. The Darkwing's airborne venom was taking effect. Cusha swayed and crumpled to the floor.

'Protect her!' Vishtar yelled, stepping between her and the creature.

'Too late,' the Darkwing snarled, belching the fatal vapour into Vishtar's face. 'This time she is mine.'

But before the demon lord could collect his prize, there were newcomers in the heaving darkness. Scabrous fingers gripped all manner of weapons, rushing at the demon lord. Familiar skeletal figures were hurling themselves at the Darkwing.

'Jackal!' Vishtar cried gratefully.

The battle swept back and forth across the cave. The Darkwing cut great swathes through the ranks of the night-striders. Soon, piles of bones lay where they had fallen. Satisfied that he had broken their power, the demon lord melted back into the blackness of the tunnels. He would wait for the remainder of his enemy in his lair, where he was at his most powerful and deadly. Nandraghiri would be their tomb.

CHAPTER 14

The Ziggurat of Ra

I

Sanjay found his master, the Emperor, pacing his apartments.

'What time is it, Sanjay?'

'It is just before dawn, Your Imperial Majesty.'

Muzal dropped wearily into a chair. 'Draw the blinds, Sanjay.'

Sanjay let in the weak, weary light of dawn. It was the final day of Buradish, the eve of Kukhala-Ra.

'I wonder, Sanjay,' Muzal said, 'will we live to see many more dawns?'

Sanjay offered no answer.

'You have been a faithful servant to me,' Muzal said. 'How many years have you been in my service?'

Sanjay did not have to think long. 'It is thirty years, Your Imperial Majesty. I was a boy of fourteen when I entered the Imperial palace.'

'Yes,' Muzal said. 'I remember you. You always were the loyal one, Sanjay, unlike the vile cockroaches swarming around our walls. We have a wonderful life here in Rinaghar, do we not?' He gazed across the golden minarets and domes of the city. 'We live in a golden age. There is law, justice, art. Great academies teach the knowledge of the world. And what is it all based on?'

'I don't know, Your Imperial Majesty.'

'It is faith, Sanjay. We are the Children of Ra. The holy face of the sun is our truth.'

The steady pulsing of drums eddied through the morning air.

'Hear that, Sanjay?' Muzal said. 'That's the Helat war host. How dare they disturb the peace of golden Rinaghar?'

He patted Sanjay on the shoulder.

'You're not like them, are you Sanjay? Oh, you're from Helat stock, but you have enjoyed the privileges of a palace slave. You understand the greatness of our Empire.'

There was a knock at the door.

'Come in,' Muzal said. 'Ah, Asun. Is it ready?'

Asun glanced at Sanjay. Muzal read the look. 'Leave us, Sanjay,' he said. 'I have matters to discuss with Lord Asun.' He waited until Sanjay had closed the doors behind him. 'Well,' the Emperor demanded, 'how is production going?'

Asun heard how Muzal hungered for destruction. 'It will be ready by the dawn, Your Imperial Majesty.'

'Dawn! You mean we have to wait another day for the stuff?'

'What is twenty-four hours, master?' Asun asked. 'If Ra

favours us at all, by then the Darkwing's plan will have been thwarted. We can celebrate Kukhala-Ra by repelling the heretic enemy from our walls.'

'Is there no way we can do it sooner?' Muzal complained. He strode to the window, jabbing a finger at the vast multitude outside the city walls. 'Do you hear that?' he asked. 'Do you hear the way the vermin insult us? I want them annihilated. I want it now!' He railed against his misfortunes. 'The Hotec-Ra must not fail me again, Asun. First Shirep failed. Then it was Linem. Now Murak and Timu have gone the same way. Don't let me down, Asun. You're a dead man if you do.'

'I won't, Majesty.'

'And there's no chance of hurrying the process along?'

'Majesty,' Asun said with a sigh, 'you must be patient. It will be another twenty-four hours before we have sufficient quantities to demoralise the foe.'

The Emperor snorted his disgust. 'Very well. Tomorrow it is.'

2

At the same moment, but two miles across the plain, Murak was attending the war council of the Army of the Free. Like the accused going before a judge, he sat directly opposite Oled. Out of shame, he kept his eyes averted.

'You have slept on the issue at hand,' Oled said. 'Tell me, priest, what is your decision?'

Murak bowed his head. 'I will make the appeal. I will call on the Sol-ket and the Hotec-Ra to throw down their weapons. I will ask for the cessation of all resistance.'

He hesitated for just a moment. 'There is still a formidable army within the walls. The Emperor is greatly feared. I am but a general. Compared to him, I barely figure in the minds of the Sol-ket. My words may have little sway.'

'But you will make the appeal?' Gardep asked. 'You are a senior man. At worst, you are bound to make them think.'

'I will make the appeal,' Murak said.

He looked around the assembly, trying to read the impassive faces of the rebel leaders.

'But can it be true?' he wondered out loud. 'Are you truly offering me a share of power, after everything I have done?'

'You will have a sort of power,' Oled answered. 'I reprieved you out of a desire for peace. You will speak for your fellow Sol-ket in whatever government we create to rule this land.'

'I thought Gardep would be your king,' Murak said.

Oled shook his head. 'You will never understand us, will you, Murak? There will be no kings after this.' He rose to his feet. 'You will represent the Children of Ra, but only if you learn to share power with those you have tortured and oppressed. You will be one man among many, a servant of the people. That is the true meaning of reconciliation.'

He met Murak's eyes with a look that would reduce many men to stone.

'Oh, I will never be your friend, priest,' he said. 'Too much blood has been shed for that to be possible. Even now, my arm trembles with the urge to strike your head from your shoulders. But I will put aside my rage and sit down at the bargaining table with you. I am prepared to make this sacrifice in order to end long centuries of suffering. Can you put aside your dreams of absolute power and be one man among many, a small voice in a chorus of millions?'

Murak nodded. 'I will do everything in my power to help you bring peace, Oled Lonetread.'

'Then the war is over,' Oled said.

Within the hour, Murak was standing before the gates of Ra. He set out the terms of peace.

'There will be no retribution against the former masters,' he said. 'There will be no looting or destruction. You need not fear for the safety of your families. The Army of the Free ask only this of you, Children of Ra. You must give up your privileges and end the practice of slavery for all eternity. I trust this vast throng to keep their word. What say you to their proposal for peace?'

On the walls, Muzal wanted to throw the traitor's words back in his face. But he was not speaking from a position of strength. He had to play for time. Just twenty-four hours and he could settle accounts with this miserable priest. He would watch his flesh melt and hear his traitor's throat scream in agony.

'Tomorrow is the first day of Kukhala-Ra,' Muzal said. 'It may be the last day we have on this Earth. It may be the first day of a new world. Destiny will decide. But, if Ra grants that the good sun rises, we will sit down by first light, Sol-ket and Helat together, to draw up a peace settlement. I will send an envoy to make the arrangements.'

At that, there was a great roar of jubilation from the Helat masses. Muzal turned away and descended the steps. 'Let them have their moment of triumph, Asun,' he hissed. 'Tomorrow, the fools will burn in the fires of Hell.'

3

It was after dark when Asun was led into the tent erected for the following day's meeting. He was accompanied by three of the rebel leaders: Gardep, Oled and Atrakon.

'It stands halfway between the Army of the Free and the city walls,' Gardep told Asun.

Asun looked around then opened the tent flap and cast his gaze towards the city walls. 'Show me where your warriors will be standing,' he said.

Gardep pointed to a long row of fluttering standards. 'Nobody will step beyond that line.'

Asun examined the distances involved for some time then professed himself satisfied. 'All we have to discuss now is when the two sides will take their seats at the negotiating table,' he said.

Oled's eyes hardened. 'What's this?' he demanded. 'Are you planning some treachery, priest?'

Asun shook his head. 'Not at all. I was about to suggest that both sets of negotiators set off from their own lines simultaneously. If this war is finally to be settled, there must be mutual trust.' He looked at each of the rebel leaders in turn. 'Do you agree?'

Gardep exchanged glances with Oled and Atrakon. Each gave a slight, if wary, nod.

'His Imperial Majesty will be accompanied by Ghushan-Ra and three senior officers. I will be the final member of the negotiating team.'

'There will be five representatives of the Army of the Free,' Gardep said, 'the three men you see here, Murima ul-Parcep and the Vassyrian Adrius. In this way, every section of our alliance will be represented.'

'As you wish,' Asun said. 'That is decided then. We will meet an hour before dawn. We will set off at the same time. All we need now is an agreed signal.'

Atrakon smiled. He found all this slightly ridiculous. 'What about a bugler from each side?' he suggested. 'After all, everything has to be equal and fair, doesn't it?'

'On behalf of His Majesty, I agree to this arrangement,' Asun said. 'By the grace of Ra, the Darkwing will perish. Then sun will rise again over our deliberations. Good evening, gentlemen.'

With that, he turned his back on them and walked back towards the Gates of Ra. He permitted himself a smile of satisfaction. His fervent wish was that, Ra willing, the dawn would rise over a devastated and defeated foe.

4

Walking back towards their own lines, the leaders of the Army of the Free expressed astonishment at the priest's easy acquiescence. As they reached the city of tents, the remaining members of the war council hurried forward.

'Well?' Murima asked. 'What did he have to say?'

Oled explained the outcome of the discussions.

'Something's wrong,' Murima said. 'When did the Solket, and especially these Hotec-Ra, surrender anything easily?'

'I am beginning to have the same feeling,' Atrakon said.

Gardep frowned. 'Oled?'

'The enemy are treacherous,' he said, glancing in the direction of Murak, sitting alone by a campfire. 'But I can't see what they can do to alter the course of events. The tent is out of range of bowmen. Besides, their own emperor would be in the firing line if they attempted some skullduggery.'

'What are you saying, Murima?' Gardep said. 'Should we call off the talks?'

Murima thought for a moment then shook her head. 'No,' she said, 'we owe it to Cusha, Vishtar and Aaliya to take the first step to peace. With the grace of the Four

Winds, they will rid the world of the Darkwing. It is up to us to secure an end to war and oppression. Like Oled, I can't see what they can do with Muzal if our negotiations are undertaken in the open before the city gates.'

'It is agreed then,' Gardep said. 'We will keep our wits about us and be on our guard. But we will go through with the talks. Does anyone oppose this course of action?' Nobody did. 'Very well,' he said. 'Tomorrow, we will meet the Emperor face to face. We will try to make the world anew.'

The assembled leaders accepted his words with a nod, more of resignation than enthusiasm. The closeness of freedom seemed to make them all numb, Gardep most of all. He walked away slowly, retreating into his own thoughts. Climbing into the saddle of his mount he rode up the winding path to the heights above the city. Finally, trotting through the chopping, snow-laden wind, he came to the spot from which he had first looked down on Rinaghar many months before. He recalled that day, when he was still a naïve cadet in the service of Rishal ax-Sol. Was it just a few months? He found it hard to believe. Since then, the entire universe seemed to have shifted on its axis. Dismounting, Gardep walked to a point from which he could see the vast, open plain. There, after watching the polar winds ravaging the city of gold for some minutes, he looked north, addressing a few simple words to his beloved Cusha.

'Can we do it, my love?' he wondered. 'Together, can we really make this world anew?'

The wind didn't answer. Instead, it roared, deaf to his questions, wild and unfathomable like some desolate beast. Gardep stood there until the driving snow blurred his vision. Then he climbed back into the saddle and rode back to his quarters.

5

Muzal couldn't sleep. He tossed and turned all night, again haunted by the many-millioned slave-demon that now pursued his thoughts through every troubled night. Eventually, he gave up any thought of rest and rose. He slipped out onto the balcony of his apartment, gazing at the vast servile throng that was washing around the walls of Ra like a human ocean.

'Soon,' he murmured, 'you will understand what fools you are to tweak this tiger's tail. You will burn on Earth, then you will burn in hell.'

The thought filled his heart with a burning stream of exhilaration. Then he remembered Sanjay sleeping in the antechamber, on hand to serve his master. Muzal decided to hold his tongue. Faithful as an old dog Sanjay may be, but he was still a Helat. Moving swiftly yet softly down the corridor, Muzal roused his bodyguards and went in search of Asun. He found him organising the recently rebuilt war machines. There were ten catapults, smelling of freshly cut timber.

'Only ten?' Muzal grumbled.

'There was not time to assemble more,' Asun informed his emperor. 'Even that meant the carpenters and engineers working round the clock.'

'And the ammunition?'

'There are five projectiles for each machine,' Asun said.

'That means, what, seven, eight thousand dead?' Muzal said. 'That is but a pinprick in the enemy multitude.'

'That depends on where we concentrate our fire,' Asun said. 'I have been observing our enemy. Hence the arrangement of our war machines. You will notice, Your Imperial Majesty that they are drawn up in a semi-circle. By pinpointing the enemy leadership, we can destroy their senior leadership and the entire cadre below them. It is a blow from which they will not recover. Trust me, Majesty, we are about to pluck victory from the ashes of defeat.'

'So many men have promised me victory,' Muzal sighed. 'Every one of them is dead.'

'I will not fail you, Majesty,' Asun said. 'The moment Gardep na-Vassyrian leads the negotiating party towards us, we will behead the rebel beast.'

'How many hours until we give the enemy the punishment they so richly deserve?' Muzal demanded.

'Four hours, Highness.'

'I can't wait for this moment of retribution,' Muzal said. 'I am going to relish every sweet, agonising moment.' He clenched his fists. 'I want you to kill them, Asun. Kill them all.'

6

Gardep didn't sleep either. The thought of Cusha facing the Darkwing without him by her side troubled him. Equally, Murima's warning words kept floating to the front of his thoughts: when did the masters ever surrender easily? By the time the Army of the Free finally gathered before Rinaghar, he had made a decision. Once they had assembled, he stepped forward to address them.

'Warriors of the Free,' he began, 'this is your victory. You have ended the tyranny of the Sol-ket. How many of you would have believed, even six months ago, that this day the Emperor would sit down with us to discuss the end of slavery? Before I speak to you about the importance of this day, I want you to bow your heads. Give a few moments to remember the fallen and to think of our comrades now entering the precincts of Nandraghiri to face the demon lord.'

Immediately, there was no sound but the snapping of the regimental banners. Some thought of a brother, a sister, a father, a mother, a fallen friend. Shamana was in many minds. Her example and her sacrifice had made this day possible. Murima thought of her dead father, Shinar, and Atrakon of his lost love, Leila. Gardep thought of Kulmat. But all, of course, thought of Cusha, Vishtar and Aaliya in their moment of peril. Finally, Gardep continued his address.

'The air grows cold,' he said. 'The Darkwing winter sweeps across the land.' He pointed to the far horizon. 'Who knows,' he continued, 'whether the sun will rise this day. By sunset we will have a new world or no world at all. But, in the hope that our comrades prevail, we must turn our thoughts to peace. It is said in the Book of Scales that there will be no king. But there must be a leader. Army of the Free, I can never be that man.'

A murmur ran through the great crowd.

'I was raised to know blood and fire, the song of the blade and the sweep of the cavalry charge. When I fought Rishal, to my eternal shame, I was without mercy. I would have allowed him to die in agony. It would have meant a wretched end. I must devote myself to the task of learning gentleness and sympathy. Over time, with Cusha's help, softer feelings will grow in me. Maybe one day I will learn wisdom. But I have not learned it yet. I will not lead you.'

He turned to the other leaders. 'I must pass that burden to another man, my friend Oled Lonetread.'

Oled looked thunderstruck.

'Yes, Oled, you are the man to lead us,' Gardep said. 'You spared Murak though he was responsible for the death of your own mother. This is the act of a man who can bring peace to this tortured and divided land. You know the arts of pity and fogiveness. Do not refuse this request, Oled. Look into your heart. You know I am right. You will look Muzal in the eye. You will be our voice.'

It took some time for Oled to speak. When he did, it was with strength and purpose. 'Gardep is right,' he said. 'The time of Kings is at an end. No man or woman was born to lead others. That right does not flow in our blood. It is not passed on from father to son or mother to daughter. It must be earned. If I am to conduct your affairs and administer justice, I must have your consent. Do I have that sacred trust?'

There was a roar of acclamation.

'Then, with humility, I will accept this honour,' Oled said. 'I will be your protector and your judge.'

'All hail Oled Lonetread,' Gardep cried, 'protector-general of the Free.'

'All hail!' came the answering chorus.

Oled smiled. 'Protector-general,' he said, 'it is a good title. I will not be king. I seek no permanence for my office. Each twelvemonth, let there be a casting of lots. The people will choose their leader anew. Yes, let the judge be judged.'

He gestured to the other four members of the negotiation team.

'Let's bring peace to this land,' he said.

7

Muzal nodded to the guards.

'There,' he said, 'twenty metres before these gates is the position from which we are meant to march towards the foe. But we will never enter their cursed tent of peace.

There will be only one road to peace in this land and that is through the crushing of all rebels and heretics.'

He glanced at Asun. 'When we reach that line,' he continued, 'the enemy leadership will be gathered facing the Gates of Ra. The moment we cross the line, you must unleash heaven's fire on the foe.'

He fired a warning glance at his soldiers. 'There must be no cheers,' he told them, 'no battle cries, nothing to warn the foe.' He winked at Ghushan. 'The moment fire begins to rain on them and spread dismay through their ranks, our brave Sol-ket will ride out and slaughter the leaderless herd. We will punish them for their impudence.'

He gave a smile of incipient triumph. 'They want freedom. We will give them death.'

As Muzal walked through the gates he noticed Sanjay in the crowd. Oddly, when he acknowledged his most faithful servant, Sanjay gave no sign of having noticed. Dismissing the curious moment, Muzal strode ahead of his fellow negotiators.

He was dressed in the Imperial white and gold, the crown of his ancestors on his head. As he walked briskly towards his line, he saw the rebel leadership set off.

'It's almost time, Asun,' he whispered. 'I'm going to enjoy watching this.'

Already, in his mind's eye, he could see the havoc the Fire Dust would wreak in the enemy ranks. He watched the insurgent leaders, focusing on each one in turn. He was surprised to see Oled walking at the head of the contingent. Behind him there were the warrior, Gardep, the slave Murima, the Vassyrian Adrius and the Selessian Atrakon. Every one of you will burn, Muzal thought. He just prayed the keen-eared Tanjur would not catch the creak of tension in the catapult ropes. He had no need to worry. The giant was too busy marching towards his place in history. Any minute now, Muzal thought. Any minute now. Finally, Muzal crossed the line. A split-second later the fire weapon exploded, engulfing thousands of men in flame.

8

Far to the north, Jinghirza led the way into the Darkwing's lair.

'Where is he?' Aaliya asked. She could see the chained prisoners but there was no sign of the Darkwing.

'He is here,' Cusha said. 'I sense his presence.'

'Stay close to me, sister,' Vishtar said. 'As always, our enemy will have murder in his heart.'

He was right. In a dark corner the Darkwing was waiting. He had forgotten Jinghirza, the girl he had tormented for so long. He could smell Cusha. He could see her. His bleak eyes hunted her through the gloom. The demon lord imagined the way her ribs would splinter, the way her flesh would tear, the way her heart would gush sweet, refreshing blood. Soon he would drain the Holy Child, leaving her as lifeless as the world would be by the end of day.

'I'm going to free the captives,' Jinghirza said.

She started to strike their manacles with her hammer. The freed prisoners barely moved. They were suffering the catatonic drowsiness of the demon lord's victims.

'He has fed on all of them,' Vishtar said, seeing the tell-tale signs. 'But where is he now?'

Nobody spoke. They listened to the squabbling crosswinds that were whipping round Sangra Peak. Outside, the gales wailed, yelped and shrieked. Filaments of trailing snow drifted across the entrance. In the tight, pulsating dark the demon lord waited. The intruders exchanged haunted looks. They couldn't hear him but they could smell him. The reek of evil permeated every atom of this terrible place. It crawled from every space, writhed and twisted from every crack and crevice. Even Jackal's night-striders were infected with the deep, numbing throb of fear.

'He's coming,' Cusha murmured.

All around her, her comrades sensed it, the intense coiling of snarling menace.

'He's coming.'

Then, with a vile, gut-wrenching screech, the Darkwing attacked.

9

The vast fireball climbed into the sky, like the black and crimson head of some ancient dragon. Men screamed as they writhed and twisted in agony, made living torches by the exploding projectiles of Fire Dust. One after another they detonated, spraying their victims with scarlet destruction. Cowering before the intense heat, those soldiers who had not been burned were thrown into confusion, their discipline and unity splintering before the searing conflagration.

'By the holy face of Ra!' Muzal exclaimed, watching the jaws of hell gape wide and swallow hundreds of cinder-black victims.

But there was no celebration in his voice. It was not the ranks of the Army of the Free that had been immolated, but his own Sol-ket.

'What happened?' he demanded.

Then, hearing loud roars behind him, he spun round to see the fury in the faces of the Army of the Free.

'Treachery!' Oled Lonetread roared. 'Why is it always treachery from these people?'

He looked at his companions.

'Whatever they had planned for us has misfired. We will not give them a second chance.' He caught Gardep's eye. 'The Gates of Ra are open. The Sol-ket planned to unleash war. We will impose peace by force of arms. I say we enter golden Rinaghar and subdue the foe.'

Gardep nodded. So did the other leaders. Taking up their weapons, they climbed into the saddle.

'For freedom!' Oled roared.

10

'Close the gates!' Muzal yelled as he re-entered the city.

'There are no gates to close,' Asun told him.

It was true. They were on fire and useless to resist the rebel throng. Muzal stared in disbelief at the firestorm that was consuming the heart of his army. 'In the name of Ra,' he demanded, 'what happened?'

Eventually, Ghushan fought his way through the screaming confusion. 'Fire arrows,' he panted. 'They were shot from within the city.'

'From *within*!' Muzal repeated. 'But how? It makes no sense.'

'It makes complete sense, tyrant,' a voice shouted.

Muzal searched for the speaker. When he located him, his face filled with rage and disbelief. 'Sanjay!'

Fifty or so Helati surrounded the house-slave. All were armed.

'I have been waiting for this day all my life,' Sanjay shouted. 'All these years I have had to put up with your tantrums and your punishments. Worst of all, I have had to swallow your mindless raving and ranting.'

'Ingrate!' Muzal yelled, drawing his sword. 'I fed you and gave you shelter.'

Sanjay shook his head. 'You gave me nothing. You worked me half to death. You treated me like a beast of burden. But I bided my time. My heart sang when my Helat brothers and sisters gathered outside the city walls. Then I heard you talking to Asun, preparing your weapon. I sought out any man or woman who wanted to strike against their oppressors. I found many Helati keen to fight. Then, ax-Sol, I struck.'

'You'll die for this, slave,' Muzal bawled.

'Do your worst,' Sanjay told him. 'I will be waiting for you at the Ziggurat of Ra.'

Even as this exchange was taking place, Gardep, Oled and Atrakon were leading the charge through the Gates of Ra. Leaping over the smouldering catapults they drove through the demoralised Sol-ket. But, even as the dogs of war were unleashed, there was a renewed appeal for peace. Murak had mounted the city walls and was shouting at the top of his voice.

'Listen to me, Sol-ket,' he cried, 'heed my words, Hotec-Ra. This is madness. You cannot resist the Army of the Free. Shrug off the influence of the Muzals. You cannot win. For Ra's sake, live to return to your families. At least then you can have some kind of future. Yes, you will have to share wealth and power. But what will you have if you're dead? Nothing!'

He threw out his arms. 'If I have learned anything from this war, it is this. Violence begets violence. Embrace the future, my brothers. We can have peace.'

Peace was the last word to leave his lips. At that moment an arrow pierced his throat. The bowman was Asun.

11

Murak's sacrifice was not in vain. His words made sense to the beleaguered Sol-ket. Defeated at the Dragon Mountains and again at Dullah, vastly outnumbered in the present conflict, they knew the war was over. Encircled everywhere by the Army of the Free, the Children of the Sun threw down their weapons.

'Disarm them,' Oled shouted. 'Stack their weapons and guard them well.'

He caught the eye of Gardep and Atrakon.

'Take over,' he said. 'I must go to Murak.'

With that, he raced to the priest's side. He found Murak dying.

'Is it over, Oled?' Murak croaked feebly.

'Yes, Murak, it is over. The Sol-ket are disarmed. There will be no more war.'

'Thank Ra,' Murak said.

Oled stared at him for a few moments, a tumult of emotions boiling in his breast. Then, making a decision, he knelt and cradled the dying man in his arms.

'Ours could have been a great friendship, Murak, but the ways of the Hotec-Ra were too strong in you.'

'I drew no pleasure from my treachery,' Murak said. 'With each act my mouth filled with a more bitter taste. If I could only run back the sands of time, Oled. If only . . .'

He spluttered blood. Oled stared at him. In spite of everything that Murak had done, he was overwhelmed with a great sense of pity. The scene reminded the giant of his own mother's death throes.

'The world is growing cold,' Murak said. 'Don't leave me, Oled.'

'I will be here to the end,' Oled said.

Murak managed a smile of gratitude. 'Tell me that I have discovered some shred of goodness in myself,' Murak pleaded.

'Yes,' Oled said, 'you did some good, Murak. You did some good at the end.'

Murak struggled with his breathing for a few moments longer, then he lost his fight for life and went limp in Oled's arms. A life devoted to treachery was over.

12

In the confused half light Muzal climbed the Ziggurat of Ra to face Sanjay. Behind him, even his Eternals had surrendered.

'You're looking old, Muzal,' Sanjay said, watching his master steadily climbing the steps.

'I'm not too old to kill you, Helat,' Muzal panted.

Sanjay waited between the unlit braziers at the summit of the Ziggurat. 'Then kill me, old man. What are you now, Muzal, an Emperor of cinders?' He pointed the tip of his sword at Muzal's chest. 'We are equals at last.'

'No Helat will ever be equal to a lord of the Sol-ket,' Muzal snarled. 'Imagine this, Sanjay. You think you have conquered. Maybe there will yet be a Sol-ket victory of sorts. I will kill you here, atop this monument to the power of Ra. With your dying eyes you will see darkness cover the world. Yes, look to the east. There is no dawn. What an irony! At the moment your Helat cockroaches are dancing in the street, celebrating their pointless victory, my monstrous son has triumphed in the Mountains of the Moon. All you have inherited, slave, is endless night.'

Then the talking was over. Their swords clashed. Up

and down the stairs they fought, striking and slashing, until the exhausted Muzal let his sword fall from his hands. With no reserves of strength or courage left, he sank to his knees. But, as Muzal awaited the deathblow, he glimpsed Asun approaching Sanjay from the rear. The priest was drawing a bow. The arrow was tipped with Fire Dust.

As the arrow left the bowstring there was a warning shout. 'Look out!'

Sanjay seized Muzal's shoulders and used him as a human shield. The moment Asun's arrow bit into the Imperial flesh, Muzal's body exploded into flames. He tumbled down the steps, burning as Shinar had burned forty years before. Appalled, Asun searched for the man who had shouted the warning. It was Gardep. With a single arrow, Gardep sent Asun to the House of the Dead. With their deaths, the Empire passed into memory. An hour later, the victorious Army of the Free gathered around the Ziggurat of Ra. Oled's words to them were simple.

'The war here is over. There is no more that we can do. It is up to the Holy Children now.'

As one, the vast throng turned to the north and prayed.

CHAPTER 15

An Innocent and Generous

I

As they anticipated the demon lord's assault, the companions could feel his presence all around them, a tangible malevolence. The coldness and savagery of his soul seemed to coat every surface with evil. Cusha led the group. Hesitant, crouching, she edged forward. Sword in hand, she searched the gloom for some sign of movement. Every fibre of her being was buzzing with apprehension. The whole place reeked of menace. She found it hard to believe that, long ago, this monastery had been a refuge. She tried to imagine it. Once there had been order and tranquillity, each of the day's devotions announced by the dull boom of the bell. Now, those sacred routines were replaced by a silence that was heavy with danger. Aaliya

289

and Vishtar followed, darting glances up at the vaulted ceiling, alert to every wheeze and moan of the wind. The few surviving night-striders came last, fanning out, weapons in hand, ready to strike when the time came.

Jinghirza shuddered. 'We must destroy this place,' she said, flesh creeping as she remembered her days of imprisonment. 'Brick by brick we must tear it down, burn what can be burned and sow the ground with salt.'

Such was the claustrophobic atmosphere of encroaching terror: few had any faith in their weapons. It would take more than weapons to defeat the Darkwing. If anything, Cusha and Vishtar were the most anxious of all. They knew the monster better than any living being, his ruthlessness, his disregard for human life. Even so, they didn't know what to expect. Then, just as the air itself seemed to be imploding with expectation, a primal, heart-melting scream drilled through the passages of Nandraghiri. Like a great, heavy blanket, the Darkwing dropped from concealed vents in the ceiling. Avalanching from the dark, he fell upon the intruders. Jackal was first to react but the demon lord hurled him out into the howling wind. It came as no surprise to anyone that the creature selected Cusha as his prey. In his lair, he was more powerful than ever. He tossed aside the rushing night-striders like so many toy soldiers; cast them aside as he had cast their leader Jackal into the glacial void outside.

He enveloped the Holy Child in his leathery wings, folding her in his black presence. In vain, the companions fought to free her, Vishtar more than anyone. He slashed at the monster, but the Darkwing seemed invulnerable. Strengthened by the foul brew in which he bathed every night, he felt their thrusts as pinpricks. Cusha struggled to get free, but the Darkwing refused to let her go. His talons closed round her waist. He was unnaturally strong. He sniffed at her throat and his lips parted revealing glistening fangs.

'Help me!' Vishtar cried as he stabbed and stabbed again without effect, his swordpoint deflected by the monster's carapace. 'He will kill her.'

'This is just too easy,' the Darkwing hissed, spearing Cusha with a fearsome gaze. 'Did you come all this way to succumb with so little resistance?'

With a desperate lunge, Vishtar succeeded in thrusting his sword up into the Darkwing's face. Gouts of black blood sprayed over the boy, making him recoil with disgust. Still grasping Cusha by the waist, the Darkwing snarled at the Holy Child. Cords of muscle stood out from his reptilian neck. The wound had barely even made him flinch. Vishtar stared into the raven-black eyes and his insides seemed to dissolve.

'Is that all you have?' the Darkwing demanded. 'Eight years I fed on you, boy. Eight years I filled your soul with torment. And what do you do? You give me a pinprick with *this*!'

Snatching the sword out of Vishtar's hand, he drove it into the ribcage of one of the last night-striders.

'Are the Helati mad?' he wondered out loud. 'Did they really think this pathetic band could triumph over me?'

Driving Aaliya and Jinghirza back with his poisonous breath, he dragged both Holy Children to the entrance, where the polar winds snapped and yelped.

'Look out there,' he roared. 'Soon it will be dawn. Tell me, where is your precious sun? Does it stain the hills yellow? Does it illuminate the valleys? No, not this day, or any other day in the future.'

The Holy Children gazed into the grey-black half-light and were dismayed at what they saw.

'Last night,' the Darkwing gloated, 'it set for the last

time. This is the day the world finally succumbs to the icy breath of the Darkwing winter.' He leered. 'Don't you think that's wonderful? Mankind has named its last days after me. This foul race's final act will be to curse *me*.'

He drew close to them, his putrid breath stinging their faces.

'How I have longed for this moment,' he grunted. 'Those who survive this battle – and I will make sure you two do – will die slowly of cold and despair. I will watch the colour drain from your flesh, leaving you grey like that sky. Next, I will see your limbs blacken and lose sensation. Then, finally, I will watch eternal night lay its black fingers on your eyelids and put you into the sleep from which no living soul recovers.'

Behind him Aaliya and Jinghirza were gagging at the effects of the venom. The Darkwing spread his wings and took to the air.

2

The Darkwing swept upwards.

'Where are you taking us?' Vishtar cried against the buffeting wind.

'Look to your left,' the Darkwing said, swooping between towering peaks. 'There are greater peaks than Mount Sangra. From the summit of the tallest of the Mountains of the Moon, you can see half the world. I wanted to show you what has happened to the land.'

Cusha stole a glance back at Nandraghiri.

'Oh, don't fret,' the demon lord said. 'I will return you to the monastery presently. First, you will witness my triumph.'

He set them down on the greatest of the range's many

cloud-raking summits. So deep and bone numbing was the cold, the Holy Children gasped like stranded fish. Their lungs heaved and their eyes blurred. Seized by the ferocious cold, their mouths sagged open, snatching wounded breaths. Oblivious to their distress, the Darkwing pointed to the south.

'Do you see?' he cried, though they were already unable to see anything. 'The Khut land shivers under endless snowdrifts.'

He spoke of things he could imagine rather than see.

'What do you think those dark clouds are that you see moving across the plain?' he asked the now senseless pair. 'They are animals. That's right, thousands of yaks, bears, wolves, deer and mountain goats are migrating towards Jinghara, searching for food. They will find none. Further south, the blizzards are swallowing up mile after mile of what was once hot, sultry farmland. Ice clings to the battlements of Karangpur, the minarets and temple roofs of golden Rinaghar, even the terracotta walls of Tiger-gated Parcep. The southern ocean has begun to freeze. Do you see, Holy Children? Do you see?'

He turned. Cusha and Vishtar were barely conscious. Overwhelmed by the glacial, penetrating wind, they lay groaning in a near coma.

'Oh no you don't,' the creature said. His face rumpled with a lethal intelligence. 'You must live to see the final darkness come.'

3

'Aaliya,' Jinghirza shouted, drawing her sword, 'they're coming back.'

Together, they stared at the demon lord. He was

carrying the limp forms of the Holy Children. To all intents and purposes, they were dead. He dropped them to the ground and swept on towards the two women fighters. Momentarily thrown into confusion and bitter dismay, Aaliya stood rooted to the spot while the demon lord closed on her. By the time she had recovered her wits enough to put up resistance, he was upon her, dashing her to the ground.

'Say your prayers to whatever gods you have,' the Darkwing told the cowering Jinghirza. 'It is time to die along with your world.'

'I may die,' Jinghirza said. 'All mankind may perish this day. But you will have no triumph. Your solitude will be your punishment. May you rot for all time in your dark coffin. This new world of yours will be your own private hell.'

Stung by Jinghirza's defiance, he came at her with primal force, spitting, snarling and stabbing. She saw his mutilated face. It was sweating dark bile. Jinghirza could only half-deflect the attack. She did her best to protect herself but the hell-creature fastened on her shoulder. With a cry of anguish, she succumbed to the torrent of agony that gushed through her veins.

'Who will be next?' the Darkwing bellowed, hurling his challenge at the remnants of the Lost Souls. 'Is there nobody worthy of my rage?'

He raised his claws to drive them through Jinghirza's heart. Lying dazed in one corner, Aaliya's eyes focused on the small packet she had concealed days earlier in a crevice in the wall. It was the Fire Dust. She drove an arrow into the packet and shot it at the demon lord. Instantly, he was engulfed in flames. For a few moments he staggered around the chamber, beating at his blistering flesh. Aaliya stabbed several more arrowheads into the Fire Dust and shot him again, intensifying the conflagration. To her horror, though he shrieked and howled in agony, when the flames burned down, he was still standing.

'No,' Aaliya gasped, 'it's impossible.'

The Darkwing lurched towards her. That's when a skeletal figure returned from the storm outside. Its legs were shattered and it was crawling across the stone floor. It was Jackal. He seized the demon lord by the ankle and momentarily slowed his progress. The Holy Children stirred.

'Return to the fight,' Jackal cried. 'No mercy, Cusha. He is beyond redemption. Help Vishtar rid the world of his evil. Do this and I will enter the House of the Dead happy.'

Even as the Darkwing mercilessly stamped him to dust, a familiar voice made him turn.

'Our business isn't done,' Cusha said, rising unsteadily to her feet.

Before Vishtar could struggle up, the Darkwing had swept across the room, enveloping Cusha in his wings. He shook her until her teeth rattled.

'I planned to let you live to see the end of things,' he said, taking her in his death-grip. 'But I grow impatient. Savour this moment, Holy Child. It will be your last.'

Seeing the razor-sharp claws glint before her eyes, Cusha screamed. The blades flashed, then a second scream, louder, more piercing, more riven with agony, blazed through her tormentor's corrupted flesh. Enraged by the destruction of Jackal, desperate to save Cusha, Vishtar had driven his sword clean through the Darkwing's body.

'Look,' the boy cried. 'The conflagration has weakened him.'

Shuddering and jolting with violent spasms of anguish, the Darkwing released Cusha from his juddering arms.

The demon lord's voice reverberated through the winding passages of Nandraghiri. 'Even weakened,' he snarled, 'I am too strong for you.'

Gripping Vishtar's weapon, the demon lord eased himself off the blade. It seemed to take an age before he slid the sword from his fractured carapace. When he did, gobbets of black gore squirmed from the wound.

'I will make you pay for that,' the Darkwing threatened.

In a final show of defiance, Cusha and Vishtar stood side by side and faced him. They were trembling. Then Aaliya's voice put strength back in their hearts.

'This is why you were destined to reach Nandraghiri, Holy Children,' she cried, 'not to redeem the creature, but to destroy him. Remember the prophecy. This is the final battle. On this feat of arms the fate of the world will rest.'

'Of course,' Cusha cried. 'Destiny was always going to lead us to this. Now I understand the prophecy.' She took Vishtar's hand. 'We are one flesh, brother. We are one heart.'

'An innocent and generous heart,' Vishtar said, understanding at last. 'I thought it meant you. You thought it meant me. All the time, it meant the two of us together.'

Vishtar nodded. Even Cusha knew Sabray was unreachable within the hideous form of the Darkwing. Supported by Aaliya, the Holy Children fought the demon lord.

The struggle was long. It raged back and forth across the inner sanctum of Nandraghiri. Sword struck claw. Enfeebled by the Fire Dust, the Darkwing was as vulnerable as he had once been as a mortal man. With a hacking blow, Vishtar struck the side of the Darkwing's head. A chunk of the creature's skull tore free. He swayed and fell to his knees.

'This is it,' Aaliya said, stamping her boot down on the

demon lord's throat. 'You must finish him now.' She gazed at Cusha. 'Can you do it?'

Vishtar twisted his sword and cracked open the demon lord's ribcage. While he lay struggling, Cusha reached into his chest cavity and tore out his still-beating heart. Black blood stippled her face. More of the stuff puddled on the floor. The Darkwing's still-wide eyes dilated and the black fire within them died. Then, behind the backs of the Holy Children, Aaliya saw a brilliant, golden dawn.

'By the Four Winds,' she gasped.

Across the room, warmed by the life-giving rays of the rising sun, Jinghirza began to stir. Aaliya helped her to her feet. 'The wound is not fatal,' she said, examing the Khut maiden's torn shoulder. 'You are young and strong. It will heal in time.'

Jinghirza smiled. 'Soon I will return to my family, and you to Jinghara.'

Together, the four turned. They saw the great, life-giving star as if for the first time.

'It's beautiful,' Cusha said.

The sun climbed steadily, burning away the greyness that had obscured the azure sky. For the world, a new age had dawned.

4

Far away, in the great city of a fallen Empire, Rinaghar was golden once more. A wondrous sun illuminated its roofs and walls, its minarets and temples, its broad boulevards and avenues. Flocks of birds, long absent from the skies, took flight and wheeled overhead in dense swarms. Most of all, the light of the dawn warmed the faces of Sol-ket and Tanjur, Helat and barbarian, freed slave and powerless master. The sumptuous light spread like a warm, welcome tide, washing away the cold and the dark, nourishing the trees and the plants, reviving the birds, the animals, the fish and the tiniest insects. The air pulsated with bright, irrepressible life.

'They've done it,' Gardep cried. 'They've conquered the monster.'

He thought of Cusha and his heart leapt with joy. Oled too laughed out loud as he dreamed of Aaliya's return. Around them, vast crowds cheered and danced. The Ziggurat of Ra, so long the site of barbarous oppression, became the epicentre of a lavish and unbridled celebration. Hour after hour, there was music and dancing. What food could be mustered was shared, no matter what the caste, creed or nationality of the person to whom it was offered. Only as sunset reddened the great Ziggurat did some realise that they were sharing their jubilation with someone who had, just hours earlier, been a bitter foe. True reconciliation would not come that day or even that year but, with the victory of life over death, light over eternal darkness, the process of healing had begun. It was Oled Lonetread, flanked by Murima and Gardep, Atrakon and Adrius, Harad, Qintu, Nikesh and Bulu, who climbed to the summit of the Ziggurat to bid the multitude good night.

'The threat of extinction has been lifted from the land,' Oled said. 'Soon, our heroes will return from the north and we will give thanks for what they have achieved. This is the first day of our freedom, my brothers, my sisters. From this moment on, we will look to grow a sturdy crop of peace from the ashes of the fallen. Take your rest. You have earned it. Tomorrow we begin the work of forging a new freedom in which all our children can live and grow in security and shared hope. By the grace of the Four

Winds, we will wake to another wondrous dawn.'

With that, the huge crowds drifted away to find a bed for the night. Rinaghar slept soundly.

5

The boulevards of golden Rinaghar were richly scented with flowering blossom on the day that a lone Khut rider reached the former Gates of Ra. Now renamed the Gates of Freedom, the charred wooden doors opened to admit him. The guards conducted a brief interview before leading him to the house where Murima lived with Harad and Qintu.

'She's on her way!' Murima squealed with delight. 'My daughter is less than an hour from the city.'

Qintu and Harad came running from the courtyard.

'Is it true?' Harad demanded.

Murima nodded. 'She'll be here before noon.' She clapped her hands. 'What are you waiting for? We've got to find Gardep.'

They discovered him in the cells of the Great Ziggurat interrogating Murak's priests, the men who had produced the fire weapon.

'How many of you were involved?' Gardep demanded.

'We are all here,' their leader said.

'You're lying!'

'We alone are privy to the secrets of Fire Dust.' The priest met Gardep's stare. 'I swear, it's true.'

'Knowledge of the material is a sin,' Gardep said. 'This is the mandate of the people.'

'Are you going to kill us?'

Gardep shook his head. 'There are some in the Army of the Free who demanded a death sentence,' he told them.

'You were responsible for a weapon which could obliterate human life. But we are not like the Hotec-Ra. You will live out your days in sealed apartments, attached to a temple. There will be gardens to walk in. You will have books and manuscripts. But you will not be allowed to speak to another living soul. The secret of this evil weapon must die with you.'

The priests lowered their heads. 'We thank you for your mercy.'

'And nobody else knows about the dust?' Gardep asked again.

'Nobody.'

Gardep exchanged glances with Oled and Atrakon. They had been listening in silence. Gardep was about to say something when he glimpsed Murima and the boys standing in the doorway. There was something in Murima's eyes that made his heart leap.

'Cusha?' he asked.

Murima nodded. 'She's here.'

Oled too had a question. 'Aaliya?'

'Yes,' Murima said. 'They all lived to tell the tale: Cusha, Aaliya, Vishtar, all of them.'

Atrakon looked at Oled and Gardep. 'Just go,' he said with a grin. 'I can handle things here.'

The thunder of five horses could be heard drumming towards the Karangpur road.

6

Atrakon oversaw the movement of the Hotec-Ra to their temple-prison. He was about to go when he saw a silhouetted figure waiting for him. 'Sanjay?'

The Emperor's former servant stepped forward.

'Don't believe them, Atrakon Ebrahin,' he said.

Atrakon frowned. 'What do you know, Sanjay?'

'When I spied upon Muzal, I learned many things,' Sanjay said. 'I counted the priests involved in the production of the Fire Dust. When I heard that you had captured the Hotec-Ra, I came to see if you had them all in custody. My heart sank when I saw them being led into the interrogation room. Two are missing.'

'Do you know their names?'

Sanjay nodded. 'I do.'

'And would you recognise them again?'

Once more, Sanjay nodded.

'Do you understand what this means?' Atrakon asked.

'Yes,' Sanjay sighed, 'for some men the task of guarding their fellow man goes on for ever. They must be eternally vigilant.'

'Are you ready for this sacrifice?' Atrakon demanded.

'My life has been one of hardship and enslavement,' Sanjay said. 'Nothing that destiny places in my path can be worse than that. I may face many dangers to pursue those who would put our freedom in danger but I will be a free man. If you are planning to arrange a party to hunt them down, I will go with you.'

Atrakon seized Sanjay by the hand.

'You are a good man. Be ready to leave at a moment's notice.'

Sanjay smiled. 'Will the fight for freedom ever be over?' he asked.

Atrakon shook his head. 'Maybe this is the meaning of the Book of Scales,' the Selessian said. 'All things are meant to exist in balance. But mortal men and women have to fight to maintain that equilibrium. There is nothing inevitable about the triumph of good over evil. Only one thing can safely be predicted: the contest will continue as long as some of nature's children seek power over others. Are you sure you are ready for that fight?'

Sanjay let the sun's rays fall on his face.

'Yes,' he said, 'I am ready.'

7

The moment Gardep saw the riders in the distance; he spurred his horse and galloped towards them. Cusha did likewise. They met on the spot where the tent of peace had been. Gardep swept his beloved from her saddle and they embraced, weeping.

'There were times,' Gardep said, 'that I was weak. I lost faith in your return.'

Cusha pressed her cheek against his. 'That is not weakness, my love,' she said. 'The same shadows often flitted across my soul. We dared to oppose the most sinister forces this cruel world has mustered. We are flesh and blood, not gods. Gardep, we are human, that's all, with human hopes and dreams, yes, and human fears.'

'I have something to tell you,' Gardep said. 'I have stepped back from the position Shamana gave me. Oled Lonetread is now protector-general of the Free. He will guide the people through the difficult first years of freedom. Are you disappointed in me?'

'Disappointed?' Cusha said. She laughed out loud. 'Oh, Gardep,' she said. 'These words fill my heart with great joy. I am coming home to a man, not a general. Let others conduct the affairs of government. Through all our trials we promised one another that, one day, there would be a time for love. This is that time.' She clung to him. 'In the darkest moments on the journey to Nandraghiri, at the most critical turning points in our struggle, it was the thought of your touch, your breath that enabled me to go on. I thank the Four Winds that you are free of the expectations of destiny.'

Gardep stroked wild wisps of raven hair from her face. 'By what miracle of Fate were you placed in my path?' he murmured.

'Why, by the providence of the Scales, of course,' Cusha said. 'Perhaps, in all the chaos of a troubled land, there is truly some sense of order, some trace of purpose.'

Gardep gazed at her. 'If I didn't know better,' he said, 'I would say that your eyes are even darker than when you left.'

Cusha shook her head and smiled. She didn't tell him that there was a reason for that deeper blackness. She had seen into a soul so cold, so lacking in mercy, so incapable of redemption, that an edge of irresistible foreboding had been added to her view of the world. The last trace of her childhood innocence had gone.

Murima, Aaliya and Vishtar joined them; Harad and Qintu hovering uncertainly at the edge of the group. Their time of great journeys and many hard struggles was over.

8

Cusha's marriage to Gardep took place at the summit of the Ziggurat of Ra. It would be their final appearance before the people as leaders. They met before a huge crowd beneath a canopy. Cusha's throat and midriff were bare and her hair dressed with fine jewellery. Their bodies had been anointed with turmeric, sandalwood paste and oils, making them pure and fragrant, ready to exchange their oaths. They swapped gifts and garlands and received the congratulations of the guests and the acclamation of the crowd. Cusha was an orphan, her parents long dead, so Murima and Jackal performed the marriage duties instead, pouring water over Cusha's bare arms – the giving away of the bride to the groom.

Cusha glanced round at Oled. 'It will be you and Aaliya next,' she said.

Oled could only huff and rub his whiskers self-consciously.

'Step forward,' Aaliya said.

Then Cusha and Gardep faced each other. Aaliya, now the senior priestess of the Scales, tied the bride's sari to the groom's shirt in a knot, symbolising their union. After that, a sacred fire was lit and sprinkled with crushed sandalwood, herbs, sugar, rice, ghee and twigs. Gardep took Cusha's left hand in his right. After all this time, he started at her touch as if pricked by thorn bushes. In that precious moment, he knew he would never tire of her touch. Squeezing her hand tenderly, he faced west while Cusha sat facing east. She too marvelled that the warmth of his body behind her made her senses swim, that his presence made her blood race in her veins. With their free hands, they pointed to north and south. Overjoyed to be united for ever with his bride, Gardep's senses were swimming. He had made the right choice. What was duty and kingship compared to this?

'By the Four Winds and the secret ways of the Scales,' he said, struggling to speak through the tightness in his throat, 'I swear that I will do all in my power to make this marriage prosper.'

In response Cusha, smiling with joy, cupped her hands, receiving grain from Harad and Qintu before offering it as a sacrifice to the Four Winds.

'This grain I spill,' she said, the words ringing from

her lips like music. 'May it bring us both wellbeing and happiness.'

Bride and groom then stood before the ritual fire and closed their eyes, remembering their ancestors and their lost friends. Finally, after embracing, they took handfuls of flower petals from baskets held by Aaliya, Murima, Harad and Qintu and scattered them over the heads of the listening multitude. Their marriage ceremony was at an end. Immediately, old friend and new acquaintance alike engulfed them. Murima, Harad and Qintu were the first to offer their congratulations, their eyes glittering with tears.

'Just imagine,' Harad said, 'my beautiful sister married and the land free. Tell me it isn't all a dream.'

'If it is a dream,' Qintu said, 'then you've been asleep an awfully long time!'

Murima hugged Cusha, kissing her forehead. 'You are my heart, my life,' she said. 'By all that is holy in this world, I knew you were special the first day I saw you. For all that, I did not dream that these tiny hands would know how to turn the world upside down.'

Cusha blinked back her tears. 'It seems such a long time,' she said, 'since that sultry night in Parcep.'

The following morning, there was a parting of the ways for the companions who had crossed the great world to make it anew. Atrakon, Nikesh and Sanjay rode to Tiger-gated Parcep, there to embark on a ship for foreign parts. There was a rumour that the rebel priests were seeking refuge in distant Lukshmir. No matter what the cost, they would pursue the escaped Hotec-Ra to the end of the Earth and bring them to justice. They had to be stopped or the terrible secret of Fire Dust could yet cost mankind dear. Bulu departed for Zindhar, from which he would govern the northern provinces. With Adrius as their guide, Gardep and Cusha would set off on an expedition to

Inbacus, the city of the warrior's birth. Gardep wanted to discover the last secrets of his origins. Oled and Aaliya watched the departures from the Gates of Freedom.

'Do you think there will ever truly be peace?' Oled said, feeling the terrible weight of leadership on his shoulders. 'Will Shamana's dreams ever be fulfilled?'

'I fear that there is something destructive in the hearts of men,' Aaliya said, 'but we can be sure of this, my love. From this time on, no mortal man or woman will hold another human being in servitude. Nobody will have to endure a life being treated as a chattel to be bought and sold, flogged and denied freedom. From the moment you led the Army of the Free through the gates of golden Rinaghar, there has been an end to demons, an end to oppression.'

She took his hand. 'You are the son of the She-wolf,' she said, 'and a worthy successor to great Shamana. With you to lead us, there will be balance in the land, between male and female, light and dark.'

They watched the sun rising steadily over the Great Ziggurat.

'There will be justice.'